THE FIANCÉ

RONA HALSALL

Boldwood

First published in Great Britain in 2024 by Boldwood Books Ltd.

Copyright © Rona Halsall, 2024

Cover Design by Head Design Ltd

Cover Photography: Shutterstock and iStock

The moral right of Rona Halsall to be identified as the author of this work has been asserted in accordance with the Copyright, Designs and Patents Act 1988.

Every effort has been made to obtain the necessary permissions with reference to copyright material, both illustrative and quoted. We apologise for any omissions in this respect and will be pleased to make the appropriate acknowledgements in any future edition.

A CIP catalogue record for this book is available from the British Library.

Paperback ISBN 978-1-83603-108-6

Large Print ISBN 978-1-83603-107-9

Hardback ISBN 978-1-83603-106-2

Ebook ISBN 978-1-83603-109-3

Kindle ISBN 978-1-83603-110-9

Audio CD ISBN 978-1-83603-101-7

MP3 CD ISBN 978-1-83603-102-4

Digital audio download ISBN 978-1-83603-105-5

Boldwood Books Ltd
23 Bowerdean Street
London SW6 3TN
www.boldwoodbooks.com

This book is dedicated to all my friends on the Isle of Man.
Thank you for your love and support xxx

PROLOGUE
TWO YEARS AGO

The words scattered in Anna's mind, like marbles dropped on a hard surface, bouncing and rolling, unable to form a sequence that made any sense. She frowned up at the doctor, a young woman, probably in her early thirties, the same age as herself. Her shiny dark hair was tied back in a low ponytail, wisps escaping around her face, framing concerned brown eyes.

'No,' Anna said, a frantic quiver to her voice. 'That can't be right.' She tucked her blonde hair behind her ears, once, then twice, then three times; a compulsive habit that appeared whenever she was stressed. And now she was more stressed than she'd ever been in her life.

They were crammed into a small office, the only free space for a quiet talk, Anna hunched on a battered chair, coffee stains on the light blue seat. The doctor was sitting opposite her in a black office chair, gently swinging from side to side, like she was nervous, her hands gripping the stethoscope that draped round her neck. It was stuffy and hot, Anna's palms clammy as her hands clasped together in her lap. Holding on tight, like they were scared of losing each other.

'I'm so sorry,' the doctor said, leaning forward and placing a comforting hand on Anna's shoulder, its warmth seeping through her T-shirt. She blinked, her body tensing. *This is real. It's happening.* Her chest tightened, her breathing became shallow and she started to feel a bit light-headed. 'Is there anyone who can come and get you? It's best not to be alone when you've had a shock like this. And you shouldn't be driving.'

Her words didn't register, Anna's mind still stuck on the first thing the doctor had said, unable to move past it. *Dead.* Her husband, Ollie, was dead.

'I... don't understand... It was a routine operation. That's what I was told. Very quick. How can he be...'

It was impossible to say the word, let alone believe that it was true. Her lovely, goofy husband, who'd been teasing her about her current celebrity crush only two days ago. How was it possible that he was no longer alive? They'd been making plans to travel, buy their own house, start a family. The next five years all mapped out.

And now she couldn't see beyond this moment, had no idea how to exist without him.

She caught the doctor's eye, gave a feeble smile, her head shaking, her whole body shaking. 'I heard you wrong, didn't I? This is me catastrophising.'

The doctor stared at her, lips pressed together. 'I'm so sorry, Mrs McKenzie, but I think you heard me right. And I know it's hard to take in, but your husband unfortunately passed away in theatre.'

The words lodged in Anna's heart, an emotional hammer blow forcing a sob from her throat. And once she'd started, the anguish poured out of her like water gushing from a broken dam. An unstoppable sadness convulsing her body, tearing at her chest. She covered her face with her hands, stupidly embarrassed to be falling apart in front of a stranger.

'But how?' she asked when she could finally catch her breath, swiping at her tear-stained face with a bunch of tissues the doctor held out to her. 'How can that have happened?'

The doctor's gaze sank to the floor. 'I'll let the surgeon come and explain in more detail. He shouldn't be long.' She gave Anna's shoulder a gentle rub. 'Unfortunately, these things happen, I'm afraid. There's always a risk with surgery, as we explain before the patient gives their consent. Nobody's fault.'

Anna's jaw tightened, a surge of anger forcing her sadness out of the way.

'I don't understand how you can say that. Him needing the second operation in the first place was somebody's fault, wasn't it?' The words forced themselves out, sharp and pointed, needing to find a target, a place to spear the blame. 'If the first operation had been done properly, he wouldn't have needed the second.' She paused, swallowed, determined to say it. 'And he'd still be alive.'

The doctor shifted in her seat, then stood, her expression blank, like she'd packed away her empathy. 'Like I said, I'll get the surgeon to come and explain the details.' She fidgeted with her stethoscope. 'I understand it's a terrible shock. Can I get you anything? How about a hot drink? Or can I call someone to come here and be with you?'

Anna shook her head, eyes staring ahead of her, not seeing anything but Ollie's face. Laughing. He was always laughing and making her laugh too. He wasn't one to worry, never let life get him down and could see the bright side in any situation. Exactly the sort of person she needed by her side. She tucked her hair behind her ears again, hands shaking. She shivered, cold now. How would she manage without him?

It wasn't fair. He didn't deserve to die. He wasn't expected to die. So why the hell was he dead?

She closed her eyes, her body rocking backwards and forwards as her arms wound themselves round her chest, fingers clasping her ribs. A keening erupted from her throat and there was nothing she could do to stop it.

Her world was broken. She was broken.

And someone needed to pay for what they'd done.

1

NOW

Anna's heart skipped when she noticed a change in Theo Heaton's profile on Facebook. *Single*, it said. Yesterday it hadn't said anything about relationships, and it had been the same for the two years she'd been following him. As far as she was aware he was married, even if he didn't like to mention it on his profile. Come to think of it, had she ever seen a picture of him with his wife? She couldn't recall anything. He didn't give much away on his posts and now Anna thought about it, she didn't know much about him outside of his work life. She enlarged his new profile picture on the screen of her phone, studying the face she knew so well, without ever having met the man.

Silver hair, cut short and styled on top to give a little bit of height. Playful, it said to her. His hair would curl, she imagined, if he ever grew it longer. His chin was square and clean shaven, his skin tanned and pretty much flawless. He was fifty-two but he looked at least ten years younger. Piercing blue eyes, with a navy-blue ring round the edge. Dark eyebrows. A straight nose, a little on the large side, maybe, but on him it looked noble. In fact, that word summed up his image. Noble, trustworthy, although there was a hint of a smile, creating little grooves at the corners of his mouth that said he had a sense of fun. She studied his lips, wondering how they could look so gentle, given everything she knew about him.

She checked out the background for clues, saw that he was at a marina, rows of boats moored on pontoons behind him. Hmm, was that Caernarfon Castle in the background? Yes, unmistakable really. Was one of the boats his?

He clearly had money; you could tell by the places he frequented. The smart-looking people he hung out with, his annual skiing trips to America, holidays in the Caribbean, the way he dressed. The black coat he was wearing in the picture was a Barbour if she wasn't mistaken. It looked good on him. But then he was one of those men who never looked shabby or scruffy – if his social media feed was anything to go by. He always glowed. You could tell he smelt fresh, just from the pictures. Clean, shiny, immaculate.

She'd started following Theo on Facebook and Instagram, about four months after Ollie's death. He seemed to use Facebook for work-related posts and Instagram for his out of work activities, so she always checked both. Before that time, she'd been in shock, names and faces all blurring together in her grief. But when her mind had cleared a little, she was able to understand that Theo Heaton was the surgeon who'd killed her soulmate. Whatever had gone wrong in that operating theatre was his responsibility, even if the internal inquiry had decided otherwise.

So, she'd started following him on social media, for no logical reason other than it made her feel like she was doing *something*. Even if there was no tangible outcome, it alleviated the over-whelming feeling of helplessness that swamped her on a daily basis. She would look at his pictures and project hate at him, hoping that somehow all her negative energy would start to interfere with his life. Obviously, she had no idea if it worked in any way, but it made her feel better for a little while.

For someone she'd never met, she knew a lot about Theo Heaton in his capacity as a surgeon.

She had an encyclopaedic knowledge of his career as a doctor. In fact, she could recite his CV like it was her own. She knew where he'd worked in the past, had searched for other instances of his patients dying, looking for a pattern of negligence or incompetence, anything she could use to ruin his career. But she'd found nothing. She knew he ran a private surgical clinic, but no wrongdoings there either. It was annoying, but it did appear his carelessness with her husband had been out of character, just as his peers and bosses had said. Somehow that made it worse.

Why did it have to be Ollie who'd died?

In her frenzy to uncover professional wrongdoings, she hadn't thought to research his private life. It didn't occur to her it might be helpful. Never had she thought to scroll back through his social media feeds to the months before the operations. In fact, until today, when she'd found out he was single, her thinking had been very woolly. She'd looked at him and hated him for what he'd done, but outside of going through official channels, which had come to nothing, she'd no idea what she could do.

Now she could see an opportunity to learn more about the man himself, a way to get close to him. And that had to be her next move because it was the only line of attack left. *Could I date him?* That would be the easiest way to find a weak spot, a way to hurt him. Everyone had things they didn't want made public. Details she could use against him to tarnish his reputation, humiliate him, cause him financial harm. Information which, if it came to light, could destroy him in some way.

Revenge is a dish best served cold, isn't that what they say? Well two years was long enough for her rage to solidify into an ice-cold block in her heart. She had despaired at finding a way to make him pay for what he'd done. But now an opportunity had been presented to her and her gut instinct was to grab it with both hands. Her heart was going at a steady gallop now, excitement building in her chest. This was it, the chance she'd been waiting for. *Is it really possible?*

* * *

She turned her phone camera on herself and gave a dissatisfied laugh when she saw the image. Tired and dull. That's how she looked, dark shadows under hazel eyes tinged with sadness, her mouth turned down, unkempt eyebrows, pallid skin, hair looking limp and lifeless. She was not the sort of woman a man like Theo would be interested in, but then she hadn't bothered with her appearance since Ollie had died.

Her hair needed a wash, and the lower half was purple, the ends split and frizzy. She'd had it cut and coloured the day before Ollie's funeral, wanting to look her best for him as she escorted his coffin to the crematorium. Just in case he was there, watching. Purple was his favourite colour, but it looked scruffy now.

She ran her hands through the grown-out cut, her hair full of tangles. It was hard to remember when she'd last given it a brush, tending to gather it into a knot on top of her head to keep it out of the way. That was the danger of working from home. Nobody who mattered ever had to see the state you were in. And when she went out to the shops, she put on a baseball cap. It made her feel invisible, just how she liked to be.

There were stains on her grey sweatshirt where she'd spilt coffee and her fried egg sandwich had dripped. The collar was shapeless and fraying. She looked like a bag lady, someone without the facilities or the money to keep herself and her clothes clean.

She sighed, turned the camera off and studied his picture again as her mind wandered.

Since Ollie's death she'd become a recluse, always cancelling invitations to social gatherings at the last minute, with what she hoped were plausible excuses, only agreeing to go in the first place to stop her friends fussing about her. Thinking about it, she wouldn't say she had any close friends now. Their knowledge of her was over two years old, the closeness a mirage created by social media and messaging. Most of them hadn't seen her in person since the funeral.

The lives of her friends had moved on. Boyfriends becoming husbands, babies arriving for a couple of them. Foreign travel, house moves, career changes, new qualifications, promotions. She'd watched it all happening, without getting involved. An interested bystander. Her life had gone nowhere, pinned to the spot by her grief and her rage at the grinding unfairness of life. At thirty-one she was too young to be widowed. Too young to have all her dreams ripped away from her.

She blinked back the tears, so salty they made her eyes sting, wondering if she would ever move past this point. Could she accept that the baby she'd imagined in her arms, the one with Ollie's smile and his sticky out ears, could only be alive in her imagination? Those trips to far-flung lands, could only be lived in her fantasies. The chapters of her life would never have *Ollie* written in their pages. Sometimes it was too much to bear, and she would sit and howl until she was all cried out. But nobody knew that because she kept everyone at bay. Even her parents, her stock answer being, 'I'm fine. Everything's fine.' But she wasn't.

Ollie had been the sensible one, the practical half of their partnership. The one who stopped her from panicking when things went wrong, like the kitchen tap leaking, or the washing machine breaking or the boiler refusing to come on. He grounded her, made everything seem possible, made life an adventure she couldn't wait to experience. Without him, she existed in a dark tunnel, with only one direction of travel, and however many steps she took, she never got closer to the light. In fact, there were times when there was no light.

She shook the dark thoughts out of her head before they started taking over. They were her constant companions, but she couldn't spend time with them now. She had things to do. Plans to make, because Theo being single had opened up a once-in-a-lifetime opportunity that she was determined to take. She'd get one shot at this, and she had to make it work. One chance to cleanse herself of the caustic rage that boiled inside her, corrosive and all-consuming.

This was her chance to make things right, to balance the scales of justice a little. Perhaps then she would stop being plagued by the nightmares and the intrusive thoughts that brought her to tears at random moments. Perhaps then she could start living again, instead of existing in this endless fug of sorrow and pain.

Looking through her photo gallery, she scrolled back to when she'd been happy, and found a picture Ollie had taken of her with a new range of scarves when she'd first opened her Etsy shop. Thank goodness she'd had a chance to get that established before she found herself on her own.

In the picture she was grinning, eyes sparkling, her hair short and shiny, with a long fringe tucked behind one ear. She was wearing big dangly earrings that she'd made from silk offcuts and twisted into loops. That was a point in her life when she'd felt everything was starting to come together.

They'd just had an offer accepted on a three-bedroomed property, where she could have a decent-sized workspace as well as there being a room for a nursery when they were ready. Ollie had been promoted at the media firm he worked for, and she had big plans to develop her online business. That future had been taken away from her with Ollie's death. She'd pulled their offer for the house and stayed in their rented apartment, unable to decide what to do once he was gone. Most of the insurance money she'd received after his death had been invested in a long-term bond. It seemed like the safest option; to keep everything the same. Life had ground to a shuddering halt.

She studied the picture of herself and let out a long sigh. Once, she'd been attractive. She'd turned heads, she knew she had, and been so full of confidence she'd thought nothing could go wrong. *Ha, how naïve. Look what could happen in an instant.*

I could look like that again, she thought, a flurry of ideas blowing into her mind like autumn leaves hurried along by the wind. *I could make men interested in me, if I tried. Men like Theo.*

A smile curved her lips as she decided this was the best idea she'd had in a long time. Theo becoming single was exactly the chance she'd been waiting for, a challenge that would give her life focus.

She gazed out of the window, planning a list of things she'd need to do. She would get her hair done first, and her nails and her eyebrows. Eyelashes as well, of course. Ditch the glasses and move back to contact lenses. She studied her face in her phone again. Hmm, maybe get her lips plumped a little. Glamorous was what she needed to aim for, because a man as well-groomed as Theo would want a woman who took the same care of herself as he did. And clothes. She'd need a whole new wardrobe of clothes. She laughed, excited now. There was some serious shopping to be done.

Having studied him for the last two years, she knew his style, knew which brands he liked to wear so that gave her some clues as to what she might need to get for herself. *It's all possible,* she told herself, the excitement mounting.

Writing notes as she went along, she started a list of things she'd need to organise and buy for her makeover. An hour later, she sat back on the sofa, smiling to herself. This wasn't going to be cheap, but she'd left some of the insurance money in an instant access savings account for contingencies. If she thought of it as an investment into her future, an investment in her mental health and peace of mind, the cost was worth it. Yes, this might be the way to finally put everything behind her, exorcise the demons and move on.

'He's not going to know what's hit him,' she murmured to herself as she started scrolling through the fashion sites, picking out items for her new look. She could almost hear Ollie laughing at her choices and that spurred her on. The woman she was going to make herself into was not going to be the person he knew. And in an instant, the memories came flooding back. The night when her life changed.

2

THEN

Ollie clinked his champagne glass against hers, grey eyes twinkling in the candlelight, his light brown hair tied in a man bun, his neatly trimmed beard a shade darker than his hair. They were sitting in their favourite Italian restaurant in a secluded corner booth, and it felt as though there was just the two of them in the world.

'Here's to us,' he said. 'Happy anniversary, sweetheart. I can't believe it's been three years already, but it's been the best three years, hasn't it?'

She beamed at him, more in love with this man than she'd ever been. He was everything she'd ever wanted, more than she'd ever hoped for and every day she woke up stunned that this was her life. 'To us,' she repeated. 'It's been... wonderful. And I love being Mrs McKenzie.'

He took a sip of champagne and shook his head, grinning. 'I'm such a lucky man.' He took her hand, his thumb stroking her palm, sending tingles up her arm. 'You know, I can't wait to see what our children look like.'

She laughed. 'Steady on, tiger. We've got dessert coming before we think about starting down that road. And a small matter of the house move to get through. I want to be settled in our new place, with all the work done before we have any children. Otherwise, we'll be like my parents and end up living in a half-finished house forever.'

He grimaced, his hand slipping away from hers to rub his stomach, his eyes screwed up in pain.

She frowned. 'Is that stomach ache back again?'

He grunted, his face contorted. 'Christ, it feels like my guts are strangling themselves.' Beads of sweat popped up on his brow, his face suddenly pale.

He'd been having stomach cramps all day and it had seemed to settle down before they came out, after he'd taken a couple of tablets for stomach acid. But now she could see from his face he was really suffering. This was different, something had changed.

He groaned, and leant forwards, both hands on his stomach now, and she jumped to her feet, rushing to his side, not sure what she could do to help.

'It's getting worse,' he said through gritted teeth, panic making her heart race. It was her job to look after him, her job to work out what to do. But she'd never felt so clueless in her life.

'Shall we just go home?' She looked around for a member of staff, wanting to ask for the bill. 'I'll get a cab.' He groaned again and she frantically waved her hand in the air, trying to attract someone's attention. Thankfully, a waitress spotted her and hurried off to sort out their bill once Anna had explained the problem.

By the time she'd paid, and organised a cab, Ollie was looking even worse. He said he was too hot and he was certainly sweating profusely and when the cab arrived, he was struggling to walk, doubled over with the pain. There was only one place they were going, and it wasn't home.

'Can you take us to the hospital, please?' she asked the cab driver, desperate to get medical help. 'Quick as you can.'

* * *

Fortunately, it was midweek, the hospital wasn't full of weekend drunks who'd started fights with each other and the triage nurse recognised that Ollie was in significant pain. Anna felt unbearably helpless, and all she could do was hold his hand, tell him everything was going to be okay, while they waited to be called into the treatment room.

It took longer than she would have liked, but the examination and tests gave appendicitis as the problem and surgery as the answer. By this time, it was the early hours of the morning, and she was so tired her eyes were dry and sore, hurting every time she blinked. She watched as he was wheeled off to surgery, telling him she loved him one last time, before he disappeared through the double doors and down the corridor. All she could do was sit and wait, reminding herself it was a routine operation, her husband was in good hands. It would be fine. Absolutely fine.

What had started as the most wonderful romantic evening had turned into a frightening whirlwind of pain and blood tests and concerned doctors. It was terrifying to see the person she loved suffering and the whole experience had left her feeling shocked, jittery and thoroughly exhausted.

Up until now, Anna would say she'd had a good life, brought up by loving parents, with a brother and sister she was still close to. Enough money in the family budget for them all to go on annual holidays, a good group of friends at school and new friends made on her fashion design course at university. She'd never had to deal with a medical emergency, never had to concern herself with the possibilities of death. It was unchartered territory and she was scared witless, unable to sit still as she paced the floor waiting for news.

'Can I get you a drink?' a nurse said as she popped her head into the empty waiting room. It was almost 4 a.m. and everyone else had been and gone. She studied Anna's face, her head cocked to one side, a concerned look in her eye. 'I don't want you to worry, love. I know it's been a horrible shock for you, but the surgeon who's on tonight has done this op hundreds of times.' She gave a reassuring smile. 'Honestly, there's nothing to worry about.'

She was back a few minutes later with tea in a paper cup, which Anna clasped to her chest, feeling cold and empty, although the cup was almost too hot to hold.

'You can head off home if you like, and we'll ring when your husband's out of surgery. There's nothing much you can do here and you won't be able to see him when he comes out because they'll take him straight to the ward. You'll probably have to wait until visiting tomorrow afternoon.'

Anna shook her head, certain she couldn't leave him, wanting to feel she was as close as she could be until she knew that he was okay, that he'd survived the operation and there really *was* nothing to worry about.

Two hours later, a hand gently shook her awake and she opened her eyes to see the nurse again, smiling at her.

'I just got word that he's out of recovery and they're ready to take him up to the ward.' Her smile widened. 'I told you there was nothing to worry about.'

Anna was unable to answer, not sure whether she was about to laugh or cry and she ended up doing both while the nurse sat beside her and rubbed her back. She was stiff and aching from sitting for so long on a hard, plastic chair, but she heaved herself to her feet, ready to go home now that Ollie was safe.

Looking back on it now, she wondered how life had managed to throw them such a curve ball. *But that's what happens, isn't it?* You think you've got everything sussed, think you're winning, then a storm blows in and all the cards you've carefully constructed your life with come tumbling down.

3

NOW

Anna already felt so much better than she had just ten days ago, when she'd first had the idea of trying to date Theo. She'd developed a new habit of swinging her head just to feel the movement of her silky hair brushing against her neck, sitting there twisting it between her fingers while she got on with whatever task she was doing. Her eyebrows were tamed and shaped and a facial had improved the tone of her skin. She was also drinking loads of water and had done a weekly shop, buying a pile of vegetables and healthy ingredients. She'd even bought herself a cookbook.

When Anna set her mind on a goal, it was full commitment, nothing less, and she was completely obsessed with making herself into a woman Theo would want to date. It had taken over her life, but it felt like a good thing, having something new to focus on. It had pulled her out of the bog of despair she'd been wallowing in and she'd actually caught herself singing in the shower that morning, something she hadn't done in years.

Obviously, this wasn't going to be a quick process; she knew transformations took a certain amount of time if they were to be convincing, but she was delighted with the results so far. Every bit of progress was a step in the right direction. She checked her watch and stood up from her work desk, stretching. It was amazing how having Project Theo to focus on had more than doubled her productivity. She eyed the pile of parcels, orders ready to post, and for the first time since Ollie's death, she felt a glow of satisfaction, a warm feeling of well-being about a job well done.

It was nearly time for her appointment at the opticians to see about contact lenses, an important part of her makeover. She used to wear them before she met Ollie, over seven years ago now. But then she found she didn't want to be bothered with them any more and Ollie said she looked cute in glasses, so she'd stopped wearing the lenses.

She was strangely excited to give them another try, convinced they'd be worth the investment. Ollie always said it was her eyes that had drawn him to her, large and round in her delicately boned face. If she was intent on snaring her man, it was only right to make the most of her best feature.

The weight she'd lost since Ollie's death had accentuated her cheek bones and given her back the figure she'd had in her early twenties. She'd thought she was getting a bit skinny, but looking at the pictures she'd found of Theo's wife, she believed that was how he liked his women. And it meant she could go for outfits she wouldn't have considered when she was carrying more weight. It was exciting dressing up in her new clothes and she couldn't wait for more of her purchases to arrive.

She checked herself in the long hall mirror, pleased with the grey skinny jeans and cream cashmere sweater she was wearing. Simple but elegant and not a muffin top to be seen bulging over the top of her waistband. Every cloud has a silver lining, she thought as she grabbed her keys and left the house, humming to herself as she walked into town for her appointment. In the past, she would have driven, although it was not that far. Now, she tried to walk everywhere as part of her new fitness regime, getting muscles back on her spindly legs.

She had other jobs to do while she was in town, not least checking out the gym where Theo worked out three times a week. He always posted gym pictures on a Monday, Wednesday and Friday and had done all the time she'd been monitoring his social media, so there was no reason to think anything would have changed.

* * *

Once she'd finished at the optician's, she made her way to the gym, housed in a re-developed retail site that had once been an Aldi before it moved to bigger premises. The front was tinted glass, but she could see the shadows of people on the treadmills, felt a twitch of nerves before hitching her fake Dior bag over her shoulder and heading inside.

The reception area was quite small but plush with a curved reception desk straight ahead. The receptionist, a young woman in her early twenties, with bleached blonde hair, looked up when she heard the door and gave her a toothy grin, her smile so white it was disconcerting.

'Oh, hello,' Anna gushed. 'I just wanted to enquire about membership? Can I pay for ad hoc sessions, or do I have to pay a subscription?' She gave a nervous laugh. 'I've no idea how these things work.'

'It's completely up to you. Obviously, it's cheaper if you're a member and then you can use the gym every day of the week if you like. But you can also pay as you go. Most people do that to get started, and when they settle into a rhythm and know what classes they like, they switch up to a membership.'

Anna's hands clutched her bag, fighting the urge to run back out of the door. But if Theo was here regularly, then this was where she had to be. What better place to meet someone? She cleared her throat. 'Okay, well that sounds great.'

The receptionist grinned. 'I can get you a tour if you like?'

Anna gave her a nervous smile. 'Fantastic.'

She waited while the receptionist made a call and a few minutes later, a young man wearing grey shorts and a white T-shirt came bouncing into reception, his hair slicked back in a style that could only work with copious amounts of hair product. He smelt wonderful though, all zingy and fresh, his scent drawing her behind him as he showed her round.

It was an impressive facility, with state-of-the-art equipment and a wide range of classes, ranging from classic weight training to yoga, cross-fit, spin classes and Zumba. They also had a couple of treatment rooms where you could book a range of massages and an in-house physio who specialised in sports injuries. This was obviously serious stuff.

Anna listened and nodded as they went round, taking a leaflet on all the available classes to study when she got home. She would sign up to a couple, she decided, then she could really familiarise herself with the place and make sure she was there at the right time to 'accidentally' bump into Theo.

Not yet though. She wasn't quite ready. Her contact lenses would take a couple of weeks to come through and she still had some beauty treatments to get booked in.

Her next job was to check out the make-up counter at the chemist down the road. She'd had to empty her make-up bag in the bin, all of it dried up and unsuitable for the look she needed. She reckoned Theo was the sort of guy who liked smoky eyes, long lashes, something dramatic, whereas she favoured understated and neutral. It was going to take a bit of practice to get it just right. And that was going to be fun.

She'd had a session with a make-up artist, and together, they'd come up with the right look. She'd also been shown how to do it herself and had a list of products to buy. It would pay, in the long run, to have the professional help because if you were going to do something, Anna's philosophy was to do it properly. No cutting corners. Full commitment, nothing less.

* * *

While her makeover was progressing, she was monitoring Theo's social media feed to see what he was up to, making sure he hadn't already snagged himself a girlfriend. That was the first thing she did when she got back home and frowned when she saw his latest post. A picture of a white room, no furniture and a caption that simply said:

Starting over

Hmm, interesting, so he's moved out of the family home. It appeared he was no longer living in the Boat House on the edge of the Menai Straits, the stunning property where he and his wife had brought up their family. Anna had been down there a few times in the past, in the months after Ollie's death, hiding in the bushes at the side of the property with her binoculars. But she'd nearly been caught out once and it had freaked her out so much, she hadn't dared go near the place after that.

Now why would he have moved out?

The Boat House hadn't been on the market. She knew this because she constantly checked new listings for that very eventuality. But if he and his wife had separated, which his single status suggested, the person who wanted the relationship to end was usually the one who left. Which suggested it was him. *Is he having an affair?* Her heart sank. Maybe her plan to date him was doomed to failure before she'd even started. Perhaps he already had somebody else. Maybe he was moving in with them.

She looked again at the photo of his new place, trying to see if she could work out where it might be. Oh wait, she could see the vague outline of mountains in the distance. Ah yes, she recognised that view, it must be somewhere up on that new estate in Bangor, by the hospital. Very nice. Some comments had started to appear on his post. People wishing him luck. She'd just have to keep checking his feed, see if anyone was blowing him kisses or leaving love hearts.

A Google search led her to a list of local estate agents and after twenty minutes checking rental properties in the area, she struck lucky. There was one house, let agreed, up on that estate. She gave a little fist pump. The pictures showed a room identical to one in his photo. She smiled to herself. Now she knew where he lived, it was time to go and check it out, just to make sure he hadn't moved in with another woman. The last thing she needed was to be wasting her time. Because if this plan was a non-starter, she'd have to go back to the drawing board and work out another way to get to him.

Excitement fizzed through her veins as she dug out her surveillance bag, something she'd put together when she'd gone to spy on him at the Boat House over a year and a half ago. She had a pair of binoculars, a little notebook, snacks and a water bottle in there. Having it all together made her feel like she was doing something meaningful, worthwhile, moving towards an important goal. It had kept her going through the tough times, but now things were moving to a new phase. Victory was getting closer; she could sense it and it lit a fire in her heart.

4

THEN

She went to visit Ollie in hospital the day after his appendix operation, laden with a carrier bag of clothes, slippers, phone charger and toiletries. And another bag with books, puzzles and all sorts of bits and pieces that he might want and need. They hadn't given her any idea how long he might be in for, but she was hoping it would only be a couple of days. Just to make sure he was healing properly. She hadn't spent a night without him by her side for such a long time, it had felt strange in the apartment on her own. Like a piece of her was missing.

For some reason she felt nervous as she walked the corridors, having never been on a hospital ward before. She came from a healthy family and couldn't remember a time when any of them had needed to be an inpatient, which seemed to be unusual these days. Even her grandparents were all in rude health. Blessed by good genes, her parents used to tell her, and for that she was grateful. Hopefully this incident was a one-off and they would soon be able to put it behind them because the background smell of antiseptic was enough to make her stomach turn.

The ward was busy with visitors, doctors and nurses all bustling about, the hum of conversations filling the air. She looked around while she waited at the central reception desk, peering into the four bays that seemed to make up the ward, each filled with a handful of beds, but none of the faces she could see were her husband's. She'd just have to wait until someone was free at the reception desk to ask where he might be.

Finally, the nurse finished her conversation and put down the phone, glancing up at Anna. 'Can I help you?' Her round face creased into a warm smile. Anna explained she was looking for her husband and the nurse consulted her screen, then her face changed, her eyebrows pinching together.

'I'm just going to have to ask what's happening,' she said, getting up from the desk as she looked around for someone to consult. Anna stood there, gripping the handles of the bulging carrier bags a little tighter, a feeling of unease building in her chest. She hadn't liked the change in expression on the nurse's face. She'd looked surprised, but not in a good way. Surely it should be easy to tell her which bed he was in?

A few minutes later, the nurse came back, followed by a doctor. A small Asian lady, with a long dark plait falling down her back, her hair flecked with strands of grey, the obligatory stethoscope hung round her neck. She gave Anna a quick smile.

'Hello, I'm Doctor Chandra, there's been a... development with your husband.' Her eyes swung round the reception area, still busy with visitors waiting to ask about their loved ones. 'Let's go into the meeting room where it's a bit quieter, and I can tell you what's happening.'

A development? What sort of development? Anna's heart started to race, a sudden heat flushing through her body.

She followed the doctor down the corridor into a small room near the entrance to the ward, fitted out with a low table and six comfy chairs. The doctor pulled out a chair indicating the one opposite.

'Please, have a seat.'

Anna sat, putting her bags down by her side, her hands smoothing the legs of her jeans, before going into the tucking hair behind her ears routine. The doctor gave her a sympathetic smile. 'So... we were monitoring your husband and we noticed something wasn't quite right. He was experiencing some discomfort after he came round, so we sent him down for a scan, just to check the operation site and we discovered a problem.'

She looked uncomfortable, hesitated.

Anna's mind raced through a terrible scenario that she really didn't want in her head and she found herself blinking, trying to rid her mind of the horrible images. 'Is he okay?'

The doctor moistened her lips, then finally spoke. 'It seems a swab was left at the operation site.'

Anna's eyes widened, her hand flying to her mouth. 'A swab? Left inside him?'

The doctor looked down at her hands as she mumbled, 'We think there might be a piece of medical equipment as well.'

'Oh my God.' Anna's brain felt like it had been jump started, working so fast it was hard to keep up with her thoughts. 'And what does that mean in terms of my husband's health? I need you to be more specific.' She wanted to leap out of her chair and shake the woman, see if that would make the words spill out of her mouth. Words that would give Anna reassurance everything was okay. 'What's happening?'

She glared at the doctor, feeling her temper coming to the boil, her body tense. She looked away, telling herself it wasn't the doctor's fault, she was merely the messenger and getting angry wasn't going to help. But this news was shocking. No, it was worse than that, it was appalling. She took a deep breath, trying desperately to calm herself down.

The doctor was obviously flustered, her hands holding her stethoscope like it was a buoyancy aid, keeping her afloat in choppy waters. It was clear from her body language that she was finding this an uncomfortable conversation. 'He needed an immediate operation to remove the foreign objects and clean the site. He was happy to give his consent and he's down in surgery now. We knew you were coming in to visit and the consultant thought it would be better to tell you in person what was happening, rather than give you a call.'

'Another operation?' Anna completely lost her cool, bouncing to her feet to relieve some of the nervous energy trapped inside her body. She walked in a circle, her hand clasped to her forehead where a headache had started to throb. 'How on earth did this happen? I thought you had to count everything these days and get things double-checked. I'm sure I saw a documentary about this not long ago.'

The doctor sighed, shook her head. 'I can only offer our apologies. I really can't comment on how it happened. I wasn't there, but I'm sure it'll be looked into. All I can say is it can be pretty hectic in theatre when it's an emergency operation, and we have been very short-staffed for the last couple of weeks, with the new wave of Covid that's going round.'

Anna blew out a long breath, not sure what to think, but certain this was all wrong. It shouldn't be happening. A sudden thought made her heart stutter, and she stopped her pacing, locked eyes with the doctor. 'He'll be okay though?'

The doctor smiled and nodded. 'Please don't worry. This is a low-risk procedure. He'll be just fine. Luckily, we discovered the problem very quickly and your husband will be on precautionary meds to make sure there isn't a problem with infection.'

Anna was finding it hard to think straight, to know what she was supposed to do. But in reality, there was nothing she *could* do. Yet again, she was a helpless bystander and she'd just have to be patient. 'When can I see him?'

'When he's out of theatre he'll be in recovery and it will be a little while before he comes back up to the ward. It might be better if you go home and we'll give you a ring when he's back with us. Would you be able to come back during visiting hours this evening?'

Anna nodded. It wasn't a problem as she didn't live too far from the hospital.

The doctor stood. 'I'm so sorry this has happened but I'm afraid regardless of the safeguards we have in place, mistakes do get made.'

It would have to happen to my bloody husband, wouldn't it?

Anna didn't say it, just thought it while her teeth clamped tight. She had so many questions, but didn't want to hear the answers, deciding she'd just have to come back later. 'Thanks for letting me know what really happened.' She caught the compassion in the doctor's eyes and knew she'd taken a bullet for whoever had been responsible for the mistake. 'I suppose you could have glossed over it and then I would never have known the truth.'

The doctor held her gaze. 'You deserve to know. And nobody wants to hide anything from you, that's not how we do things here.'

Anna sighed. 'I'll be back later then.' She went to grab her bags, but the doctor put a hand on her arm to stop her.

'It's okay. I can take the bags for you, and put them in his bedside cabinet, if you like?'

Anna handed them over, her body shaking now her anger had subsided. It was such a shock. She'd never imagined there would be a problem with the operation. Not when the nurse she'd spoken to the previous evening had stressed how competent the surgeon was and how routine the operation would be. But she supposed it wasn't just the surgeon involved, there was a whole team of people and there was no point second-guessing what had gone wrong. She just had to hope they could put it right.

* * *

The afternoon dragged, minute by minute, as she constantly checked the time. Evening visiting hours were seven until eight and she was getting herself ready to set off when her phone rang. It wasn't a number she recognised and she hesitated before realising it was probably the hospital.

'Hello, is that Mrs McKenzie?' A female voice.

'Yes,' she said as she searched for the car keys.

'This is the Ogwen Ward, at the hospital. We just wanted to check that you're coming in this evening?'

'Yes, I'm on my way now. Is my husband back from surgery? Is he okay?'

There was a silence and Anna wondered if the call had been disconnected for a moment before the woman came back on the line. 'The consultant wants to speak to you, so if you make yourself known at the reception desk when you get here, he'll give you an update.'

'Thank you. I'll be there soon.'

She disconnected thinking how nice it was that they were making sure she'd be coming in to see her husband. Maybe he was awake and asking for her. She smiled to herself as she set off, singing along to the radio as she drove.

When she got to the ward though, she knew there was something wrong as soon as she told them at the reception desk who she was. Staff members flashed her horrified looks as they bustled in the opposite direction, until there was only her and a nurse who was talking on the phone at the reception desk.

She finished her call and met Anna's gaze. 'Mrs McKenzie?'

Anna nodded. 'Yes, I've come to see my husband. I had a phone call earlier saying he was on the ward. I just need to know which bed he's in.'

The nurse gave her a tight smile. 'I'm Julie Bennet, the staff nurse in charge of the ward. The consultant was wanting to speak to you, but I'm afraid he's been delayed.' She walked round from behind the desk. 'Unfortunately, it's a bit busy this evening and the meeting room is being used. Let's go into my office, it will be quiet in there. And you can wait for the doctor to come. I don't think he'll be long.'

'Could I see my husband first?' The muscles at the back of Anna's neck tightened, her heart rate speeding up. This didn't feel right at all.

The nurse put a hand on her back, gently guiding her down a different corridor. 'It's this way.'

With no other choice, she had to go along with her suggestion and was left sitting alone in the nurse's office while she waited for the consultant to turn up. She busied her mind by studying the posters on the walls. Tried to memorise the warning signs for sepsis. The flow chart for resuscitation.

Despite the promises of the staff nurse, the consultant surgeon in charge of the operation never came to speak to her. A junior doctor came to speak to her first. That was the moment her world turned on its head. When she discovered her husband was dead.

Then Doctor Chukwu came to speak to her. He'd been in theatre when Ollie had died. His voice was deep and full-bodied, with a slight accent. Nigerian she would guess, having shared a house with a couple of Nigerian girls at college. He gazed at her with compassionate brown eyes, his voice full of apology, answering her questions as best he could. Except for the most important one: *why did my husband die?*

She noticed evasiveness, his eyes sliding away from hers at several points in the conversation.

And that was the moment when Theo Heaton became important to her. Because Doctor Chukwu told her that was the name of the consultant surgeon who'd operated on her husband. Unfortunately, he was tied up with another patient at present and couldn't speak to her himself, so Dr Chukwu had been sent instead. That, in itself, made her furious. Why wasn't her husband's death important enough for him to come in person? In that moment, she hated him with every fibre of her being.

* * *

Later, there'd been an internal investigation, but even though Ollie's death had been the result of a severed artery, no wrongdoing was found on the part of Theo. Or anyone for that matter. Lessons were learned, of course, and procedures tightened up, an apology given, but that was about it. Nobody was sanctioned in any way, there was no disciplinary action. Nothing. There had been no consequences for the man who'd devastated Anna's life. His own life had gone on unfettered by blame, his lucrative private clinic, which he ran alongside his NHS work, earning him a fortune from other people's misery.

The initial mistake was understandable, they'd said. *Mitigating circumstances.* There'd been a road accident on the A55, the dual carriageway that ran up the coast. A lorry had skidded and gone across the carriageway, causing a pile up and creating an influx of badly injured people who needed urgent care. On top of that, the staff had been working beyond their twelve-hour shifts due to so many of their colleagues being off ill with Covid.

The overall conclusion was an unfortunate series of events. Everyone doing their best in a difficult situation.

Anna had been incensed then and she was still incensed now, carrying that fury in her heart. A smouldering rage that had poisoned her mind, making her into someone she'd never been. Someone filled with hate, looking for revenge, because that was the only way to make things fair. Why should Theo walk away unscathed? Of course he was to blame. He was in charge of that operating theatre on both occasions, and he'd failed miserably.

Ollie's death was Theo's fault. No question. And something horrible needed to happen to him to balance out the scales. The question she still needed to answer was: what?

5

NOW

Finally, Anna was ready for her reconnaissance mission. It was the end of October and she waited until seven, when she knew it would be dark and he was likely to be home. The night was cool, a stiff breeze sending clouds scudding across the sky, a half-moon appearing intermittently. If she picked her moment, she would have the cover of complete darkness. It was a good night for a recce.

Excitement buzzed through her as she drove into the estate and found the house to let, with the agent's board still in the front garden. It was a standard semi-detached with three bedrooms. Nothing special and nothing like the house he used to live in. Something drastic must have happened for him to move out, she thought, making her theory about an affair more likely. She parked just down the road a little way, out of the glare of the streetlights and turned off her headlights. His car was in the drive. A metallic blue Porsche Carrera. Very nice.

The lights were on in the living room, so she knew he was in. But was there someone else in there with him? His profile still said single, but he'd recently posted photos of himself with a couple of different women. No clues as to who the women were, just bland comments stating the obvious, like 'enjoying the afternoon sun in Llandudno' or 'dinner at my favourite Indian restaurant'. The appearance of women in his posts was a new development, so he was definitely up for dating. But had one of them already won him over?

She pulled out the binoculars, but the angle was all wrong and she couldn't see anything. She huffed, annoyed with herself for even thinking this would work. It wasn't like she could park right outside his house and peer in. But she *could* walk past, spec out the area and see if there was access round the back.

Thankfully, she was in her joggers and trainers, so she could pretend she was out for a run. She pulled her water bottle out of her bag, thinking she would look more authentic if she had that in her hand, and got out of the car. As she neared the front of his property, she bent, pretending to tie a shoelace. She was directly opposite now and the curtains were open, light spilling onto the lawn at the front. He was there, she could see him, framed in the downstairs window. He was hammering something into the wall, then he disappeared, reappearing with a picture, which he hung up, standing back to admire his efforts, leaning forwards to straighten it.

He must have sensed her outside because he glanced towards the window, his eyebrows pinched together in a frown and she stood, making a point of not looking in his direction as she jogged up the road. *Phew, that was close.* Her heart was flip flopping all over the place and she stopped when she reached a junction, puffing hard as she tried to catch her breath.

Looking back down the estate, she could see there was no way to get round the back of his house; the garden backing onto another house directly behind and bordered by houses on either side. Not much potential for spying on him here. And the estate was relatively new so there were no large trees or bushes or even garden walls to hide behind. Her shoulders slumped with disappointment. She'd have to find another way to discover what was going on in his life.

She jogged back down the road to her car, allowing herself a glance towards his house as she passed, but he'd drawn the curtains now, so there was no point hanging around. Better to focus on other potential points of contact, but at least she knew where he lived now.

* * *

On the way home, she did a quick shop, keen to keep up her healthy diet. Now she'd started it, even after only three weeks, she was beginning to feel different, more energised. She was also sleeping better, and her skin was a healthier colour. Project Theo was doing her good and soon she'd be ready to meet him for the first time.

Back at home, she made her evening meal then sat down to do a bit of research. She needed to know more about Theo as a person if she was going to get close to him. The secret to successful dating, she believed, was to make her interests align with his so he believed he'd found his soulmate.

First though, she was curious to find out what had happened between him and his wife. He seemed to use his Insta feed like an online photograph album, with the comments meaning little to anyone other than him, which suggested he liked to keep his private life private. Maybe she could look at his wife's social media, see if she was the one who'd found herself a new partner. She wriggled in her chair. Time to discover a bit more about Mrs Emilia Heaton.

Google was her friend, throwing up a whole list of search findings and she skimmed through, building a picture of Theo's wife.

Italian-born Emilia Heaton had been a paediatric doctor at the hospital. So that was their common ground: both she and Theo were in the medical profession, and it no doubt explained how they'd met. But she didn't appear to have any social media, which was odd. Anna carried reading on down the list until she saw something that made her do a double take. A news report from two years ago with the headline:

Local doctor drowns

Anna's eyes widened. She hadn't been expecting that. She skimmed through the rest of the article then went back and read it more slowly to make sure she wasn't mistaken.

In a tragic accident, local paediatric doctor Emilia Heaton, aged 49, wife of surgeon Theo Heaton and mother to Luna (29) and Gino (27), has drowned. She had been off work for some time with health issues but had been due to return to her post at the hospital next week. The family home is situated on the banks of the Menai Straits, where it appears she may have fallen from the jetty. Her daughter came home to find her missing and raised the alarm, but it was only today, almost a week later, that her body was found by local fishermen.

Anna sat back in her chair, cradling her wine glass, shocked by her findings. Theo's wife had died just weeks before Ollie.

That would explain him not being focused on the job and some of the 'mitigating circumstances'. But still her heart didn't thaw, her certainty didn't waver. He was the one who'd left the swab and surgical implement inside Ollie's body in the first operation. He'd had a chance to put it right and had just made matters worse. Surely he shouldn't even have been back at work after his wife had died so tragically, or he should have handed over to somebody else if he wasn't in the right frame of mind. Then Ollie might still be alive.

Anger lodged in her chest, all those terrible times coming back, sending a wave of emotion crashing over her, crushing her until the tears started to fall. It wasn't one of the anguished sobbing fits she used to experience, but a quieter, angrier sadness that had its own voice, its own plaintive howl.

Sometimes it was too hard being half of a whole, living half the life she should have had, experiencing everything by herself instead of having someone to share things with. Theo hadn't just taken Ollie's life, he'd taken her future too.

It shouldn't have happened. There was no two ways about it. *It. Should. Not. Have. Happened.* She wiped her tears with the back of her hand, more determined than ever to get her revenge. But she mustn't get ahead of herself, this plan of hers was going to take patience and there was no way of knowing if it would work.

It was time to dig deeper. Time to actually think about meeting the man face to face. But even as she daydreamed about their first encounter and how she would present herself, one thought kept swinging back into her mind like a boomerang. *If you live by a body of water and are used to the dangers, how on earth do you manage to fall off a jetty and drown?*

6

The next morning was her appointment at the beauty clinic and she came away with plumper lips and Botoxed areas around her mouth, eyes and forehead. It felt weird, numb and she wasn't sure she would put herself through the same procedures again. She studied herself in the mirror, thinking she did look younger, her lips more luscious, although she'd only had a little bit of filler, nervous to overdo it.

When she got back home, she found more of her new clothes had arrived and she spent a while trying everything on, wondering if she had enough now or whether there were still gaps in her wardrobe. She pulled on her new gym outfit, slate-grey leggings and a matching crop top, something she wouldn't have dared to wear a few months ago. But she didn't care now because this wasn't about being herself. This was about playing a part and that made it different.

She was slender enough; that was never going to be a problem after she'd turned into a walking skeleton over the last two years. However, her new diet had encouraged her to eat more and put on a bit of weight, so she looked relatively healthy now. However, her ribs were still visible, and her arms were stick thin, lacking any sort of shape. A bit of time in the gym was going to be good for her, she decided, even if her plan didn't work out.

Deciding there was no time like the present, she kept her gym kit on, slipped a hot-pink fleece jacket over the top and shoved her feet into her new, bright-white trainers. She checked herself in the mirror, smiling at the end result. Not bad, she decided, things were going in the right direction in terms of her improved appearance. She took a picture and uploaded it onto her new Insta account, in her maiden name, Anna Meadows, captioning it:

Day 1 at the gym

The gym was quiet, it being a Thursday afternoon and not yet stuffed with the after-work crowd; exactly what she wanted for her first session. A young man, Gethin, probably mid-twenties, greeted her and said he would do the induction tour. He had amazing shoulders, and biceps that Popeye would have been proud of, and she had to stop herself from staring as he demonstrated all the equipment and sorted out a training programme for her. He also introduced her to another of the trainers, a young woman called Tanya, who would be there to help if Gethin was not available.

'You want to start slow and gradually build up the reps,' Gethin said, as he set up the leg press machine. 'Then we can up the weights. But don't be impatient or you'll end up hurting yourself, then you'll have to stop coming for a bit and I can tell you now, it's a nightmare to get started again.' He rolled his eyes. 'Believe me, I'm speaking from experience. I used to be the world's worst at trying to do too much too soon.'

Anna laughed. She actually laughed, for the first time in two years and it felt so alien she wondered what was happening. As she did her first ten reps on the machine, Gethin corrected her technique and shouted, 'Good job,' when she'd finished, giving her a high five before telling her to go again. This could be fun, Anna thought, once she'd done her three sets and moved on to the next machine.

The routine Gethin had organised for her covered all the big muscle groups in her body and by the end, she knew she'd done some exercise, her legs a little shaky, her arms feeling like she'd struggle to pick up a tin of baked beans. But she was glowing, and it was in this state, rounding the corner to the changing rooms, that she ran slap-bang into Theo. Literally walked into him.

She was too shocked to speak, panic freezing her brain. They weren't supposed to meet yet. Her timetable had given her three weeks at the gym to get a bit of shape into her body before their first encounter. Her heart was racing, her mind searching for ideas as to what she should do. She was hot and sweaty, her hair stuck to her forehead, her cheeks glowing red.

I'm not ready.

'God, I'm so sorry,' he said, his hands grabbing her shoulders to stop her from slapping into the wall as the collision sent her off balance. 'Are you okay?'

She glanced up at him and could see only concern in his eyes. And what lovely eyes they were, even more striking than in his photos. This is the opportunity you've been waiting for, she told herself, giving him a broad smile, showing off her newly whitened teeth. 'It's okay,' she said, 'no harm done.'

She returned his gaze, confident that he wouldn't know who she was. They had never actually met after Ollie's death, with Theo sending one of his minions to break the news that her husband had died. How cowardly was that? A spark of anger fired in her heart, and she quickly smothered it, keeping the smile plastered to her face. *Cool it*, she told herself. *Now is not the time for anger.*

'I'm such a klutz,' he said. 'Honestly, I can't apologise enough.'

He had a lovely mellow voice, the sort that would calm you down if you were having a bit of a moment. His eyes were appraising her, holding her gaze a little longer than she would have thought necessary, and she was aware she'd piqued his interest. He had big hands, was taller than she'd thought and when he let her go it was as though he'd left indelible handprints on her skin.

'It's fine,' she said, her cheeks aching now because she was unused to keeping a smile on her face for this long.

He finally broke his gaze and moved to the side to let her pass. She thought he might still be watching her as she walked towards the ladies' changing rooms, but she couldn't look behind to check. Men like him enjoyed the chase. She had to play it cool, not be too eager and anyway, it was too soon.

Thinking it over as she got showered, she decided bumping into him like that was actually a good thing, because it had happened naturally, nothing fake about it. It was a nice bonus, she thought, as she dressed in the jeans and jumper she'd brought with her, a satisfied grin on her face. Maybe this was going to be easier than she'd thought. *But it's a Thursday*. She frowned. He was never here on a Thursday. Monday, Wednesday and Friday, those were his days. Then she corrected herself. Those were the days he posted, which wasn't the same as being the days he was actually here. Hmm, perhaps she'd have to change her planned schedule, if she was going to 'accidentally' bump into him again.

* * *

In the end, she decided to go to the gym every day at the same time and hope she might see him again at the end of her session, when she wouldn't be embarrassed by how easy her routine was. If that didn't work, she could try going later or earlier in the day. There was no real rush, because it would be better if her body had gained a bit of muscle definition before she started her charm offensive. The problem was, she had no idea what sort of working hours a surgeon would have, so it was going to be hit and miss for a bit.

Still, she thought, as she headed home, feeling weary but cheerful, she'd taken the first step. She'd actually met him, and she was sure he'd remember her, given his lingering look. In fact, she couldn't have engineered a better first meeting if she'd planned it.

'Thanks, Ollie,' she muttered, looking up at the sky, sure that he'd have her back in this project. He always had when he was alive. That was probably one of the reasons why his death had hit her so hard. He was the sensible one in their relationship, the organised one, the person who made the difficult decisions. Once he'd gone, she was left with all that to do by herself and it had been a shock because she was naturally scatty. 'Blame my artistic brain,' she'd told him so many times when she'd locked herself out again or misplaced her car keys. It was like she'd had to retrain herself to be a competent human being, now she didn't have him to lean on.

Every cloud has a silver lining though and being forced into singledom, she'd found ways to manage. Project Theo was an additional step forward, giving her a new sense of purpose and she was sure she was functioning better. Maybe it was because she was looking forwards now, rather than living in the past. And eating better. Sleeping better. Whatever the reason, she decided it was a gift from the universe, possibly from her husband, that she would enjoy.

Is Ollie really helping me do this? She stopped and considered that question for a moment. *Would he even approve of my plan?*

She started to question herself when she arrived back at the apartment, her stomach muscles quivering like jelly now. Ollie had been all about fairness, hated injustice and had dragged her along to many marches and demonstrations when they'd been students. She'd admired his principles, his willingness to be open and honest about his values. But how would he feel about her involvement in a scheme that was inherently dishonest, leading a man on purely to be able to gather information that would allow her to break him in some way?

She shook the question out of her head. The truth was, she was a helpless minnow in life. Theo was in a different situation, having money and power. How was she supposed to make him understand what he'd done? The only power she had was her femininity, and using herself as a lure was the best that she could do. And if she was doing her best, then surely Ollie would understand.

7

Three weeks later, Anna had upped her weights and was starting to
look different. Her belly muscles had tightened, her legs had a bit of
shape, as did her buttocks and arms. She even had the slight swell
of shoulder muscles. She really hadn't expected a result quite so
quickly, but she'd been exercising daily, and Gethin had been
pushing her all the way.

'You're my star student,' he announced when Anna managed
proper press-ups, something she could only dream about when
she'd started.

She laughed, delighted. 'I'll let you into a secret, I've been practising at home as well.' She'd sorted out a bedtime exercise routine
for herself and once she'd got into the swing of it, she found she
liked it, and it helped her feel relaxed last thing at night.

Gethin gave her a high five. 'That's what I wish all my clients
would do.' He checked his watch. 'Perfect timing. I've got another
client due now.' He gave a dramatic sweep of his hand across his
brow. 'No rest for the wicked, you know.'

Anna laughed again and grabbed her towel, giving her red,
sweaty face a wipe before heading towards the changing rooms.

Tanya, the other trainer, was in there, washing her hands. 'Hey, how are you doing? I saw you in there, really going for it.'

Anna smiled, surprised Tanya had noticed while she was working with another client. 'I know. I can't believe the difference in such a short time.' She grinned. 'Three proper press-ups.'

Tanya gave her the thumbs up. 'That's brilliant. You go, girl.' She dried her hands and came and sat on the bench beside Anna. 'Hey, I don't suppose you fancy a drink before you head off? I'm on my break now and we never seem to have time for a chat.'

Anna's immediate reaction was to say no, but she caught herself before the words were out of her mouth and smiled. She liked Tanya and had done a few sessions with her when Gethin had been on a different shift. She could be a useful source of information because Anna hadn't seen Theo at the gym again, but Tanya might have a better idea about his routine. No harm in asking. She grinned. 'That would be lovely.'

* * *

The on-site cafe was next to the reception area with windows looking out into the street. They served all sorts of healthy snacks and drinks and Tanya bought them a couple of energy balls to go with their green smoothies. Anna eyed hers suspiciously.

'What's in this thing?'

'Try it. I'm not going to tell you till you've had a bite.'

It looked like a dung ball, but Anna didn't say that. Instead, she nibbled a tiny mouthful, surprised that it tasted of chocolate and peanuts and salted caramel. She took another bite. 'Oh my God, that's delicious.'

Tanya laughed 'I know, right? Looks disgusting, tastes amazing. That seems to be the theme with the snacks in here and believe me, I've tried them all. This is raw chocolate, so pretty healthy. It'll give you a boost after the hard work you put in today.' She smiled at her and took a sip of her green smoothie. 'I'm so proud of your progress and I was wondering...' She hesitated, looked a little uncomfortable, her hands fidgeting with her napkin. 'Would you mind if I used you as a case study? I'm in the middle of an online course and need to show what I'm doing with real clients to put what I'm learning into practice. I know Gethin is your trainer really, but we've done a few sessions now, haven't we? So I'm claiming you as mine as well.'

Anna thought for a moment, but could see no reason to refuse. 'Yeah, no worries. I don't mind if you do. But... would you mind using my maiden name instead of my married name?' When she'd registered at the gym, she'd had to produce ID and only had a driver's licence in her married name, so had registered under that, which she could now see was a mistake if she wanted to be incognito.

Tanya, shrugged. 'Makes no difference to me.' She leant towards Anna. 'I sense a story here.' She settled back in her chair, raised an eyebrow in question.

Anna thought for a moment, then decided Tanya could be a useful ally and was more likely to be on her side if she knew a bit more of the truth. It didn't mean she had to tell her everything, did it?

'Okay, so I'm a widow.' She sighed and glanced down at her drink, while she let the inevitable wave of emotion wash through her. It always happened, every time she mentioned Ollie's death. But she'd learnt to ride the wave, let the emotion go, then she was able to speak without breaking down. 'There's nothing untoward going on, I can assure you. But there's this guy...'

Tanya gave a sympathetic smile. 'I'm so sorry for your loss, that must have been hard at such a young age. But I'm glad to hear you're ready to move on.' She leant towards her, clearly intrigued. 'Come on, tell me more.'

'I bumped into him the first time I was here. I mean we literally walked into each other and he was... cute. And I thought he was interested in me. But I haven't seen him here since.' She got her phone out of her bag and pulled up Theo's profile picture. 'This guy. Do you know him?'

'Oh, I see you've done a bit of detective work already.' Tanya reached for her phone and looked at the screen. 'How did you manage that? I'm impressed.'

Goddammit. Anna couldn't think of what to say, having backed herself into a corner. What would be a legitimate reason for having Theo's profile on her phone?

'I... um. I thought I recognised him from the hospital. When my mum had an op. She remembered his name and then I found him on Facebook.'

Tanya didn't need to know that Anna's mum lived in Spain with her dad. Her explanation sounded plausible and that was all that mattered. She ate the rest of her energy ball to give herself time to calm down while Tanya studied the picture.

'The handsome Theo.' She gave a harsh laugh. 'Many others have tried and failed to attract his attention, I can tell you.'

'Really?'

'Well, look at the guy. Who wouldn't want a piece of that?'

'He's... single?'

Tanya popped the last of her energy ball into her mouth. 'Shall I put you on the list?'

Anna laughed, her eyes on the street outside, watching people walking past. Her face was burning and she felt a bit stupid. This was a crazy idea of hers. 'I suppose if he's that popular, I don't have much of a chance.'

Tanya took a sip of her smoothie, shook her head. 'Why should you have less chance than anyone else? You're gorgeous and we'll have you looking totally toned in no time.'

Anna gave a wistful sigh. 'I've been hoping to bump into him again, but I haven't seen him.'

'That's because he's been away. Off to Sicily with his kids to visit their grandparents.'

Anna's heart skipped and she seized the opportunity to learn more. 'Oh, with his children.' She feigned ignorance, thinking she might get more information that way.

'Grown up. I think his daughter is thirtyish, and the son is a couple of years younger. He dotes on his kids.'

'Right.' Anna took a sip of her smoothie and had to make an effort not to spit it back out again. It was green and bitter with the consistency of pond slime. 'Sounds like you know him quite well.'

Tanya shrugged. 'I've known him since I started work here about three years ago. We even went on a date. Well, it wasn't a proper date. He needed a plus one for a work dinner, so I said I'd go. It was only a couple of months after his wife died, and he wasn't in great shape emotionally, so I went along for moral support.'

Anna sensed an opportunity to fill in some of the gaps in her knowledge about Theo. Maybe get answers to questions that were bothering her.

'His wife died?' she said, acting like she didn't already know. 'I'd just assumed his marriage had broken down.' It was an unavoidable lie; how could she admit she'd been researching the guy without coming across as stalkerish?

Tanya pursed her lips. 'She drowned, poor woman. The family home is on the Menai Straits. Honestly, it's fabulous, but anyway... she jumped off the jetty. That's the theory. She'd been off work with stress, and things weren't great between them.' She sighed, finished off her smoothie. 'The coroner gave a verdict of suicide. There was a note.' She looked Anna in the eye. 'The police were happy there were no suspicious circumstances in case you were wondering. Because foul play had to be an option, didn't it?'

Anna stayed silent, letting the information percolate into her brain. A slightly different story to the news report. She didn't think she could push for more. Probably best to eke it out of Tanya over time, than bombard her with questions now. 'That's really sad, but it seems like he's moved on now.'

Tanya laughed. 'Oh, he'd moved on well before his wife drowned. Their relationship had completely broken down. They'd been talking about divorce, but neither of them wanted to give up the house.'

Something about that house was making her curious to know more, but it sounded like Theo was a bit of a player.

'Oh, talk of the devil,' Tanya said, looking over Anna's shoulder and beckoning to someone behind her. 'Theo, you're back.'

Anna tensed, her eyes wide in horror, making Tanya giggle. She turned and there he was, looking tanned and relaxed in a white shirt and grey chinos. A blush suffused her skin and she felt suddenly awkward, like being back at school.

'Theo, this is Anna, our star client.'

He looked at her for a moment then laughed. 'I remember you. We bumped into each other, didn't we?'

She gathered herself and gave him a full wattage smile. 'That's right. At least I know your name now, Theo.' It sounded weird saying it out loud, making a more definite connection.

'It's lovely to meet you properly.' His hand dropped to her shoulder, and she felt a tingle radiate through her body.

'Why don't you join us?' Tanya asked, a mischievous smirk on her lips.

He shook his head. 'Sorry, I would but I can't stop. I was just looking for Jez, but I can see he's not here. I've got to head up to the hospital.' His eyes lingered on Anna. 'Another time though. I'm here most days, but it depends on my shifts. They've been all over the place.'

A man came in and slapped him on the back. 'Theo, been looking for you, mate.'

Theo said his goodbyes and left the cafe, deep in conversation with the man who was presumably Jez.

'Hmm, I think he's got the hots for you,' Tanya said with a wink.

'Don't be daft,' Anna blustered, secretly hoping she was right. He'd held eye contact and made a point of touching her, though. That was a good sign, wasn't it? It was almost ten years since she'd dated and she felt out of her depth, floundering in waters that were so deep she couldn't see the bottom.

Tanya was due back from her break, so she left Anna at the table with the rest of her pondweed smoothie. She waited until she'd gone before leaving her untouched drink on the table, the memory of its taste sending an involuntary shudder through her body. She wouldn't be falling for that one again. But there was a spring in her step, knowing that she'd moved forwards with her project, with useful information assimilated and introductions made. That had to be a win. And he knew who she was now.

* * *

At home, as soon as Anna walked through the door, the weight of her sadness hit her out of nowhere. It was weird how it happened like that sometimes. Ollie's shoes were still on the rack in the hall, his coats hanging on the hooks above. She buried her nose in the fabric, but all the scent of him had gone now. Her shoulders dropped and she stood for a moment, overtaken by a deep malaise, reminded of what she'd lost.

She sighed and walked into the living room, noticing for the first time how dusty it was, the windows grubby and smeared.

Ollie's picture sat on the mantelpiece, next to a wedding photo and another she'd taken on their wedding anniversary, the day he'd been taken ill. She went over and picked them up, one by one, giving him a hug and a kiss, the emptiness in her heart no less than the day he'd died.

'I love you, sweetheart,' she whispered, stroking his face. 'This is for you, making it right so you can rest in peace.'

In her heart, she knew this was the crux of it all. It wasn't just about *her* being able to move on once justice was done. Ollie needed it so he could move on too. How could his spirit possibly be at rest when his life had been so cruelly taken from him? She thought this was why she was finding it so hard to let go, wanting to do this last kindness for him, to find some means of reparation. Something to make up for the disappointing response of the health board who'd decided to turn a blind eye and pretend that nobody had done anything wrong. They'd brushed the incident aside like his death didn't matter. Just one of those things, and she'd been unable to argue with the system, unable to persuade them there was a case to answer.

She'd reached a dead end going down the formal complaints route and although senior staff had listened to what she had to say and had been very sympathetic to her plight, she felt they'd lost patience with her and eventually stopped responding.

I'm doing this for you, Ollie.

That night, she went to bed feeling unsettled, her mind full of everything she'd learnt about Theo. She even dreamt about him, but her romantic dream turned into a nightmare when hands shoved her from behind and she realised she was in dark, swirling waters, the force of the currents dragging her under, as she struggled to breathe.

8

Anna decided to keep to her routine for the time being and just hope she might see Theo at the gym again. The following week, she was on the leg press machine, totally focused on doing her reps, when his voice cut into her thoughts.

'Anna, I was hoping I might bump into you again.' His voice reminded her of a Radio 2 DJ, easy to listen to, nothing jarring.

She was so flustered, the strength went out of her legs and the weights clattered down with such a crash, several heads turned in alarm. He held up a hand, looked around at everyone. 'Sorry, my fault,' he called out, laughing. 'Everything's okay.'

Her turned and gave her a cheeky grimace. 'Oops.'

She laughed. 'I'd almost finished, anyway. Are you waiting to come on this one?'

'No, I saw you when I came in and thought I'd come and say hello. I'm starting on the treadmill to warm-up.'

She glanced over, noticed two treadmills free next to each other, and smiled at him. 'Oh, that's a coincidence. I'm ready for a cool-down. I'll walk with you if you like?'

In reality, she was only halfway through her routine, but this was an opportunity too good to miss.

'Yeah, great. Why not?'

She could feel his eyes appraising her as she got up off the machine and walked over to the treadmill, adding a more exaggerated sashay to her hips. Her bum looked good in these leggings and Tanya had commented that her glutes had tightened up. She smiled to herself as she hopped onto the treadmill and adjusted the settings to the right speed, thinking her muscle structure had been a complete mystery to her before she'd started training. Now she knew where everything was and what she had to do to make it look good. Who knew that's where her mind would be at?

She glanced at Theo who was walking at twice the speed she was, his arms pumping, eyes focused on the wall ahead.

'That's fast for a warm-up,' she said, surreptitiously upping her speed a little.

'I do a couple of miles at this speed, then I jog for another couple of miles.' He was already puffing, and she wondered if he was trying to impress her. She had an inkling he might be.

'Are you training for anything in particular?' She gasped, not sure how long she could manage at this speed.

'No, I just like to keep in shape. I'm a surgeon and see so many people who haven't looked after themselves, it sort of rams it home how important it is.' He laughed. 'I think I've become a bit obsessed.'

'A surgeon,' she said, as if she didn't know. 'Tough job.'

He glanced at her. 'Yeah, sometimes. But I like being able to help people. That's why I do it.'

And what about when you kill someone? she thought, her lips pressed tight to stop the question from blurting out. How on earth was she going to stomach being close to this man when she knew what he'd done?

It's not going to work. This is a stupid idea. What the heck was I thinking?

He ramped up his speed and she slowed hers down. Sod trying to impress him, she decided. A few minutes later, she stopped her machine while he was still pounding away on his, completely in the zone, seemingly oblivious to everything around him. She picked up her towel and made her way across the gym towards the changing rooms.

'Anna!' She turned when he called her name, watched him hurrying towards her. He stopped in front of her, puffing hard, sweat trickling down his face. She could smell him, an earthy muskiness that awakened a basic instinct, warming her from the core of her being. 'I was wondering if you fancied grabbing something to eat this evening? I should be finished at seven if that works for you?'

No, she thought, anger burning in her chest. *That will never work for me.*

'I'm sorry, I've already got something on tonight.' She gave him a quick smile. 'A friend's birthday.'

He looked a little confused, clearly not used to being turned down. 'Another night then?'

She wondered what it was about certain men who liked a woman they had to chase. It seemed Theo was that sort of guy. Through the red haze of her rage, she realised she'd done it. She'd achieved her goal. He'd asked her out on a date. Her plan could work after all, if she could stomach being near him for any length of time. *It's for Ollie,* she reminded herself, knowing she would walk to the ends of the earth and back to get justice for her lovely husband. *I can do this.* She did a mental fist pump.

'I've got quite a lot on,' she lied, flashing him an apologetic smile. 'It'll have to be next week now. How about Tuesday?'

He nodded, wiping the sweat from his eyes. 'That sounds great, but I'll need your number. Just so I can let you know if my shifts change.'

Smooth, she thought, *very smooth*.

They exchanged numbers and she walked back to the changing rooms with a spring in her step, feeling proud of herself.

* * *

Making him wait to see her would suggest she had an active social life, but she realised her social media would need some attention to back up that image in case he looked her up. To that end, she made herself go to a local Indian restaurant and photobombed a table of people enjoying themselves, pretending she was with them. Then she went to a nightclub and got one of the bouncers to pose with her for a selfie while she wrapped herself around him as if they were pals. At least she hadn't had to go inside. A few snaps of scenery, cups of coffee and cake. Finally, Tanya took some pictures at the gym, which she wanted for her course work, but they were good for Anna to post as well.

Her profile was coming along nicely, and she had almost a thousand followers now. Tanya's pictures of her had generated a lot of interest. They were close-ups of different parts of her body while she was using the machines. Lots of men seemed attracted to those for some reason and she'd ended up having to block a few after inappropriate comments.

'How's it going with Theo?' Tanya asked when they were having lunch together a couple of days later. 'Have you managed to catch up with him again?'

Anna laughed. 'It just so happens I did. But I decided maybe I wasn't interested after all, then he came running after me, asking me out to dinner.'

'Oh yes, he loves the chase. Not sure he's committed to anything after that though. I said no to him a few times after I went to that work meal with him.'

'So why didn't it work out between you two?'

Tanya smiled. 'Oh, I met somebody else. And it was never going to be the start of a relationship. For me, it was never a proper date, I just felt sorry for the guy.' She checked her watch and picked up her bag. 'I've got a client coming in soon, so I've got to dash, but I'd just say... tread carefully and watch your back. You might find there's three people in any relationship with Theo.'

Anna felt unsettled by her words. What on earth could she mean?

9

On the evening of their first date, Anna was a bundle of nervous energy, telling herself it would be fine, absolutely fine, while not believing a word of it.

'Why am I doing this to myself?' she asked her reflection in the mirror as she applied her make-up, in a rush now because she'd taken so long to decide what to wear. In the end, she'd gone for smart casual and the understated elegance of midnight-blue capri pants and a silver-grey silk shirt. She'd never worn silk before and it felt so lovely against her skin, all slinky and soft.

Not bad, she decided, looking at the finished effect, allowing herself a smile.

Her stomach grumbled. She'd been too nervous to eat much today, oscillating between wanting to tell him she couldn't make it and being keen to go. This was the first big step for her. The first chance to get close and have a proper conversation with the man. Maybe she'd learn all she needed to know tonight, find a weak point that she could use for his destruction, then she wouldn't need to put herself through this again. She clung to that thought, needing every ounce of the mental strength it gave her. How was she going to behave normally when all she wanted to do was gouge his eyes out? Scream at him that he was a murderer?

The doorbell rang. Her heart jumped. *Oh God. This is a stupid idea.* Another one of her impulsive, idiotic decisions. What had happened to her brain since Ollie had died? She couldn't understand what she was thinking half the time and had made so many stupid decisions.

You're doing it for Ollie, she reminded herself as she took one last look in the mirror before gathering her red jacket and slipping her feet into matching shoes.

'You look beautiful,' Theo said, when she opened the door. A compliment that made her feel so flustered she couldn't think how to reply.

'Thank you,' she mumbled, turning to lock the door behind her. She felt hot and bothered and totally unprepared.

Calm down, she told herself. *It's a meal. Just a meal. You can call time on the whole thing after this if you want.*

She followed him to his Porsche, parked on the double yellow lines outside her house, embarrassed by the shabbiness of the area. *This is so not going to work.*

Theo was taking her to a restaurant in Menai Bridge on Anglesey, which looked out over the Menai Straits.

It was December, but relatively mild, and he led her outside to a seating area on the decking. The patio heaters were on and they wrapped blankets round their legs, watching the moonlight sparkle on the water, turning it into a river of stars. They were sitting next to each other on a sofa, and his arm had snaked round her shoulders, his fingers stroking the back of her neck. Despite herself, she couldn't deny it was a delicious sensation and, if she was a cat, she knew she'd be purring. The whole thing was romantic with a capital 'R'.

It doesn't mean anything, she told herself. *Purely a chemical reaction.*

'It's so beautiful, isn't it?' she said, sipping her gin and tonic, trying to sound relaxed.

'I love it. There's no better place in the world. That's why we moved into the Boat House, even though it was falling down when we bought it.'

He didn't know she knew he was living by the water, on the Bangor side of the Straits. Here was her opportunity to delve a little deeper into that particular mystery. Why was he renting a house in Bangor if he already had a house? Was it something to do with his wife's death?

She frowned. 'What's the Boat House? Is it down this way? I thought you said you lived up near the hospital.'

'Oh, I'm just renting while I have the kitchen and bathroom re-done. And the decorators are coming in to give the place a freshen up. A full makeover really and we've only got as far as the ripping everything out stage.'

'Sounds like a good idea to be out of there while they make a mess. I've watched the TV programmes and I honestly couldn't cope with all that dust and dirt and noise.'

He laughed. 'I'll admit I feel the same, that's why I decided to move out.' He took a sip of his beer. 'I suppose I should have done it a while ago, but I didn't have the heart after Emilia...' She glanced at him, saw him staring into the distance, or was he staring at his house. It was definitely in that direction. 'It was my daughter's idea. Luna thought we might feel more comfortable if we made some changes. "Refresh and renew", she said. So, I've given her a budget and left her to it.'

Anna was curious to know more about his children. Perhaps *they* would be his weak spot. 'That's very trusting. What if you don't like it?'

He laughed. 'Oh, she's told me what she's doing, and I've seen the plans and we've chosen the general colour scheme together. But I don't want to have to make decisions on where the plug sockets need to go and what the worktops are going to be made of and what shape of taps to get.' He took another sip of his drink and she glanced at him again, noticing how the moonlight gave his face an air of mystery, half in the light, half in darkness. 'I had enough of that when we did it up the first time. But Emilia thrived on the project and Luna is very like her mum.'

His eyes were still on the water. The same body of water that had claimed his wife's life. Was that what he was thinking about? 'Hopefully she'll settle better once it's done.' He sighed. 'She's struggled since her mum died, can't seem to decide what she wants to do with her life.'

Their conversation up to this point had been light-hearted and jokey but he was in a serious mood now and a thrill of excitement thrummed through her body. Could this be the night she made a breakthrough? She needed to keep this conversation going, see what more she could find out.

'So... you live with your daughter?' Was that what Tanya meant about three people in a relationship?

He nodded. 'Usually, yes. But I'll admit I'm enjoying having my rental to myself. Luna's stayed at the Boat House so she can micro-manage the builders and decorators and whoever else she's got coming in.'

Anna laughed. 'She's brave taking on such a big project.' Theo didn't respond, lost in his thoughts. She decided to prod him a little on an earlier part of the conversation, her voice gentle. 'That must have been hard, your wife passing away.'

He gazed up at the night sky, the moon playing hide and seek behind the clouds. 'It was a terrible time for the whole family. We were all living in the house at that point. Gino was about to leave to start his new job, Luna had just come back from living with her grandparents in Italy for a year. It was a fun time, all back together. But Emilia hadn't been well and then...' His eyes dropped to his lap, and he took her hand, linked his fingers with hers, like he needed a bit of comfort. The warmth of his touch sent an unexpected flush to her skin.

Without thinking, she squeezed his hand, feeling a rush of compassion for the man. 'I'm so sorry. I didn't mean to bring up such a painful subject.' She hesitated. 'I lost my husband too.'

He caught her eye then, looked surprised. 'Really? I was wondering how a lovely woman like you could be single.'

She shrugged, concerned she might have given too much away. 'It's taken me a while to be ready to date again.'

He looked away, possibly because, from what Tanya had said, the opposite had been true for him.

'He was involved in... an accident,' she volunteered, thinking the deaths of their spouses would be a solid piece of common ground that might allow them to bond at a deeper level. Lead to more personal revelations. Then she realised he worked in the emergency department and if Ollie's accident had happened locally, he might well have been involved. 'We were on holiday,' she added, quickly.

Theo's hand tightened round hers and he leant in for a kiss, soft and gentle. She froze, not expecting a kiss so soon, but then her body was responding, and she was kissing him back, hungry for him, like he was the main course and she'd been starving for a week. It had been so long since she'd kissed someone she'd forgotten how it felt, how it could transport you away from time and space into another realm altogether. A place where all you had were your senses and the heightened awareness of another person. Someone who wanted you. For a moment she forgot who he was, relishing the kiss with a desire that consumed her.

The guy was an excellent kisser, she'd have to give him that, and, for a ridiculous moment, she wished things could be different. A cough made them spring apart, the waiter standing at their table with their meals, the scent of the food bringing her back to reality.

I kissed him. I bloody kissed him. Revulsion twisted in her stomach as Ollie's face appeared in her mind. *I had to kiss him,* she told herself. *Otherwise, he won't want another date and Project Theo will be over before it's begun.*

It was a solid justification for her treachery, and she swallowed her distaste for what she'd done, refusing to acknowledge how much she'd enjoyed the kiss. The trick was to keep herself emotionally distant, while giving the impression she was interested in him. Not easy. Not easy at all.

She asked about his daughter while they ate, wanting to learn more about the family dynamics.

'Luna kept me going after Emilia died,' he said. 'She's been my rock, helped me to carry on. Honestly, I don't know what I'd do without her.'

'That's lovely you're so close. I think I'm probably closer to my mum. My dad's all about football and he and my brother travelled all over the place watching Wrexham play.'

Theo didn't respond to her, carrying on with his own train of thought.

'We've been close since she was a baby.' He laughed, enjoying the memory. 'It was love at first sight.'

Like Ollie and me, she thought, her knife slicing through her steak and scraping on the china underneath, setting her teeth on edge, switching her focus back to her goal.

This is not a date. This is the first step in your destruction, she said to him in her head while giving him a warm smile. *Just you wait.*

10

Two months later, Anna had been on six dates with Theo. They went for walks on the beach, trips to the cinema, drives to wonderful pubs tucked away in hidden corners of Snowdonia and fancy meals in expensive restaurants. To her confusion and annoyance, she found she looked forward to their dates.

He was attentive, caring and entertaining with lots of funny anecdotes about patients, which she was sure he shouldn't be telling her. And, although she couldn't help but laugh, because the way he told the stories was hilarious, it felt wrong. She kept voice notes on everything he told her as soon as she got the opportunity, and did more research when she got home, but there was no sniff of any wrongdoing.

He didn't mention names, so she supposed he was keeping the most important elements of patient confidentiality intact, but it felt like he was making fun of people. It was the only thing she could criticise about him, but she was thankful for it, because she needed things she didn't like about him, otherwise she'd be distracted from her objective of ruining the man.

She kept herself elusive, no more than one date a week, hinting there might be other people in her life. Which there was in the form of Tanya, who'd invited her out for drinks a few times, so it wasn't a complete lie. And she let him do most of the talking, because her aim was to get information out of him. She figured the more he talked, the more likely it was that she'd find a weakness to exploit.

He was the type of guy who had a lot to say. A natural entertainer who liked being the centre of attention. But she also gave him crumbs of information about herself to keep him interested.

Now, as she got ready for their dinner date, she decided she should up her game, let him get closer. Because she needed to get into his house and have a snoop around, see what she could find. So far, he'd always taken her to places, rather than them enjoying quiet nights in at home. And although that had suited her, because it meant the question of them enjoying anything more than a kiss hadn't arisen, she was making no progress in digging up any dirt in his life. She was starting to get impatient.

Would she be willing to spend the night with him if it meant she could find out more about him? Initially, she'd squashed the thought, appalled that she'd even allowed it to enter her head. But, as time went on, she knew it was something she had to consider. *A means to an end. Nothing more.*

There's was no doubt her body responded to him, even if her mind had built a wall to keep him out. Asking herself whether she'd sleep with him had set up a squabble in her head as she kept giving herself different answers. It would be worth it if it gave her a lead, a hint of a secret he didn't want the world to know, wouldn't it? All sorts of secrets came out in pillow talk, in the glow of post-coital contentment. *But he killed Ollie, how could I even think of doing such a thing?* Then again, being in the house would give her access to his personal paperwork. Maybe he had some dodgy financial dealings going on that she could investigate while he was asleep. *I can*

*pretend he's someone else during the dreaded deed, can't I? Pretend he's
Ollie?*

On and on her thoughts went, backwards and forwards, round
and round, until she was feeling slightly sick. It would help if she
knew what she was looking for, but she had to be open minded and
cast the net wide at this stage in the project. With a heartfelt sigh,
she told herself she was getting too far ahead, and needed to focus
on what was happening tonight. That was all. She might *never* have
to sleep with him. The important thing was to delve a little deeper
into Theo's life each time they met, until she found the weakness
she was looking for.

Her head buzzed with anticipation as she looked at her glowing
reflection in the mirror. She knew this challenge had been good for
her. It had ignited a spark, awakened her from a zombie state and
she was enjoying this feeling of purpose.

In fact, it had kick-started every area of her life, including her
creativity. She'd been busy with her Etsy shop, creating a new range
of T-shirts ready for the summer season. And she found herself
singing along to music as she worked, playing songs that reminded
her of Ollie, always mindful to keep his memory alive. This felt like
their project, and she would even talk to him about it sometimes,
when she was mulling things over, trying to work out how to find
that elusive pearl of information that would bring Theo down.

* * *

They enjoyed a delicious meal at the local Italian and then, because
it was a lovely night after a week of solid rain, they had a wander
down Bangor Pier. The air was fresh and clear, the night sky lit with
a thousand stars, and she was feeling pleasantly tipsy after a few
drinks. They sat on a bench at the end of the pier, watching the
lights twinkle in the water, a breeze ruffling the surface. The smell

of brine took her back to holidays with Ollie, surfing on the Gower Peninsular, eating hot dogs from the kiosk near the beach.

It focused her mind, stopped her behaving like she was on a real date. Oh, how her foolish body tried to trick her into doing stupid things. Thank goodness Ollie was watching over her, bringing her back into line. She smiled to herself, changed the conversation, because she needed to be able to see an end to this thing before it sent her crazy.

'How are the renovations coming along? Do you think you'll be able to move back into the Boat House soon?' This would give her an idea about her timescale, and how long she had to get herself into his rental to have a snoop. Because once he was back in the Boat House, she had a niggling feeling that Luna's presence might put snooping out of the question.

'I've got the rental for six months, up to the end of April. But I think I'll see if they'll extend it for a few more months. I don't want to put her under any time pressure because she gets a bit flustered when she's stressed. Anyway, it seems to be coming along well.' He caught her eye. 'I can take you to see the house if you like? Introduce you to Luna at the same time.' He grinned at her. 'I think you two would get along great.'

Oh my word, that's a big jump forward. Having willed something to happen she didn't feel ready now that it had. *But I can't say no, can I?* And what did that tell her about where he saw their relationship going? It meant he trusted her, didn't it? Oh, this was turning out to be a very good night indeed.

She beamed at him. 'I'd love that. She sounds so impressive. I mean managing a renovation project is amazing. And your house sounds fantastic, like it's in an idyllic spot.'

His hand settled on her thigh, the warmth of his touch travelling up her leg, bringing sensations to her body she hadn't experienced in years. But she didn't want it to be *his* hand. *It should be*

Ollie's. The thought made her tense, wanting to brush his hand away, until a little voice in her head reassured her. *This is good. All part of the plan.* Ollie would understand that it meant nothing to her. Nothing at all, just part of the game she was playing.

She glanced at Theo, saw that his eyes were on her, his pupils dilated, an expression on his face that left her in no doubt what he wanted. She leant towards him, let her lips brush his, her eyes catching his gaze, lingering.

His hand caressed her leg, his fingers stroking the inside of her thigh now, bringing an immediate response from her treacherous body. 'I've been wanting to ask you this for a while now,' he murmured. 'But... will you come home with me tonight? Will you stay?'

Up until now, they'd done a lot of kissing, but not much else, she'd made sure of that. But she would have to admit that Project Theo hadn't progressed. Here was her chance to step things up a level. She hid a cringe. *Can I really, though?*

'Yes,' she whispered, before she'd even answered her own question in her head. She kissed him again. 'I'd like that.'

Oh my God, she thought. *It's happening.* She'd just agreed to go and have sex with a murderer. She'd agreed to stay the night. But in her heart, she wanted him to be dead instead of Ollie and that was the thought she would cling to. Her jaw tightened. That would get her through.

11

Theo was a considerate lover, skilled in the art of giving pleasure. His lovemaking was slow and gentle and despite herself she was lost in the moment, forgetting where she was and who she was with as she fell under his spell. She hadn't realised how lonely she'd been, how much she'd missed the intimacy and her body responded as though his touch was all she'd ever wanted.

That night, she had the first full night's sleep since Ollie had died, waking up to the smell of fresh coffee, as Theo placed a mug on the bedside table.

He gave her a lazy smile. 'I don't know about you, but I'd like to do that all again sometime very soon.' He bent down and gave her a lingering kiss, before straightening and stretching. 'Unfortunately, I've got to get ready for work, so it'll have to wait.' He pulled a sad face, making her smile.

In truth, she'd like to do it all again too, despite telling herself she hated him. Oh, how she'd loved being wrapped up in a man's embrace, the warmth of skin on skin, the whisper of his breath giving her goosebumps of pleasure. This was what he'd taken from her, but it was also what he'd given her back. Life was full of ironies and now her brain was a mess of clashing emotions.

She lingered in bed, her body listless with sleep, her mind dopey. In another world, this would be a version of heaven. But in her world, right now, she had to wake up, get with the programme. She cursed herself for sleeping so soundly, having no chance to look around. A wasted encounter. Guilt made her heart feel heavy.

It didn't mean anything, Ollie. You know that, right?

She couldn't hear his voice, there was no reply in her head, and she wondered when that had stopped. For a long time, she'd been asking him questions and talking through decisions as if he was sitting on the sofa beside her. Sometimes she thought she could feel him encouraging her in a certain direction or reassuring her she was doing great. Now there was silence. A cold emptiness. Was he angry? Did he hate her for what she'd just done as much as she hated herself?

It had been an impulsive decision, agreeing to spend the night with Theo, the latest in a long line of decisions that she'd made and instantly regretted since Ollie had died. There was something about grief that made her not care as much as she should sometimes. That's why she'd taken out a loan for a new car she couldn't afford, and been stopped three times for speeding. And there were more instances, so many more she didn't like to think about them. This was another to add to the list.

However, this felt like a step too far, especially when it hadn't progressed her cause. Mind you, she had noticed that his possessions in the property seemed very sparse and she wondered if he'd just brought essentials with him. Perhaps all his private papers were back at the Boat House and there was nothing to be found anyway.

And I just slept with him, she shouted at herself, appalled now at what she'd done.

With a sigh, she clambered out of bed and got dressed, taking a big slurp of her coffee. She wanted to go. Right now, she wanted to be home, have a good hot shower and wash the scent of this man off her. Christ, she hadn't thought it would be this hard, or that the act itself would have been so easy, hadn't anticipated these conflicting emotions tearing her heart to shreds.

On the surface, Theo appeared to be a good man. He'd certainly been lovely to her, but then he did have an ulterior motive. He wanted sex. What would he be like if she refused? Or if they got closer, when the barriers came down and she saw him on a bad day? She was intrigued to find out. His team at the hospital had certainly all stood up for him, and protected him when she was sure one of them could have told the authorities what had really happened. Then he would have been in trouble, then she would have had her justice. Something had kept them bound together, all supporting each other. They could have ruined him, but they didn't. So why was that? Was it because they loved him, or because they were frightened of him?

Perhaps she needed to engineer some conflict, see how he reacted. But then, that wasn't going to suit her purpose. If she was going to find an opportunity to delve deeper into his life, she needed to be low maintenance. Someone who would be there for him, who could give him all the emotional support he might need.

God, this is exhausting.

He came back into the room as she was pulling on her shoes, her bag ready by her side.

'Can I drive you home?' He checked his watch. 'I've just got time to drop you off.'

She shook her head. 'No, it's okay. I'm going to walk.' She laughed. 'Got to get my ten thousand steps in, you know. And I could do with some fresh air to clear my head.'

When she stood, ready to go, he pulled her to him for a last, lingering kiss, his arms encircling her, holding her close.

'Oh, what you do to me,' he murmured, as he looked into her eyes, the back of his hand stroking her cheek. 'I can't stop thinking about you.' He laughed. 'It's ridiculous. I'm like a bloody teenager. But it's also wonderful as well. I never thought I'd feel this way about anyone again.'

Her heart was pounding, his words sounding sincere, but maybe he said this to all his conquests.

'Neither did I,' she replied, giving him one last kiss before pulling away.

'Can I see you tomorrow?' he asked, catching her hand, stopping her from leaving. This was a new development and for a moment she was flustered, unsure what to say. They normally saw each other once a week and he'd seemed happy with that.

Oh God, he wants more sex. The thought made her feel nauseous.

'We could go over to the Boat House, if you like. I'm supposed to be catching up with Luna to confirm some decisions.' He rolled his eyes. 'I'll need moral support. That girl can wrap me around her little finger, so if she's telling me she's going with leopard print wallpaper, I'll be depending on you to pipe up and suggest that might not be a good idea.'

'Oh, right, like a wicked stepmother type of person?' she teased, appalled by her choice of words.

'No, no, no. You'd be a wonderful stepmother.' His eyes met hers, a twinkle of laughter making them sparkle. 'The voice of reason, that's all I need.'

'Okay,' she said, slowly taking her hand from his. 'That sounds like fun.'

'Brilliant. I can't wait for you to meet her.'

* * *

The next night, a persistent drizzle hung in the air, making them run from the car into the house. She'd been here before, at the height of her grief, wanting to confront him, but her timing hadn't been right. When she'd complained to her mum, she'd had a stern word with her.

'Look, love, I know this is hard. I know it seems so unfair and I understand that your heart is broken. But you can't live your life blaming people. All that does is keep you stuck in the same place. The hospital has investigated, and they've said it was an unfortunate accident.' She sighed, her mum's face looking more creased and careworn every time they did a video call. Anna knew she was worried about her and now her voice was firm, her tone saying she needed to listen. 'I think you have to accept that. Of course you must grieve for Ollie, but don't dwell on the surgeon. He was doing his best. Everyone has a bad day, but it doesn't mean he should be punished. You need to leave the poor guy alone.'

Anna's bereavement therapist had said the same thing. Then her dad had repeated the message, said he didn't want to hear another word about Theo. And at that point, she came to her senses, and she did stop her stalking activities. But it didn't help her to move on. Not even a tiny step. All she could hear was Ollie's voice saying, 'I shouldn't have died. I should still be with you, moving into our new house, having adventures, starting our family.' So she moved her stalking online instead and stopped talking to anyone about what she was thinking.

She shook the thoughts from her head, telling herself she needed to pay attention as she followed Theo into a huge open space. The furniture was huddled in the middle of the room, covered with dust sheets, leaving the walls clear to be painted. To the right was the bones of a kitchen, an L-shaped run of white marble worktops, with a matching island, still under construction.

A giant American style fridge sat against the far wall, a fitted oven and microwave at the other end, a sink in the middle. There were boxes and bits of wood and piping all over the place and the floor was covered in a fine layer of dust.

To the left was a floor-to-ceiling window, the full width of the house, looking out over the Menai Straits. The view was breathtaking, over the water to the wooded banks of Anglesey on the other side. She could see the jetty, jutting out from a thin strip of lawn beneath the window and wondered again how Emilia's death could have happened. It must have been suicide, mustn't it?

Poor woman. Was it Theo's behaviour that had driven her to take her own life?

'Dad!' a voice shrieked, and she turned to see Luna barrelling towards her father, flinging her arms round his neck in an enthusiastic welcome, her black ponytail swinging. She was dressed in denim overalls and a paint splattered white T-shirt, streaks of paint in her hair. It was a moment before she let him go and turned to Anna, brown eyes appraising her. She was a stunning looking girl, even more beautiful in real life than in the few photos on Theo's social media. 'And this must be your girlfriend.'

Theo grabbed Anna's hand, a welcome show of solidarity. 'Luna, I want you to meet Anna. She's a designer.'

Luna smiled, holding out a hand, which Anna shook. It was very formal and distant, compared to the welcome she'd just given to her father, her grasp limp and short-lived. But then she was bound to be wary of the new woman in her dad's life. Anna knew it was up to her to make a good impression and try and generate some warmth between them.

'How lovely to meet you,' she gushed. 'And what a fabulous house. Theo's been telling me what a great job you're doing managing the renovations.'

Luna smiled. 'Thank you. It's been a lot of fun but trying to get Dad to make decisions has been real hard work.' She gave her dad a playful punch on the shoulder. 'It's a bit of a mess down here still but let me show you what I've done upstairs.' She grabbed Theo's hand and tugged him towards the back of the room. He followed her lead, Anna tagging on behind, sneaking a look in the rest of the downstairs rooms.

At the back of the living area was an office, with a treatment bed in the corner opposite the door. It was decked out in bright colours, with a seating area by the window and a box of toys on the floor. The size of the seats suggested it had been used by Theo's late wife for private paediatric patients. Next door was a toilet and shower room and next door to that a utility room, with a door no doubt leading into the garage at the back.

She hurried upstairs, finding Luna and Theo in the family bathroom, the fittings in place but the walls bare and newly plastered. Theo glanced at her as she stood in the doorway, two tiles in his hands. 'What do you think, Anna? You're the designer so I know you've got an eye for these things.' He showed her the tiles, both of them types of stone. 'Do we go for the blue/grey or this sandy colour?'

Nerves stirred in her belly, and she glanced at Luna who was giving her a curious look, waiting to hear what she had to say. *Oh dear, this is difficult.* Luna probably had a favourite, and she didn't want to contradict his daughter's choice. 'It's a matter of personal preference,' she said with a shrug. 'I mean, they're both gorgeous. Whatever decision you make, you can't go wrong.'

He laughed. 'You're not helping. Luna likes the sandy colour and I like the blue. You get the casting vote.'

She pretended to study the tiles, already knowing her answer. 'The blue might make the room feel a little cool and dark maybe.

The sandy one would be lovely and warm. So, I'm going with Luna's choice.'

Luna winked at her, and she felt the tension ease in her shoulders. At least she'd got that right.

He considered the tiles for a moment. 'Okay, you might have a point. Let's go sandy then.' He gave the tiles back to Luna who flashed Anna a satisfied smile. Anna gave her the thumbs up behind Theo's back before Luna led them out of the room.

'Okay, let's have a look at your en suite now, Dad.'

They followed her into a magnificent double bedroom at the front of the house with a wall of windows looking out over the water. The view was even more breathtaking from the first floor, the mistiness of the weather giving a haunting quality to the scene, the eddies and currents more obvious from up here.

'I've got the fitted wardrobes being installed next week, halfway along this wall here,' Luna was saying, although Anna wasn't really paying attention, bewitched by the view. 'That'll be enough storage space, won't it?'

Theo tapped Anna on the shoulder to get her attention. 'What do you think? Half a wall of wardrobes should be more than enough, shouldn't it?' He laughed. 'I don't think I've got enough clothes to fill even a quarter of that space.'

'Yeah, well it's not just for clothes, Dad. We can have a shelving unit in there as well if you like. You know, it's just storage so you don't need lots of free-standing furniture cluttering the place up like you used to have. It'll look more spacious and elegant and be easier to clean.'

'Yep, you're right,' Theo said.

'Not that you ever have anything to do with the cleaning.'

Theo's expression turned to mock horror. 'Cheeky madam.' He scanned the room and Anna could tell by his body language that he'd already had enough. 'Okay, so what's next? What else do you need me to decide?'

Luna gestured for him to follow and walked into the en suite. It wasn't big enough for all of them to fit in and Anna was reluctant to be pressed into making any more decisions. This was Luna's project, not hers and she didn't want to be seen to be interfering. However, this might be an opportunity to have a bit of a nosy around, while they were occupied.

'Can I just use the downstairs bathroom?' she asked, popping her head into the en suite.

'Yes, of course,' Theo said, his eyes on a brochure of bathroom fittings, Luna pointing something out to him. It looked like shower heads, and she didn't want to be drawn into *that* conversation.

She hurried downstairs and into the back office, aware that she didn't have much time. A filing cabinet stood by the desk, and she tried to open it, but it was locked. Quickly, she turned her attention to the desk and had a frantic rummage through the drawers, acutely aware of seconds ticking away. But she couldn't find the keys to the filing cabinet or anything else of interest, the drawers being practically empty. She scanned the surface of the desk. It was an antique, walnut she thought, looking at the grain and the warm glow of the wood. A big old-fashioned blotting pad sat in the middle, covered with random jottings. She pulled the paper out and folded it, stuffing it in her handbag before hurrying to the bathroom before she was caught out.

There was probably nothing useful on there, but it was the only thing she'd been able to find that might throw up something of interest and she was loath to leave empty handed. Her heart was racing, sweat sticking her shirt to her back. She wasn't designed for covert operations, but it was the best she could do in the time available.

When she made her way back upstairs, she could hear their

voices, but the tone of the conversation appeared to have changed. And the subject.

'Look, Dad, there's no need to get all defensive. I'm just concerned, that's all.' Luna's voice was low and urgent. 'She's about the same age as me. So, I'm just thinking, what's she doing with a guy who's old enough to be her father?'

Anna stopped to listen, thinking Luna had a point. But would Theo take any notice of her? She held her breath, trying to keep as quiet as possible so she could hear what they were saying.

'It's not for you to tell me who I can have a relationship with,' he snapped. 'And a lot of young women find older men attractive. She's a widow, she's been through a lot, and age is just a number. We have fun together and that's all that matters.'

'Okay, Dad. No need to get so worked up. I'm just looking out for you. Got to be careful of gold-diggers, you know.'

Anna supposed the age gap might look a bit odd to his daughter, but when she was with Theo, she didn't even think about it. And he was right, they did have fun. Even though it hadn't been her plan, and despite herself, she had come to enjoy his company.

She was nervous about walking in on their conversation but knew she'd been away a while now and they'd be expecting her back. Talk about awkward. She crept back downstairs and then made sure to make plenty of noise as she stomped back up to the landing, so they knew she was coming.

Theo met her in the bedroom doorway and steered her back towards the stairs. 'Time to go.' His jaw was set, a hard glint in his eyes. 'I've had enough of decisions, and I've got an early start tomorrow.'

'Oh, okay. Bye, Luna,' she called. But there was no response.

Theo was already halfway down the stairs, and she hurried after him.

'Did I upset Luna in some way?'

'No, no, nothing like that. She's engrossed in deciding which shower cubicle we should have. I told her I didn't care.' He smiled and waited for her to catch up before taking her hand. 'Let's go home, shall we?'

Home.

She chewed her lip as they drove back to Theo's house, wanting to stay with him for the night again, but hating herself for even thinking it. The feeling of being desired though was too much of a pull, the draw of knowing she would have the warmth of another body next to hers. It was quite astonishing, the way her mind was able to separate the man who was making love to her from the man who'd killed her husband. How she yearned for the touch of a hand against her skin, lips on hers, limbs entwined. Now that she'd experienced it once, she craved the comfort of it again.

It's part of the process, nothing more, she told herself, putting her doubts to the back of her mind. Surely it was okay for her to enjoy a bit of physical pleasure after all this time. *But with him?* The voice in her head was horrified.

'Oh, shut up.'

'Pardon?' Theo turned to her, a quizzical look in his eye.

She laughed, a blush burning her cheeks when she realised she'd said it out loud. 'Nothing, just telling myself off for forgetting something.' She sighed. 'How do you think it went with Luna, then?'

He gave her a tight smile. 'She's fine.'

Anna knew this was a lie and decided to push for a more honest answer.

'I'm not sure she likes me being in your life, does she? I overhead the tail end of your conversation when I came back upstairs.'

Theo flashed her a concerned look before turning his attention back to the road. 'She's just not good with change. But I'm confident she'll warm to you the more she gets to know you.'

Anna wondered if Luna's wariness might jeopardise her plan. But then again, it could be something she could use. Her brain set to work. This might be exactly what she'd been looking for. Was it possible to drive a wedge between Theo and his children? Now *that* would cause him significant pain. Whether it was enough, she'd have to consider, but at last she'd found a weakness to focus on.

Ideas started forming in her mind. She smiled to herself. *Oh, this could be fun.*

12

Seven weeks later, things were going well between Anna and Theo. Her reservations had been whittled away to the point where they were the merest sliver, a quiet whisper in her mind rather than the strident shouting of dissent. If Luna was against their relationship, the way to create a distance between him and his daughter was to make Anna's bond with him stronger. So that was her mission; a change in focus for Project Theo.

She stayed over at his house a couple of nights a week now and he'd encouraged her to move clothes and personal belongings in, so she always had what she needed. Usually, they'd meet up at the gym after he'd finished work, do their training sessions, then go out for something to eat before heading home and maybe watching a movie. They were fun evenings, light-hearted, with plenty of banter about their respective performances at the gym. He certainly didn't take himself seriously and it gave her the confidence to have a laugh with him and be herself. Surprisingly, he seemed to like the real Anna, rather than the one she'd thought she'd have to pretend to be.

The thing she enjoyed most though, was the comfort of snuggling up to someone on the sofa, watching a boxset or a movie. She revelled in being part of a couple again, having someone to make her a drink, fetch the snacks, laugh with her, cover her eyes with a cushion at the scary parts. Companionship was such a valuable commodity, and she was starting to realise how lonely she'd been without Ollie.

It appeared that her plan was working, because Luna was rarely mentioned and there were no more visits to the Boat House. She hadn't yet answered the question of how long she would allow this to go on for. How she would know that her objective had been achieved but she decided it would be a little while yet. These things took time and she wanted to be certain.

The next weekend, he whisked her away on a surprise trip to Paris for her birthday, which was the most romantic thing anyone had ever done for her. They stayed in Montmartre, famous as the home of generations of French artists, in a fabulous five-star hotel.

The whole trip was about her and what she wanted, to a level she'd never experienced in a relationship before. Even Ollie had never put her preferences before his when they went away on trips. But Theo made sure they only did things she would love, things she'd talked to him about, experiences she'd had on her bucket list. In the months they'd been together, he'd really been listening and somehow, she didn't expect that from any man, let alone this one.

A highlight of the trip was when he took her shopping to the high-end fashion boutiques, where she tried on amazing outfits, marvelling at the fabrics and the cut of the cloth. He wanted to buy her a special dress but when she saw the price tag she refused. It was far too much money. Even though her aim was to break him, she found herself unable to accept that sort of gift. Which was stupid, she'd decided when she thought about it later. Why not let him bankrupt himself trying to woo her? Wouldn't that be a good thing? But she hadn't seen it at the time. Instead, she'd been fully immersed in a romantic get-away.

'I can't believe you did this for me,' she said on their final evening as they sat in a beautiful restaurant overlooking the River Seine. Her gratitude threatened to overwhelm her in an unexpected flood of tears. It had been unbearably lovely of him to be so considerate and even her mum wouldn't have been so patient. He'd also appeared to have as much fun as she did, even though art and fashion weren't really his thing.

'It's because you deserve it,' he said, taking her hand across the table, his eyes meeting hers. 'You've no idea how much I enjoy your company. And that's the best thing about you, Anna. You are unaware what a beautiful and special person you are.' He gave her a shy smile, his thumb stroking the back of her hand, sending shivers up her arm. 'I've never met anyone like you before. Never felt like this about anyone.'

She thought her heart might explode, her words stuck in her throat as she struggled to find an appropriate response. Thankfully their dessert arrived at that point, giving her an excuse to drop her gaze and change the subject.

The holiday had been a step up in their relationship. A shift to another level and she felt confused about her goal and how she could best move towards it. He'd dazzled her with his kindness, befuddled her with his good humour and the fun they'd experienced together. To her surprise, he'd given her everything she'd been missing in her life.

It had been no hardship to gaze into his eyes, to hold his hand, to make love to him. No hardship to pretend she was falling in love. And it *was* only a pretence she reassured herself on the plane home, when the holiday was spinning in her mind, a carousel of lovely pictures, happy smiles, and romance.

It isn't real.

The thought pulled her back to where this had all started. Hurting Theo. That's what she should be focused on. Somehow, she'd managed to follow a diversion rather than stick to the path leading towards her goal of getting revenge. She needed to take stock and reassess.

In that moment, her mind recalibrated, and a new idea started to form. *Can I push him further,* she'd wondered, looking at his sleeping face in the seat next to her? Was this the real endgame – to make him fall so hard for her that he proposed? Then she would dump him. Preferably at the altar. *Ooh, that would hurt.* That would hurt a lot. And in the meantime, Luna would be horrified. There would be arguments between father and daughter, a rift opening between them because Theo would be made to choose which side he was on. Anna's or Luna's. She didn't think there was an option to have both.

Yes, she thought as her heart hardened against the man sitting next to her. *That's what my plan should be.*

13

She started acting on her revised plan immediately after they got back, suggesting Theo invite Luna and Gino along for Sunday lunch at a local gastro pub in Beaumaris. He thought it was a great idea and she couldn't wait to see how his children would react. Their weekend away had brought them closer and Theo was always touching her, like he was checking she was still there. She decided to play on this, make sure she always had his attention, because she knew Luna would hate that.

The pub was crowded, a loud hubbub of conversations filling the air, creating a warm and inviting atmosphere. It was hot for April, and she peeled off her jacket revealing a low-cut top, worn with the express intent of annoying Theo's children. She was going to be sexy and clingy and let them know she was the main event in Theo's life.

Luna and Gino were late and came in squabbling about something, heading straight to the bar. Theo saw them and went over to show them where they were sitting, giving both of his children a kiss and a hug. They were clearly still close as a family. Luna glanced over at Anna, her face wearing a frown and she didn't know if the frown was for her or if it was a leftover from her disagreement with her brother.

Anna smiled and waved. Gino, who she hadn't met before, didn't even look her way. He was a younger version of Theo, but larger in every way and more interested in attracting the attention of the barman.

Finally, they got served and came to the table with their drinks, the two siblings still having a go at each other about something.

'Dad, can you tell him to shut up, please? I can't bear to hear another word about the bloody wallpaper for his room being the wrong colour.'

'It's pink,' Gino complained. 'Why would you choose pink for my room?'

'It's not pink. It's rose. And it's not your room. It's the guest room, isn't it Dad? That's what we agreed. And you just happen to be using it whilst you're home.'

'How come you get your own room, then?'

'Because I bloody live there.'

'Kids, please can you stop it.' Theo's voice had an instant impact, his tone stern and they obviously recognised they had crossed a line with their behaviour. *Hmm. Interesting.*

Anna laughed and grabbed his arm, leaning in for a kiss. 'That was like magic. Who knew you could be so masterful?'

He kissed her back, and she could almost feel his kids recoiling in horror. Oh, this lunch was going to be fun, and she mentally rubbed her hands together in delight.

The conversation moved on to general questions from Anna about how they both were and what they were doing. Gino, it seemed, hated his job. Something to do with finance and he was looking for something new. He was home on a flying visit for an interview the following day, and it was clear Luna resented him being there. So, it looked like there was discord in the family already. How hard would it be to sow more seeds of discontent? Make them angry at their father. And each other.

Lots of possibilities to work on.

At the end of the meal, Luna went to the ladies' room and Anna made a point of following her in, glad to have a chance to talk to her one-to-one. When Luna came out of the cubicle, Anna was touching up her lipstick in the mirror and caught the unguarded expression on Luna's face, like she'd drunk sour milk. She finished her lips, gave Luna a big smile.

'I'm so happy we got to spend some time together today. I need to know you and Gino better if we're going to be almost family.' She laughed, putting inverted comas with her fingers round the almost. 'I'm practically living with your dad now.' She gave a dreamy look. 'We're so happy, honestly I can't believe how lucky I am.'

Then she walked out of the room without looking back, thinking that should start the unravelling of his little family very nicely.

14

She'd hoped to hear that Luna was being difficult, her objections to their relationship getting stronger. But Theo never said a word and despite her suggestions, they didn't repeat the family gathering. So, in terms of splitting up the family, she'd come to a halt. Maybe it was enough just to build her relationship with Theo and focus on her main goal. Jilting him at the altar. Patience was key. This was a long-term project, after all, and the result would be worth it.

Since their weekend away, Theo had appeared distracted at times, and she caught him on a couple of occasions giving her a strange look. She couldn't work out what he might be thinking and when she asked him straight out, his answer was, 'You're beautiful.' But the expression on his face didn't match his words. *Very odd.* She wondered if there was a problem at work, as he seemed to be late home more often. And when they were at home, he was taking more work calls, shutting himself in the kitchen so he could talk confidentially about his patients.

A month after they returned from Paris, he said he wanted to take her out for a special meal. It was a new Michelin starred restaurant that had recently opened in the area, and she was excited to go and try the food. He'd made a point of asking her to dress up and she'd had her hair cut, her nails done, and her make-up professionally applied, thinking this must be some sort of special occasion. Was it to do with work, maybe meeting some of his colleagues? She knew it wasn't his birthday and hers had just been, and although she quizzed him about it, he remained coy, refusing to elaborate. 'You'll love it,' he said. 'Or at least I hope you will.'

The restaurant was in a country house hotel just outside Caernarfon and they had the most fabulous meal, with very attentive service. She felt like a princess. At the end of the night, when they'd finished their dessert, the waiter brought a small plate to her, with a mini silver cloche and put it down in front of her, then backed away.

'What's this?' she asked, curious that she had a plate and he didn't.

He shrugged, his tongue wetting his lips and she thought he looked nervous. 'Have a look.'

She lifted the cloche and there was a blue box. The sort of box a ring comes in. Now her heart was galloping. Was this really what she thought it might be?

Hardly daring to imagine she might be right, she picked up the box and carefully opened it, casting a glance at Theo, who was watching her every move. A stunning solitaire diamond ring sat on a white silk cushion. Before she knew what was happening, he was down on one knee, reaching for her hand. 'My darling, would you do me the honour of being my wife?'

She was genuinely speechless, her hands covering her mouth to hide her gaping jaw. This was the new goal of Project Theo, exactly what she'd wanted, but she'd never imagined it would happen so soon. Strangely, it was what she'd dreaded too. Because it meant she was headed towards her endgame and that would mean she'd be on her own again.

With a shaky hand, she took the ring from the box, the stone sparkling in the light of the candle on their table. She let out a long breath.

Say yes, the voice in her head shouted at her. *Come on... What are you waiting for?*

She blinked her eyes closed, knowing what she must do, but feeling a stab of guilt. Theo had been nothing but loving towards her. Could she be this dishonest? Could she hurt him in the way she'd planned?

This isn't about me, she reminded herself, as she chewed at her bottom lip, so conflicted she couldn't speak. *It's for Ollie.* And her love for her dead husband knew no bounds. She would have died in his place, given the chance. And this was about showing Theo that actions had consequences. It was about stopping him from doing the same thing to someone else. *In a way, it's about saving lives.*

With that thought in her head, a rallying cry for justice that she couldn't ignore, she swallowed and opened her eyes, to find Theo gazing up at her.

'Please say yes.' There was desperation in his voice. 'I know there's an age gap, but I've always looked after myself and I think I'm good for a few decades yet.' His words raced out of his mouth as fast as her heartbeat. She was enthralled, hooked by his sincerity, unable to look away. 'If you want children, I'm up for that and if you don't, I'm up for that too. I just know I want you to be by my side for the rest of my life.'

He sounded like he meant every word he said, and her heart melted, her stance on the moral high ground slipping. She could pretend, for now, that this was real, couldn't she? That she was in love. Wasn't this what she'd been working towards? It had happened faster than she'd thought but he'd been telling her he loved her since they got back from Paris, and she'd been dropping hints that she'd be happy to get married again.

Only a few days ago he'd commented that, at his age, he was more decisive in his life choices because, as he knew from his job, there was no telling how much time you had on this earth. If he wanted something, he would grab it, like the new Porsche he'd just bought, an impulsive upgrade on his older model. Strangely, she hadn't seen a proposal coming just yet.

This is your chance, go grab it. She could organise the wedding quickly, something simple at the registry office, and the whole pretence could be over and done with. Theo could have his comeuppance and she could walk away from him at the altar and get on with her life. The duplicity was killing her, but it would be worth it, she reassured herself.

'Yes,' she said and burst into tears as he slipped the ring on her finger and the remaining diners in the room gave them a round of applause.

15

In the car, on their way back to his rental, sitting in what felt like a bubble of euphoria, his hand was holding hers until he pulled it away and turned off the main road.

'Let's go and tell the kids. Gino is back for the weekend, and he said he was staying at the Boat House with Luna.'

Anna tensed, needing a bit of time to mentally prepare herself to meet his kids again. Decide how she should play it. Her brain was frozen, unable to click into the gear she needed. Christ, she hoped they were out, and they could do this another day. But the lights were on, and they could hear music blaring as they parked up. Theo glanced at her and rolled his eyes. 'Good job we don't have neighbours, isn't it?'

He went to get out of the car, but she pulled him back. 'Theo, I... just thought of something we need to be clear about with Luna.' She hesitated.

He frowned. 'Go on.'

'Where are we going to live?'

He gazed at her for a moment. 'Here at the Boat House, of course. Unless you'd rather a fresh start, in which case we can sell up and buy whatever you want.' He laughed, still on a high. 'Honestly, it's not a problem. Whatever you want is what we'll do.'

She grimaced. 'Would Luna be living with us?'

He pursed his lips as he thought. 'Well, yes. I suppose she will at first. But she's like a butterfly, that one, flitting here and there and coming back between projects.' He squeezed her hand. 'It's time she found her own place. I've been thinking that for a while, and this will be a good motivator to make her sort out a starter home.'

Anna had a strong sense of foreboding. She didn't believe Theo had really thought this through. 'I don't think Luna sees things that way. Why would she spend all that time and energy on the renovations if it wasn't for her? She sees this as her home and I don't think she's going to be too happy, whatever we decide to do.'

'I'll handle Luna, don't you worry. Anyway, I think they'll be delighted their old dad has found himself a new wife. Now they won't have to worry about who's going to look after me when I get old and doddery.' He leant towards her and gave her a gentle kiss. 'Come on, let's tell them the good news.'

Anna climbed out of the car and followed him into the house. The living room was empty, although all the lights were on, the music so loud Anna clamped her hands over her ears, the bass beat vibrating through her body. Theo turned it off and the silence cushioned her for a moment before she heard disgruntled voices from upstairs.

'Technical hitch,' she heard Gino say as he ran down the stairs, stopping when he saw them standing in the middle of the room.

'Dad.' He turned to Anna, and she could tell he'd forgotten her name, probably forgotten he'd ever met her because it had only happened once, and he'd been roaring drunk by the end of the meal. Theo had defended him, telling her that his behaviour was completely out of character. A one-off. But he'd seemed a bit too defensive, and it had made her wonder if he was the problem child.

'Come on, Gino, what's taking so long?' Luna shouted.

'Dad's here,' he called up the stairs. 'With his woman.'

She felt Theo bristle beside her, his hand clasping hers and holding it tight. Footsteps came running down the stairs, Luna stopping behind her brother.

'This is a— surprise,' Luna said, carefully. 'We weren't expecting visitors. We're just doing the finishing touches on Gino's room while he's here.'

'Gino doesn't have a room,' Theo said, his voice calm and even, but relaying his authority. 'He's moved out. We agreed his old bedroom would be a guest room, didn't we?'

'You're behind the times, Dad.' Luna scowled. 'Tell him, Gino.'

'I lost my job, so I'm coming home for a while, just to get my finances sorted out and see what opportunities come up next.'

Theo held up a hand. 'Wait just a minute. We're going to have to talk about this because... Anna and I are getting married. This will be *our* home. Or maybe we'll sell up and find something new.'

Luna's jaw dropped. Gino slowly walked down the rest of the stairs, his sister behind him, their faces a picture of confusion. Luna frowned. 'Do you know, I think I must have drunk too much because I thought you said you and... whatshername are getting married.' She frowned at her dad. 'What did you really say?'

Anna wanted to disappear, her cheeks burning, sensing the rage emanating from Theo's children. Never had she been in a more uncomfortable situation in her life and the urge to run away was getting stronger by the second. But Theo was holding her tight. She could feel the tension in him and knew there was no way he was backing down.

'You heard right. We're engaged.' He held up Anna's hand to show them the ring.

Luna's smile dropped from her face, her eyes narrowing. 'You think I've spent six months of my life renovating this house, so she can swan in here and take over? Or tell you to sell it?'

'Oh, come on, Luna! You know being here is just a stop-gap for you. I've seen the renovation as work experience, a project for your CV. But you've always known this is my house and it's my decision whether I want to stay living here or not. We've talked about it several times. Whether memories of your mum's— accident would always hang over us.'

There it was, she thought, picking up on his hesitation, the way he said the word 'accident' so carefully, suggesting that the manner of Emilia's demise was not clear cut. Adrenaline was flowing round her body now, and she was desperate to leave, the sour atmosphere in the house unbearable.

'It's not just your house, Dad.' Gino sounded aggrieved. 'It's our family home. This is where our memories are. Growing up with Mum.' His voice cracked. 'You can't sell it.'

'I haven't said I'm going to sell it. I'm just trying to make the point it belongs to me and will be home to myself and my new wife, unless we decide we want a fresh start somewhere else.'

'That's not right,' Luna snapped. 'You're not being fair. Mum would hate you for this. I mean, look at this woman. She's the same age as me, for God's sake.'

'She is a grown-up, just like you, Luna, so don't pull that one on me.' Anger sharpened Theo's words. 'Age is just a number and we're happy together and that's all that matters.'

Anna could feel herself shaking now, hating the way everyone was talking about her like she wasn't a real person, not actually there. Theo held her a little tighter and the feeling that she was trapped intensified.

'Did you hear that?' Luna said, turning to her brother. 'We don't matter.'

Theo sighed. 'That's not what I meant and you know it.'

'You are being ridiculous,' Luna snapped, her hands on her hips as she leant towards her father, eyes sparking. 'Do you really think she loves you?' She gave a derisive snort. 'Loves your money, more like. I always had her down as a gold-digger. Nobody my age, in their right mind, would marry a guy twenty years older than them. Nobody.' She jabbed a finger at Anna, making her shy away like it was an actual weapon. 'She's a fake with an agenda and you're a fool.'

Christ that was close to the bone.

Did Luna know what Anna's agenda was? Had she guessed? Anna couldn't bear much more of this, and she prepared to squirm out of Theo's clutches and run. But he put a protective arm around her shoulders and pulled her close. Anna folded herself into him, wanting to make herself small and invisible. Never had she been so viciously attacked by anyone's words.

'Luna, stop it! Stop it now.' Theo was in full-on angry parent mode, as if speaking to a small child. 'Why are you being so horrible? What I choose to do with my life is my decision, not yours and sometimes I think you forget that. You are not the boss of me, young lady.' He was breathing hard, impressively controlled in his anger. 'We're getting married and that's it.'

Silence filled the room for a moment as Luna and Gino glared at their dad.

'Over my dead body, you are,' Luna spat, before turning on her heel and storming off up the stairs with Gino running after her.

16

'I'm so sorry,' Theo said, his breath in her hair as she clung to him. 'Oh God, you're shaking.' He led her to the sofa, where she sank into the cushions, not trusting her legs to keep her standing. 'Look, you stay here for a minute. I'm going to go and talk to them.' There was a hardness to his jaw, a steely glint in his eyes. 'That was unforgiveable behaviour and I'm not having it.'

She watched him thunder up the stairs, folding her arms around her chest to try and calm the shaking. She was shocked by his children's animosity towards her. Indifference she could accept, supposedly forgetting her name was a childish slight, but that verbal attack had been another level of nastiness altogether.

A door slammed shut, muffling their voices, and it seemed like they might be having a reasonable conversation until suddenly they were shouting at each other. Luna and Theo, she thought, Gino filling in here and there when Luna fell silent. Two against one. Was that how this family dynamic worked? Was Theo bullied by his children?

Clearly, they were not impressed, but she felt for Theo rather than them. He was right, it *was* his life, and he could do with it what he wanted. He shouldn't be beholden to his children now they were adults with their own lives to lead. It wasn't up to them who he had a relationship with. And it was no longer his responsibility to provide a home for them either. It seemed to Anna that they took him for granted, just assumed he'd help them out in whatever way they deemed fit.

Her outrage on his behalf was almost greater than her own outrage at the way she'd been spoken to, the way they were so dismissive of her. Any sane person would walk away, she told herself. But if anything, their terrible attitude made her more determined to be engaged to Theo. It was his choice after all. They didn't deserve a father like him. So generous and kind to them. They needed to be taught a lesson. Above everything else, they needed to grow up and stop behaving like spoilt brats.

It put her in even more of a moral dilemma now. On the one hand, wanting to protect Theo from his children, on the other, determined to break his heart and find a measure of justice for her dead husband. She'd wanted to drive a wedge between Theo and his children, and it seemed she was succeeding, but it felt so wrong. She hung her head, covered her face with her hands. It was all too much. Too much emotion swirling round her body, too many decisions that conflicted with each other. And definitely too much shouting.

There was banging now, the odd yelp, like they might actually be physically fighting and she sprang to her feet. She crept closer to the stairs, unsure what to do for the best. Not wanting to get involved but concerned for Theo's safety. In the end she couldn't bear it any longer, and hurried up the stairs, throwing the bedroom door open to see Gino and Theo grappling on the floor in front of her. The guest room had been an empty shell when Anna was last here, but now it was fully furnished, the walls freshly papered, one curtain half-hung at the window. Luna was urging her brother on and Anna gasped when she saw he had his hands round Theo's neck, while his father bucked and thrashed in an attempt to free himself.

'What the hell are you doing?' she shouted, the shock of her entrance making Gino turn and loosen his grip, allowing Theo to throw him off balance. She grabbed Gino under the arms, kneeing him between the shoulders to distract his attention, allowing Theo to wriggle free. Luna scowled at her in a way that suggested if looks could kill, she'd be dead. But Luna didn't try and obstruct Theo's escape. She kept herself away from the action, at the far side of the room, sitting on a set of steps they'd been using to put up the curtains.

Theo was struggling to catch his breath, an ugly red wheal looping round his neck. Anna grabbed his arm and pulled him towards the door, desperate to be out of there, thinking the time for talking was over.

'I meant what I said.' That was Theo's parting shot, before Anna got him through the door, which he slammed behind them. She hurried him down the stairs and out of the house towards the car, where they slumped in the front seats, both of them breathing heavily.

'That went well,' she quipped.

'You have no idea,' he murmured, his jaw set as he fastened his seat belt and started the car.

* * *

Two days later, she was starting to get an idea. Theo was having lots of private conversations with his children, scurrying out of the room with his phone if they called when she was there. From what she could see, things didn't seem to be settling down in the way Theo had assured her they would. Finally, her curiosity got the better of her and she decided they needed to talk about what was happening, rather than pretending there wasn't a major issue forcing its way between them.

'It's just a shock for them,' he told her as she brought up the subject that evening. They'd eaten their meal and were finishing off a glass of wine at the table and she decided the atmosphere was as relaxed as it was ever going to be. 'My marriage had not been in a good place when Emilia died. In fact, I'd been seeing someone else for a while and we were about to start divorce proceedings. The children didn't like that either.' He sighed. 'But after my wife's death, I ended that relationship. I wasn't in the right place emotionally. The children were distraught about Emilia, so I felt I had to give them all my attention.' He pursed his lips, his fingers playing with the cork from the wine bottle, spinning it round on the table-top. 'I'd only just started dating again a few weeks before I met you. I realised I was lonely, and decided it was time to try and move on with my life.'

He glanced up and Anna caught his eye, a shiver of unease running through her. A thought flitting through her mind so fast that her body responded, but she couldn't catch it. Unable to work out why his story had unsettled her. 'I'm not sure your children want you to move on.'

He gave her a half-hearted smile. 'Oh, they'll calm down. I know it looks bad, but it's the Italian in them. Their mother was the same. Fiery. Loved a fight then it would blow over as fast as it started.'

'Hmm, I'm not sure. It's been two days now and they're constantly ringing you. And I thought Gino was actually going to strangle you the other night. I mean, what would have happened if I hadn't come looking for you?' She sighed and reached for his hand to stop him from fiddling with the cork again. 'Are they ever going to accept me?'

She'd never seen him like this, fidgeting, unable to keep still.

This conflict with his children had made him agitated in a way work problems never did.

'We've just got to give it a bit of time. Let them get used to the idea because there's no way I'm changing my mind. We're getting married whether they like it or not.'

He gulped down the rest of his wine, and got up to start clearing their dinner plates, methodically filling the dishwasher. She watched him, wondering what her next move should be.

'Have you thought about a date?' she asked.

'For the wedding?'

She nodded. 'I don't know what timescale you have in mind.'

He stopped what he was doing and straightened up. 'I haven't thought about it.' He looked pensive, quiet for a moment. 'My first goal was getting a ring on your finger, but I suppose I hoped you might be the one driving the wedding arrangements.' He gave her an apologetic smile. 'I'm so mad busy at work I'm not sure how involved I'll be able to get.'

He hadn't really answered her question. She finished her wine and tried again.

'Yeah, but are you thinking a long engagement, short engagement? Are we talking months or years?'

'Months,' he said, firmly. 'In fact, let's just do it. As soon as you can get it sorted.'

'But you just said we needed to give your children time to get used to the idea.'

'Yeah, well, I've changed my mind. I think the sooner the better, then it's done and there's nothing they can do about it, so they'll *have* to get used to it.' He picked up her empty glass and went back to stacking plates and pans and cutlery into the dishwasher. 'To be honest, I'm sick of repeating myself to them. They're not listening to a word I say, just focused on trying to convince me you're not to be trusted.'

He banged the dishwasher shut and switched it on, turning to look at her as he leant on the worktop. There it was again, that flash of something making her anxious. *Does he know something?* She couldn't meet his gaze, her eyes fixed on his feet, but she could feel the heat of his stare boring into her.

'I told them you're the most honest person I've ever met.'

He said it carefully. Slowly. And she wondered if it was her guilty conscience reading meaning into innocent words. She got up from the table and carefully pushed her chair back in place. 'That's very sweet of you,' she murmured, welcoming his embrace as he took her in his arms, because at least he couldn't see the lies in her eyes, the dishonesty written all over her face.

Can I really go through with this?

Now that her fantasy had become reality, she couldn't imagine causing Theo any hurt. She wasn't that sort of person and she understood now that her grief had made her vengeful in a way Ollie would have hated. She didn't want to be that person any more. Wanted to stop the pretence, but was unsure now how to move forwards. It was easier to spite his horrible children, so maybe she should shift her focus back to them. Shift her thinking again. If they were so against their marriage, perhaps that's what she should do. She would marry him after all, rather than jilting him at the altar. That would serve his awful children right.

Perhaps she should have listened to her mother when she'd told her she had to accept Ollie's death was a tragic accident. That nobody was really to blame, and she needed to let it go and move on. Then she could be enjoying this moment, could relish the idea of her wedding and a life with Theo rather than being wracked with guilt and uncertainty.

* * *

Later that evening, when she was back in her apartment, her phone pinged with a message. It was from Luna through Anna's Instagram page.

> I know what your game is, and I'll prove it. No way are you marrying Dad. Ever!

17

The following day, Anna was walking back from the shops having stocked up on groceries, her arms laden with two heavy carrier bags. She would be spending at least a couple of days on her own because Theo was working late with his private clinics, and she'd decided to take the opportunity to catch up on work. But that wasn't the real reason she wanted some time on her own. Luna's message had left her feeling jittery and she needed some space to really think about everything.

She'd changed her plan so many times now, she'd lost sight of what she wanted as an outcome for Project Theo. What would be enough to make her feel happy that Ollie had received the justice he deserved, and give her the closure to move on? She didn't know the answer to that question, no longer knew what was right because her mind tied itself in knots every time she made a conscious effort to think about it.

It would be good to catch up with her own life, she decided, settle herself down and see how she felt after that. A bit of admin, updating her Etsy shop, photographing her new product range, and packing up things for the post would be therapeutic and calming.

And it would ground her in the real world, instead of being swept up into the drama of Theo's family life. Tonight she was going out for drinks with Tanya, so she was looking forward to that, being able to kick back and enjoy her friend's company. That would be a very welcome distraction.

She was almost home when she had an uneasy sensation that she was being followed. She turned and looked behind her, and although she thought there might have been a movement to her right, she couldn't see anyone. Putting it down to an overdose of adrenaline making her jumpy, she carried on towards her apartment, which was on the ground floor of a converted terrace on the edge of town.

Her apartment was cold, as she'd hardly been there the past week, and she turned on the heating, made herself a coffee and was just about to get on with some work when she glanced out of the living room window. Her heart leapt in her chest because there, looking straight at her, was Gino.

He was standing against the wall, across the road, hands in his pockets, just staring at her. She pulled the curtains and sank into a chair while her pulse raced. *What is he doing?* Was she going to confront her? Warn her off marrying his dad? That could be the only possible reason for him being there, but after she'd seen the way he dealt with conflict, she had no intention of speaking to him on her own. He could push her inside, strangle her, like he'd been doing to Theo, and nobody would know there was anything amiss.

Gino was big and powerful. A rugby player. She'd watched him attacking his father and Theo was fit and strong. What would happen if he decided to attack Anna? She shivered and grabbed the throw from the back of the sofa, wrapping it round her shoulders. Things were starting to get scary now.

Don't be ridiculous, she scolded herself. *Of course he's not going to kill you.*

She was being melodramatic. Families fought, especially fathers and sons. Plus, he was at risk of being seen if he made a move on her, given she lived on a road with terraced houses on both sides. That was a lot of possible witnesses. Still, she vowed she would not be opening the door, not even a chink with the chain on.

She waited, thinking he might ring on her bell, but after ten minutes, that hadn't happened. She peeked through the gap between the curtains, stepping back when she saw he was still there. He hadn't moved. Even though it had started to drizzle, and his hair was plastered to his head, his clothes soaked through. He wasn't wearing a coat and seemed totally unprepared for a long wait outside in bad weather. This must have been a spur of the moment thing.

What's his game? Intimidation? Giving her the message he knew where she lived? Whatever his goal, he'd succeeded in shaking her up and it worried her enormously that he knew her address now. Throughout the morning she kept checking if he was still there, giving up on any thoughts of work, and resorting to cleaning and doing laundry instead. Two hours later, to her relief, he'd gone, and she felt able to breathe properly again.

At last, she could concentrate on her work, and she settled down to what she hoped would be a productive afternoon. She checked on her business social media, ready to upload photos of her new range of scarves and noticed her last Facebook post had many more comments than she'd usually get. Clicking on the comments, she found a cryptic post from @nightmaregirl.

This woman is a scheming thief. I have evidence. Don't have anything to do with her. DM me for details.

Anna's jaw dropped as she read through all the responses. There was nothing like a cryptic comment to spark people's interest, and people were definitely interested in what this mystery person had to say.

It could only be Luna.

Anna checked the profile, finding an avatar of a cat for a profile picture. The sure sign of a bogus account. She sent her a message.

> I know this is you, Luna. I'm reporting you to the police.

She wasn't sure if the police would be interested in malicious activity on a business Facebook page, but she hoped the threat would be enough to make her stop. Quickly, she deleted the post, blocked @nightmaregirl and reported her to Facebook, but she was sure some damage had already been done. And there was nothing to stop her setting up another bogus account and doing it all over again. Her reputation was being ruined, potential customers lost. She rubbed at her neck, the muscles tight and knotty, glad she had a gym session organised for that evening, followed by drinks with Tanya.

It was no good worrying about it, she decided, her teeth grinding together. There was nothing she could do, except be vigilant and make sure she checked her business social media more regularly so she could minimise damage.

Helpless, that's how she felt. Completely and utterly helpless and it was a very unpleasant feeling. It took her back to the time of Ollie's death and how she'd felt entrusting his life to someone else. And afterwards, trying to deal with the local health board, struggling to find anyone who would talk to her. She'd been passed from pillar to post and in the end, what she got in response was a letter.

She tried to put it out of her mind, and got on with the job of packing up orders. Sending her products to their new owners always lifted her spirits, and once she had a pile of parcels ready to post, her worries had been replaced with a glow of satisfaction. She packed everything into a couple of carrier bags, ready to take to the post office and grabbed her door keys, looking forward to getting out of the house.

Her good mood didn't last long. As soon as she walked out of the front door, she saw Gino. He was sitting on the front wall now, right outside her apartment. He didn't move when he saw her, just stared, the intensity of his gaze as unnerving as a physical attack.

Her legs threatened to buckle, her heart rate shocked into a gallop, and she staggered back inside, slamming the door and fumbling the chain into place. She leant against it, the way she would if he was actually trying to force his way in. How long was he going to stay there? Was he trying to make her a prisoner in her own home, unable to get past him?

She paced the floor, unsure what to do. Her parcels still needed posting, otherwise customers would start complaining and calling her a cheat. If they left bad reviews, her rating would go down and she'd no longer have her Star Seller designation, then her visibility would be reduced. No, she couldn't put it off, however much she didn't want to go outside.

Her keys were still clasped firmly in her hand, digging into her skin. Usually she walked to the post office, but she'd drive. Then she'd feel safer. And her car was parked at the back of the apartments, so she could sneak out and Gino would be none the wiser.

With her heart pounding, she dashed to her car, making sure the doors were locked from the inside, just in case Gino should appear, while she fastened her seat belt and manoeuvred out of her parking space. When she returned home, a little while later, he'd gone.

But he'd done that earlier in the day and reappeared later. She chewed at a nail as she gazed out of the window. *Is he coming back?*

By evening and with no further sign of Gino, she was starting to feel calmer. But her anger hadn't abated. If anything, it had grown stronger. Both Luna and her brother seemed intent on causing her damage, if not physically, then to her business, her reputation, and her peace of mind. It was completely out of order, and she was desperate to talk to Theo about it, but knew that she couldn't just yet, because he had to keep a calm state of mind if he was operating. It was something he often talked about, and he'd specifically asked her not to call him when he was at work. It would have to wait until she saw him again. In the meantime, she would go to the gym and see if she could exercise her way to a better state of mind.

'Hey, Anna, good to see you.' Tanya ran up to her and gave her a hug. 'Where have you been, stranger? I take it you've been busy with lover boy?'

Anna laughed. 'What do you mean *stranger*? It's not been that long since I saw you.'

'Yes, but you used to be here every day. Now it's maybe three times a week and you keep changing the times, so I'm not always here. And Theo is normally with you, so I don't like to intrude.' She cocked her head, frowning. 'And we're not having our lunches any more. Or going out for our regular drinks.' She rubbed Anna's shoulder. 'I miss you. It feels like ages since we had the chance for a proper chat.'

Anna realised with a jolt how much she'd neglected her friend while she'd been focused on Project Theo. She gave Tanya another hug. 'I'm so sorry I've been a bit absent. I promise I'll do better.'

Tanya squeezed her tight. 'You'd better,' she said, before pulling away.

Anna grinned. 'I have news,' she said, holding up her hand, her engagement ring still a surprise every time she saw it on her finger.

Tanya's jaw dropped. 'Oh. My. God. You've got to be kidding me?' She took Anna's hand, studied the ring, 'Wow, that's lovely.' She shook her head. 'I'm finding this hard to process but you've got to give me the low down. Tell me everything.' She led her to the treadmill. 'While you do your routine, of course.'

Anna laughed, delighted to be able to tell her friend what had been happening. If anyone could understand the Luna/Gino situation it would be Tanya. Thankfully the gym was quiet, so she felt able to talk and it took her the full routine to get to the end of the story.

'I can see why you've been hammering the exercises tonight,' Tanya said, when she'd finished, and they were sitting on a bench while Anna caught her breath.

'I've been so angry with the pair of them. Honestly their behaviour is shocking.'

'Yeah, I did sort of try and warn you. But then I thought maybe it was just me they didn't like.'

Anna turned to her friend. 'So they were horrible to you too?'

'Not Gino. Just Luna. I met her the night Theo took me out as his plus one and she was horrible to me even though we'd just met and it wasn't even a proper date. So rude it really took my breath away. Theo tried to brush it off as grief but there was something in her eyes that was quite terrifying.' She held up a finger as though she'd just thought of something. 'I also know someone who went out with Gino for a while.'

'You do?'

Tanya nodded. 'They'd been going out for maybe six months when Luna invited them to a family meal at the house. She was so sick afterwards she thought she was going to die. Took her days to get over it. She thinks Luna gave her food poisoning.'

Anna's jaw dropped. 'You're kidding. She actually poisoned her?'

'Gino tried to convince her it was norovirus or something similar, but she saw Luna watching her while she was eating, this smirk on her face and she thought it was odd at the time. And the rest of the family were fine, so she must have put something in there.' She sighed. 'Anyway, she never went back to the house after that and refused to have anything to do with Luna. It sort of ruined her relationship with Gino because she worried about his sister trying some other stunt.'

Anna was quiet for a moment. 'It's not normal behaviour, is it?'

Tanya gave a derisive snort. 'It's so far from normal it's scary. Luna is all about herself and Gino does what she tells him. He also has money problems, and he can't seem to keep a job, so he boomerangs backwards and forwards.' She gave a huff. 'He's a man-child.'

Anna couldn't argue with Tanya's summary, and it gave her a clearer picture of Theo's children, a third-party perspective to balance against her own observations.

'I think they've been spoilt and the way they talk to their dad is shocking.'

'I know. I tried to speak to Theo about it, but he didn't want to hear. In fact, he became quite nasty. It's okay for him to criticise his kids, but you just try it and see what happens. Honestly, he'll make all the excuses under the sun before he'll admit the truth.'

Anna wiped the sweat from her face, her head feeling clearer for a workout. 'There's no way I'd ever speak to my parents like that. It's so... disrespectful.'

'And entitled. They strongly believe what's his is theirs.'

Anna nodded her agreement. 'They do. You're right. His home is their home, for them to use as and when they want. That's what started the row. The idea that Theo might want to sell up and buy us somewhere new for a fresh start.'

Tanya's brow crumpled in a frown, her eyes clouded with concern. 'Can you imagine staying there when both Luna and Gino are at home? At best you could describe it as awkward, at worst it could be downright threatening.'

Anna thought about that. 'I felt threatened by Gino today. He was just staring at me, but it felt so intimidating. Honestly, I was so jittery my legs wouldn't work properly.'

Tanya gave her a hug. 'I don't think you need to worry about Gino. He's harmless. The problem with Gino is the hold Luna has over him. Big sister is boss. It bugged the hell out of my friend. They all jump to Luna's tune, and I really struggle to work out why.'

Anna was so relieved to be having this conversation, being able to share her concerns with someone who'd had similar experiences. Because Theo's attitude to his children had been confusing her. Sometimes he'd back them to the hilt and at other times, like with the wedding arrangements, he wanted to forge ahead with plans despite their concerns.

'I'm not sure I agree with you about Gino being harmless. Seeing what he was doing to his dad worried me. Honestly, he was trying to strangle him, and Luna wasn't doing anything to help.'

Tanya pursed her lips, thinking. 'My friend never felt threatened by him, but then I suppose she was his girlfriend, not his enemy.

Even when they split up, he wasn't nasty. He knew it was his fault
and seemed to accept it without much of a fuss. He even apologised
for being so crap.'

'But if I hadn't barged into the room when I did, he might have
killed his dad. It was that bad. And now Theo's having to make up
all sorts of excuses to explain away the bruises to his colleagues.
They probably think we're into kinky sex or something. I don't
know.' She dropped her gaze to the floor, surprised to find tears
stinging her eyes, a lump in her throat. 'I'm... a bit scared.'

'Oh, hun, I'm so sorry this has happened to you.' Tanya put a
comforting arm round her shoulders. 'On such a happy day as well.
It must have taken the shine off the idea of marriage if those two
come with the deal.'

Tanya had said what Anna had been thinking in her darkest
moments. Wondering if it was all worth it. *Remember Ollie*, a voice in
her head piped up. *It's all for him. Hang in there for a few more weeks.
You can do that, can't you?*

She sighed. 'Yeah, it has a bit. We haven't had much of a chance
to talk about it really because Theo's had some private clinics after
his shifts and I don't want to disturb him at work.'

'I'm sure it'll sort itself out given time.'

'That's what Theo said, then he contradicted himself and said
he wanted to get married as soon as possible because it would be a
done deal and they couldn't complain.'

'You know, I think he's a bit wary of his kids,' Tanya murmured,
bending her head towards Anna's. 'Would I go as far as saying
frightened?' She pulled a face. 'Possibly.'

Anna stood, feeling cold now and ready for a change of subject
before she completely freaked out. She hooked her towel round her
neck, her hands clinging onto it as though it was her life source.
'I'm just going to have a shower.'

Tanya nodded, her face still clouded with concern. 'Okay.' She glanced across the gym. 'Here's my next client now.' She nodded towards a lanky young man hovering in the doorway. 'It's his first session, so I'm doing his induction today. But after that I'm free.'

'That's okay. I'll meet you in the cafe, shall I?'

Anna went to get changed, lingering under the hot water, feeling chilled to the core by the conversation she'd just had with Tanya. After hearing that Luna had tried to poison Tanya's friend, it was easy to believe that she might have done other malicious things. Could she have pushed her own mother off the jetty in a fit of rage? Or got Gino to do it for her? *What might they do to me?* It didn't bear thinking about. But there's no evidence, she reminded herself, just a whispered conversation with someone she'd only known for a few months. Although Tanya had no reason to lie, did she?

She was getting to the point where she wasn't sure who to trust. That's why it was more important than ever to believe in herself and what she was feeling. There was nobody she could share her plan with, nobody she could trust with the whole truth of her situation and that made her feel more isolated, more wary about what the future might hold.

* * *

It was after ten when she arrived home, having gone out for something to eat with Tanya and she was still smiling to herself when she pulled into her parking spot in the lane at the back of her apartment. It was exactly what she'd needed; a bit of a laugh and some female company for a change. It had made her realise how much time she'd been spending with Theo and she made a decision to adjust the balance. From now on she would get back into her own gym routine and make arrangements to go out with Tanya more often.

As she gathered her gym bag from the passenger seat, her eyes noticed something that made her pause, the hairs lifting on the back of her neck. The kitchen light was on. She could see it through the gap between the back gate and the wall and she knew she'd switched it off before she came out. She grabbed the torch, which she kept in her car, and turned it on, flicking the beam into all the dark corners before she got out of the car. With adrenaline coursing through her body, she crept towards the back door.

Her breath caught in her throat when she realised the door was open. The lock had been broken.

19

She dumped her gym bag and hurried back to her car. Ollie's hockey stick was still in the boot. He'd been a keen player and his stick had been so dear to him, she hadn't had the heart to get rid of it. Now she was glad she hadn't. With the torch in one hand and the hockey stick in the other, she crept towards the door, kicking it open. It banged against the wall. Loud enough, she thought, for someone to hear if they were still inside. Hopefully, if she made sufficient noise, they would run away because the last thing she wanted was a confrontation.

'The police are on their way,' she shouted, realising it would have been a good idea to ring them. But she couldn't hear any movement and she had a feeling whoever had broken in was long gone. She stood still and listened. Silence, except for the whoosh of her pulse in her ears as her heart raced. She crept into the kitchen. Nobody there. Holding her breath, she moved into the living room, coming to a halt when she saw what the intruders had done. She slumped against the wall, blinking back tears, unable to believe what she was seeing.

The place had been ransacked. Everything that had been on a

flat surface – all the things with sentimental value, the pictures and trinkets she and Ollie had picked up on their travels, were on the floor. Many of them smashed. Pictures with the glass broken, like they'd been stomped on. Likewise, a favourite vase had not just been broken, but ground into the carpet. Everything had been emptied from her desk, and from the files on top, papers all over the place. Her laptop had gone. The boxes of stock that she kept in a corner had been ripped open and some sort of liquid thrown over them. She picked her way over to the boxes to investigate further. Sniffed. *Oh God*, she stepped back; it smelt like piss.

The air was still and quiet, but she tiptoed, not wanting to make a noise just in case her movements could be heard. Cautiously, she moved into the hallway, her hands tightening round her weapons.

She poked her head into her bedroom, which had also been turned upside down, the mattress pulled from the bed, the duvet ripped, like it had been slashed with a knife and the stuffing thrown around the room. Clothes pulled from the wardrobe, cut into pieces. There was the same level of destruction in the spare room, where she had her work bench, her stock of materials lying in a shredded heap. Hundreds of pounds worth of damage. Tears rolled down her cheeks, her body shaking as she stood in the doorway in a state of shocked disbelief.

Whoever had done this really hated her. It was not about stealing. This wasn't a burglary. This was malicious damage. A hate crime. And there were only two people on her list of suspects.

Fury erupted in her chest, and she let out a wail, like a demented demon, needing to do something to release the pressure. A few minutes later, when she'd finally calmed down, she rang the police, who promised they'd send someone round and told her not to touch anything.

There was nothing she could do but wait, surrounded by the smashed-up remnants of her life. She couldn't let Theo's children do this to her. Couldn't let them destroy her. The best thing she could do was use her anger to fuel her crusade.

What doesn't kill me makes me stronger, right?

But it was hard not to mourn the loss of all her precious things. Gifts from Ollie that couldn't be repaired, memories from trips together, now reduced to shards of glass and crumbs of pottery. Clothes that he'd bought her, or that reminded her of special occasions. Every single framed photo in the apartment had been stamped on, some of the pictures ripped out and torn to pieces. She picked her way round the carnage, every step compounding her misery.

What terrible, terrible people.

Although her anger was burning hot, her mind was drawing a blank as to what she could do to retaliate. Her frustration fuelled her rage, making her feel like she might explode. How could she teach them a lesson, apart from reporting them to the police? The police would be obliged to check them out, and that process would be difficult enough for the siblings to get through unscathed. But they were clever. She had no doubt they would have planned their alibis, and they were the children of a well-known surgeon. Of course they would never dream of doing such a dreadful thing.

They'd brush it off and move on, tell people that Anna was being vindictive because she wanted them out of her life. Out of their family home. She'd read that narcissistic people did that to you. They flipped everything round to make it your fault. Made their failings, your failings. Re-framed their motivation as your motivation. Well, she wasn't going to fall for that.

She gritted her teeth, a hollowness in her chest, a feeling of desolation like her heart had been ripped out. *Is it worth it?* She asked herself. *Should I stop this relationship with Theo now? Call it a day?*

Getting revenge for Ollie was one thing, but facing vindictiveness like this in the process was making her doubt her plans. It would take weeks to sort this out and get an insurance claim organised. In the meantime, she wouldn't be able to fulfil any orders, so wouldn't be making any money.

God knows what they'd done with her laptop, the lifeblood of her business and the place where everything important was stored. It felt like she was standing at Everest base camp and a return to normality was only possible if she reached the peak, way up in the sky. So far away she couldn't even see the top. Overwhelming didn't even begin to describe it.

Her phone rang and she snatched it up, thinking it would be the police. But it wasn't.

'Hey, darling.' Theo's voice. 'I just got back and thought I'd call to see how you're doing. It feels lonely without you.' Normally, she found his voice soothing, but tonight it was like pouring oil on the fire.

Her hand tightened around her phone. *His children did this.* She wasn't in the mood for her fake persona, the one that pandered to him. Anyway, did she even care any more? She wasn't sure she did. All she wanted was an end to the hate crimes against her.

'My flat has been broken into and completely trashed,' she snarled, like he was the one who'd done it. 'I'm just waiting for the police.'

'Oh my God, no. That's dreadful.' His voice was full of concern and she could imagine his expression, his eyes full of sadness on her behalf. It made her even angrier. If it wasn't for him, she wouldn't be in this situation. If he hadn't killed her husband, she'd still be happily married. Probably pregnant by now and— She blinked, snapped her mouth shut, stopped her thoughts. This wasn't going to get her anywhere, she had to stay in the present, stay in control.

'They've completely vandalised the place. Taken my laptop.

Trashed all my stock, all my personal things.' Her voice hitched in her throat as she tried not to cry. 'It's... a mess.'

'What is this town coming to?' He gave a heartfelt sigh. 'Honestly, I despair sometimes.'

Her jaw tightened. 'The problem is not this town,' she snapped, her voice fiery with rage. 'The problem is *your* children. This is *their* doing.'

Silence for a beat.

'Come on now, that's a big jump. How can you possibly say such a thing?' Instantly, he was on the defensive, his tone different now he'd taken a step back and decided to throw a shield around his kids. Just as Tanya had said he would. 'I know we had a difficult time with them the other night, but I've seen Luna today. She apologised. Said she was sorry she overreacted and of course it's my life and I should be with whoever I want.'

Anna grunted, shocked by Luna's cunning. 'Yeah, I bet she did. Covering her tracks.'

'Come on Anna, don't be like that.' Now he was snapping back. Gone was the concern, he was ready for the fight. 'I think her apology is very positive and it wouldn't do for you to hold a grudge.'

'Theo, you're not listening to what I've been saying,' she shouted, completely out of patience. 'My apartment has been vandalised by someone who clearly hates me. Only your children fit that bill. And Gino followed me home from the shops this morning. Then he stood outside for hours in the rain before he finally went away. Then he came back again later. He was trying to scare me.'

Another silence. *Yes, that's a tricky one to explain away, isn't it?*

'The fact that he's watching you doesn't mean he broke in and vandalised your apartment.'

'Oh, for God's sake!' Anna gave an exasperated growl. 'I can't speak to you. I can't. This isn't going to work if you always put their version of the truth ahead of mine. You go and speak to your son, ask him what he was doing today. And we are over. That's it. I want you and you despicable children out of my life.'

She disconnected and unable to contain her anger any longer, put her head back and screamed, as long and as loud as she could. Sod the neighbours, she needed this. When she'd finished, she closed her eyes and took some deep breaths, only opening them again when she heard a firm knock at the door. The police were here at last, and she was going to tell them exactly who was to blame. And then she was going to work out how to get her own back.

This is war.

But as she opened the door to the two officers and invited them in, a thought wormed its way into her head. *If this is just the start of what they might do, should I really go on the attack?*

20

She gave a detailed statement to the police, two female officers just a bit older than she was, sitting in the kitchen as it was the only room that had escaped unscathed. One of them listened to her story and wrote everything down, while the other checked for evidence and took lots of pictures.

'Have you got somewhere you can go?' the officer asked when she'd finished her questions.

'Well, I would have gone to stay with my fiancé, but given it's his children who did this, I don't think I can. I'm too angry.' She sighed, as she remembered her furious words. 'And I just ended our relationship.'

The officer's lips disappeared into a thin line. 'Yes, I can see it's a difficult situation.'

Understatement of the day, Anna thought.

Tanya's face popped into her mind, and she brightened. 'I've got a friend I might be able to stay with, though.'

The officer smiled and looked relieved. 'You give them a ring, see if that's possible. If not, we'll have to think of something else. And while you're doing that, I'll get in touch with the emergency locksmith, see if they can come over and secure the place for you. We'll be here a while yet, so we can secure the premises if you want to get off. I mean it's late now, and you've had a traumatic day, probably best to see if you can get some rest.' She closed her notebook and tucked it back in her pocket. 'You can pick the keys up from the station in the morning.'

Feeling weary beyond words, it sounded like the best idea and Anna rang Tanya, who immediately invited her to stay for as long as she needed.

* * *

Tanya made up a bed for her on the sofa in her bedsit and they sat drinking hot chocolate with a shot of rum while Anna ranted and cried and ranted some more.

'Look, I can't say I'm surprised,' Tanya said, sipping at her hot chocolate. She was at one end of the sofa, Anna at the other, their legs tucked up, so they were facing each other, a fleecy blanket draped over them. 'I know that doesn't really help, but at least it was only your possessions that got trashed.' She leant forwards, rubbed Anna's knee. 'After my friend's brush with Luna, I was worried for you. Especially after you told me how they reacted to your engagement.'

Anna finished her drink, put her mug on the coffee table and pulled the blanket up to her chin. 'God, I'm worried too after what you told me earlier about the poisoning incident.'

'Did you mention that to the police?'

Anna shook her head. 'No, I wasn't really thinking straight. But maybe I should say something in the morning, when I go and pick up my keys from the station.' Fresh tears rolled down her cheeks. 'I wish Ollie was still alive, then none of this would be happening.'

'Oh, hun, I know.' Tanya looked like she might start crying too. 'It must have been hard for you, losing your husband so young.'

Anna pulled a couple of tissues out of the box Tanya had put next to her and blew her nose. 'It was so sudden. That was the thing. I suppose if he'd been terminally ill or something then I would have had a bit of time to get used to it.' Anna had never opened up to Tanya about Ollie's death, not wanting to put a dampener on the sunny relationship they'd developed.

'Was it an accident?' Tanya asked, then looked horrified. 'Oh God, I'm so sorry. Don't answer that. You're upset enough as it is. I don't want to drag it all up again.'

Anna pulled more tissues out of the box and wiped her eyes, debating whether to tell her the truth. 'No, it wasn't an accident,' she said eventually, deciding their friendship was solid and she was desperate to share. 'It was an operation that went wrong.'

Tanya's face crumpled. 'Oh no, that's terrible.'

'Yep, it really was.' She hesitated. 'Theo was the surgeon.'

Tanya blinked a few times, clearly lost for words. 'You are kidding me. And you're going to *marry* him?' she spluttered. 'What sort of twisted world are you living in?'

Anna realised she'd boxed herself into a corner now but decided it would be good to tell someone her plans. And talking it over with Tanya might help her decide what to do next. What were friends for if it wasn't for sharing secrets? *A problem shared is a problem halved*, as her mum always said. If Tanya knew the full story, Anna could be open and honest about what was going on. Then she'd have an ally, someone to properly talk to and even help.

Her mum had ruled herself out of that role when she'd told her she needed to move on. Insisted that she should, in fact, refusing to entertain any conversations about Theo. Her siblings were busy with their families and she didn't want to burden them. Her old friends didn't know her any more. This was an opportunity to share the load and she decided to take it.

'Christ I've done some stupid things in my time,' she started. 'But trying to get justice for Ollie's death has been the worst decision I ever made.' Her secret was bursting to reveal itself and it felt like such a relief as the story tumbled out of her mouth. The botched operations, the internal investigation, how Theo's team must have protected him. The stalking in real life followed by a more indirect stalking on social media.

'Something changed when I saw his status was single.' She frowned, trying to remember her thought processes at the time. 'My mind cooked up this crazy plan to start dating him so I could get closer and find out more about his personal life. I thought I could maybe discover a weakness that I could use to ruin him.' She sighed, the whole thing sounding stupidly naïve when spoken out loud. 'After a while I realised that wasn't working because there was nothing obvious. But then he took me to the Boat House and introduced me to Luna and I realised I could use a different plan of attack. I overheard Luna talking, telling Theo I was too young for him. She obviously wasn't keen on me, and I could see there might be a way to cause Theo emotional pain by driving a wedge between him and his children.

'So I went down that track for a bit, but I thought, why not push it further? Why not try and make him fall in love with me and propose. Then I could cause him maximum heartache by jilting him at the altar. I wanted to hurt him liked he'd hurt me, you see. Take away something he loved, so he knew what that felt like.' She gave another heartfelt sigh, annoyed with herself. 'It was ridiculous. The whole thing has been so *stupid*! But when it started working, when he started telling me he loved me, I couldn't stop. I wanted to push things a bit further, then a bit further still.'

She stopped talking and looked at her friend. 'Now it's

completely backfired. Totally out of control, and I don't know what to do.'

'I can understand your thinking,' Tanya murmured, looking sympathetic rather than shocked. 'And I have to say I like your style. It was a ballsy plan. Unlikely to succeed, but you know what, you actually did it. He proposed. And how cool is that?'

Anna picked at the blanket, pulling off little balls of fluff, while Tanya stayed quiet, deep in thought. 'I'll admit – and this is going to sound even more ridiculous – but I found myself... really liking the guy.'

Tanya's eyes grew round. 'Oh no. Don't say you've fallen in love with him?' Her mouth dropped open. 'You have, haven't you?' She rolled her eyes. 'Talk about ironic.'

Anna's heart stuttered in her chest. 'No, I'm not...' She shook her head. 'I don't...' She was blushing, blustering. 'I don't think it's got that far.' She chewed her lip, aware that Tanya had seen through her. 'Despite myself, and what he did, there's this spark between us. It's real, you know, not something you could fake. We have genuine... chemistry.' She looked at the balled-up tissue in her hand. 'God that sounds cheesy, but I don't know how else to explain how he makes me feel. And now I've seen for myself how he works and how careful he is to not get disturbed when he's operating and how much he cares about his patients.' She pulled a face. 'I sort of see things differently. It's not so black and white. Plus, I've got my mum's voice in my head telling me to accept Ollie's death was a tragic accident.' She shrugged, her voice cracking. 'I don't know what I think. But it doesn't matter any more because I just broke up with him anyway.'

'Oh, Anna.' Tanya got up from where she was sitting and came and sat next to her, pulling her into a hug. 'It's been so hard for you.'

Fresh tears welled in Anna's eyes because her friend was right. It was ironic that she'd become emotionally attached to the man she'd intended to hurt. And it served her right. Her plan had been wrong on so many levels and now she was paying for it.

She sniffed. 'He's been lovely to me, I can't fault him. Until his kids got involved and now it's turned into a disaster, because he won't listen to me, just like you said. Already they've robbed me of so much. All my mementos that reminded me of Ollie. Things that really mattered. Not to mention ruining my business. Can you believe Gino actually pissed all over a box of T-shirts I'd just had printed?'

Tanya pulled a face, looking horrified. 'Eew, that's disgusting.'

'Tell me about it. And I've got the whole place to clear up now to make it liveable again.'

'Hey, I can help you. It's my day off tomorrow. Honestly, I'd be happy to help.'

Anna shook her head. 'Oh no, I can't let you do that. Not when you work so hard. It's okay, I'll manage.'

'But you don't need to manage. I'm going to help. I insist.' Her voice was firm, and she held her tighter. 'I learnt something a while ago from this older guy who started coming to the gym. He was eighty, his wife had recently passed away and he wanted to keep himself fit and healthy. He was so easy to talk to, we ended up having all these deep and meaningful conversations.' She smiled as she remembered. 'Anyway, when I broke up with a guy I was seeing, I tried not to take my emotions to work, but I was struggling. He caught me crying and asked what was wrong. I wasn't going to say anything and then you know what he said? He told me it would be an honour to sit in the mud with me. Obviously, that was metaphorical, but as my friend, he said he wanted to sit with me while I worked through my pain.' She caught Anna's eye. 'And I realised that's what true friends do. They sit in the mud with you until you can get yourself out. And that's what I want to do with you. You are not a burden, so don't you ever think that, and it would be an honour to be able to help.'

Anna burst into a fit of ugly crying, touched by Tanya's words. Her friend held her as she cried, passing her handfuls of tissues, resting her head against Anna's. 'It's okay. You cry if you need to. I'm so angry on your behalf. Angry with Theo, the system, his kids. You don't deserve any of it.'

'I just want Ollie back,' Anna sobbed. 'I miss him so much.'

'Well, I can't help you with that, but I can help you come up with ideas for ways to get back at Theo's children for what they've done.' Her voice hardened. 'They won't know what's hit them.'

21

The next day, Tanya was true to her word, up early and making them both a cooked breakfast to give them energy for the clean-up ahead. She was bouncing around, full of energy, putting Anna to shame with her own sluggish start. She hadn't slept well on the sofa. Too hot then too cold, woken by nightmares of Gino following her, staring at her, breaking into her home when she was asleep. She had a crick in her neck, her limbs felt leaden, and her brain was still half asleep. The last thing she felt like doing was facing the devastation in her home, but it had to be done because she wanted to sleep there tonight and get her life back to normal as quickly as possible. Each day lost was costing her money.

Tanya's energy was exactly what Anna needed and once they got to the apartment, her friend took charge, deciding where they would start and which jobs each of them would do. Her system worked a treat and, after a busy morning of cleaning, Tanya had just popped out to grab some lunch for them both, when the doorbell rang. Thinking it might be the police, who'd said they would try to call round to give her an update on their investigations, Anna opened the door. She almost closed it again when she saw who it was. Theo. Looking sheepish and a bit drawn. In his hand was a bunch of beautiful red roses.

She stared at him, unable to think of a single thing to say, appalled at the way her body wanted to throw her arms around his neck and sob into his chest.

'Can I... come in?' he said eventually, handing her the flowers.

Her jaw clenched tight. 'Yes, yes, please do,' she said, her voice staccato and unfriendly as she opened the door wider, dumping the flowers on the hall table. She'd sorted out her battling emotions now, allowed her anger to win. 'Come and see what your wonderful children have done to my home.'

He sighed and followed her into the hallway, peering into the living room. It was tidy now, with a heap of bulging bin bags stacked by the door. There was a little pile of broken objects on her desk that she hoped to glue back together, stains on the carpet where a half empty coffee mug had been tipped over. The faint aroma of piss in the background.

'We've tidied up in there but come and see what they did to my bedroom and workroom.'

He followed her round, not saying a word as she showed him the appalling level of destruction. She stood in front of him, amid the decimation in her workroom, arms folded across her chest, chin jutting forward. 'What I want to know is... what are you going to do about it? They took my laptop too. I can't work without that.'

He gave another sigh, his hands in his coat pockets. 'I understand that you're upset. It's awful what's happened. But it wasn't Gino and Luna.'

'What? How can you say that?' she snapped, bristling like a hedgehog, wishing she had a protective layer of spikes. 'Of course it was them.'

He shook his head. 'I know for a fact it wasn't. The police have spoken to them and accepted their alibi. They were eating at a restaurant. They have CCTV of them going in and going out again. Witnesses to say they were there. It covers the time you were broken into. So, you see, it couldn't have been them.'

Anna's mouth opened, then closed again. Of course they had an alibi, she'd figured that out straight away, but it didn't mean they weren't the ones who'd orchestrated the crime. There was nobody else in the world who would want to do her harm like this. It *had* to be them. But she had no evidence and she knew Theo wouldn't listen.

He stepped towards her, a hand reaching for her shoulder. His touch sent a wave of longing through her body that shocked her. *I don't want him,* she told herself. *It's over.* But her body hadn't got the message. There was a magnetic pull, a force she was finding hard to resist. She stepped away from him, pushing his hand from her shoulder, noticing the hurt on his face.

'I know why you would think it might be them, and I don't blame you for pointing the finger. I mean, their behaviour the other night was appalling, but in their defence, they had been drinking.' He shrugged. 'They're good kids. Just protective of me since Emilia died. That's all it is. They think I'm emotionally vulnerable and don't want anyone taking advantage.' He gave a derisive laugh. 'It happened before, you see, just before Emilia died, and they don't trust me not to allow it to happen again.'

Anna still couldn't speak, so conflicted she had no idea where to start.

'Don't break up with me, Anna.' He took a step towards her, his eyes pleading with her to change her mind. 'Please give us another chance. I promise you it wasn't my children who did this. It wasn't.'

She didn't resist when he gathered her to him, kissing her hair, his arms holding her against his body. She could feel the beat of his heart, racing almost as fast as her own. He was running on adrenaline as much as she was. He'd been genuinely frightened she'd ended their relationship and his heartbeat was telling her she mattered to him. Really mattered. She lay her head on his chest, too exhausted to fight, not sure what to think about anything. She wanted to be loved, wanted that closeness she'd had with Ollie, and was now finding with Theo. She didn't want to be on her own any more.

The back door banged, Tanya's voice calling to her from the kitchen. 'They only had white bread for your sandwich, I hope that's okay? I'll put the kettle on.'

Theo's arms dropped and he sprang away from her, his demeanour changing. 'I didn't realise you had company.'

'Tanya's been helping me tidy up. She's been a godsend because I couldn't have done it on my own.' She remembered then why she'd been mad at him. Remembered what his children had done, and her anger returned.

He glanced at the hallway. 'Look, I've got to go, but I wanted to ask you...' he hesitated then his words came out in a rush. 'I want you to move in with me. I'm too worried about you being here on your own. Whoever did this might come back.' She studied his face, could see the concern in his eyes. 'What if it escalates?'

'I'm fine,' she said, not feeling fine at all, but not sure she could keep up the pretence with Theo either. If she decided to go through with her marriage to him, at some point the truth would come out because it would be too hard to live with her secret. Then he'd hate her. So, the relationship was doomed from the start.

Better to end it now.

It was harder living a lie than she'd ever imagined. But then... part of the problem was her confusion over her feelings for this man. He'd touched her heart in a way she hadn't anticipated, she liked being with him more than being apart from him, and life had become complicated from an emotional point of view.

She dropped her gaze to the floor, scuffing the carpet with a toe. 'I don't think so,' she mumbled. 'I need to get sorted out here.'

He pressed a key into her hand. 'This is the front door key. If you change your mind.' She glanced up and their eyes met, sending another spark through her body. There was nothing but concern in his gaze. 'I love you so much, Anna. I don't know what I'd do if something happened to you. Please, give us another chance.'

She looked intently at the floor again, and she felt his fingers brush her cheek, then a gentle kiss. Her treacherous heart skittered. 'Tell me things are okay between us. I can't focus on anything else.'

She sighed and kissed him back while a voice in her head shouted, *what are you doing?* 'I'm sorry, I'm really shaken up after the break-in. My business has been destroyed. My livelihood ruined. My sanctuary invaded.' Her voice cracked. 'It's a lot to deal with.'

'Oh, I know, darling. I know. But... look we're engaged now and hopefully it won't be too long until we're married. What's mine will be yours, but that can start now.' His voice was urgent, pleading with her. 'You don't have to work. I don't want you to struggle.' He kissed her again. 'Move in with me. Right now. There's no reason to wait. Then I know you'll be safe and you can have a breather while you sort everything out.'

She'd never intended moving in with him. That was not part of her plan. The goal was to get him to the altar and jilt him, never to get as far as co-habiting. But she would admit that she no longer felt safe in her own home. Because if it wasn't Gino and Luna who'd trashed her apartment there was someone else out there who really, really hated her. And that was terrifying.

It could be a temporary thing. Go and stay with him for now.

She could feel herself wavering.

'I've made us a cuppa,' Tanya said, walking into the hallway, stopping when she saw Theo. The smile fell from her face, replaced with a frown. 'Oh, sorry. I didn't know *he* was here.'

'I'm just going,' Theo said, bending to give Anna one last kiss. 'I'll see you later?' It was a question not a statement and she found she didn't have an answer, the key gripped in her hand. She slipped it into her pocket.

'I'll call you,' she said. A cop-out if ever there was one.

He turned and left, skirting round Tanya who was hovering in the hallway, while Anna stood rooted to the spot.

'You okay?' Tanya asked, handing her a mug of tea and a takeout sandwich. 'Shall we sit in the living room?'

Anna puffed out her cheeks and followed her friend, gratefully sinking onto the sofa. 'I really don't know if I'm okay or not. Oh God, I'm so confused now. He reckons it wasn't Gino and Luna. Apparently, they have a cast-iron alibi. CCTV, witnesses, and the police have spoken to them, ruled them out.'

'That's handy,' Tanya said, sitting next to her. She took a bite of her sandwich and chewed for a moment, thinking. 'You know, people like them don't tend to get their hands dirty. They pay other people to do that.'

Anna took a sip of her tea and stared at her sandwich, not sure if she was hungry any more. 'Yes, I did wonder about that.'

'Just throwing it in the mix,' Tanya said as she wolfed down her food like she'd not been fed in a week. 'The fact they have an alibi is very useful, don't you think? I mean, some people might wonder if they'd engineered that to put themselves in the clear, because those two would never choose to go out for a meal together, just the two of them.'

Anna couldn't help but laugh. 'You really don't like them, do you?'

'I'm just looking out for you, that's all.'

They were quiet for a moment while Tanya ate and Anna

sipped at her tea, lost in thought. Tanya had a point. A good point, which meant she was back at square one.

They got on with the tidying and by the end of the afternoon, they had the place pretty much cleaned up and a pile of bin bags to take to the tip. Once Tanya had gone, and with all her ornaments and pictures no longer there to decorate the walls and shelves, the place felt desolate. Sullied. It no longer felt like her cosy home. She felt the key in her back pocket and made a decision.

It would be daft not to take up his offer, she told herself as she packed a bag of clothes and picked up her essentials. *It's not safe here.*

But if Tanya was right, and Gino and Luna had organised for someone else to trash her apartment, they were still a problem. *Is there anywhere I'll be safe?*

22

To be on the safe side, she parked her car around the corner from Theo's house and walked. Then his children wouldn't know she was there. She let herself in, standing in the silence for a moment just to make sure she was on her own.

You're being neurotic. She drew all the curtains before switching on the lights. That made her feel more secure. *Nobody knows I'm here*, she reassured herself, putting some music on to help her relax. Theo had a fabulous sound system, and it wasn't long before she'd lost herself in her favourite songs, singing as she unpacked her bag. She found some spare hangers in the wardrobe and stood back, thinking it looked a little odd, her tops hanging next to his clothes. She sank onto the bed. Not odd in a bad way, she decided. Odd in an unfamiliar way. Perhaps she could grow to like it.

It had been a long, lonely two years without Ollie. She'd been brought up in a big, sociable family and the house was never empty. Then she'd shared houses with several other people when she was at university. After that, she'd moved in with Ollie. Until his death, she'd never spent much time on her own. And after his death she was too consumed by her grief and misery to socialise. As time went by, she'd got used to being alone. But now she'd found she liked being part of a couple again. Enjoyed the days out, the dinners in restaurants, the surprise gifts Theo liked to buy her. The conversations. The laughs. The intimacy. She liked having someone to cook for. Liked having someone who cooked for her too. Someone who wanted to please her and make her happy. Theo gave her all of this.

Is he actually the bad guy?

That was the question she seemed to be coming back to over recent days. Could she blame him for accidents which happened under pressure? Especially when he was working as part of a team and surely other people were there to check everything was being done properly. Although the focus of her anger had been on him, Ollie's death couldn't just be *his* fault, could it? She lay back on the bed as she considered her question, tired after a long day sorting out her apartment.

* * *

The next thing Anna knew, a hand was shaking her shoulder, and she woke with a start, Theo smiling down at her.

'Hello, Goldilocks,' he murmured, dropping onto the bed next to her and folding her in his arms. He nuzzled her neck and she felt her insides start to melt. *Is this really wrong?* She decided she would work on the answer later, unable to help herself from responding to his touch. 'I love you, Anna.' His breath was like feathers stroking her neck, arousing her senses.

'I love you too,' she found herself saying and this time, she thought she might mean it.

Much later, they roused themselves and Theo organised a take-away while she had a shower, smiling as she shampooed her hair. A new start was what she needed. What they both needed. Hopefully, he'd sell the Boat House and they could buy a new place for the two of them. Or could that be three? Was a family out of the question? A baby. Her pulse quickened, hope flooding her heart. It was a future she hadn't considered after Ollie had died. A future she realised she wanted with all her heart.

It was the first time she'd allowed herself a daydream that extended beyond an aborted wedding and her excitement mushroomed inside her spilling out in a bout of singing at the top of her voice. It was a relief to have thoughts not soured by ideas of revenge. And when she took that out of the equation, she had so many positive things to look forward to.

Her mum had told her to move on, not just once but many times, and maybe that's what she needed to do. She hadn't told her anything about Theo or her engagement. But now she was desperate to talk to her, wanted to see what she thought of him. Her dad would love him, she was confident of that, because he ticked all the boxes. A surgeon who wanted to provide her with a comfortable life and look after her. *Would that really be so bad?*

It seemed her mum might be right after all. But she wouldn't tell her just yet. Because Tanya might be right too, about Gino and Luna organising the trashing of her apartment. And if that turned out to be the case, their inevitable presence in her marriage to Theo would potentially be a deal-breaker.

She sighed, brought back down to earth with a devastating thud. She turned off the shower and grabbed her towel. Why was life so complicated? *It'll sort itself out.* That was her dad's favourite saying when things went wrong and he didn't know what to do. It wasn't in her nature to sit back and wait, though. She wasn't patient and liked to play an active role in her destiny, not wait for the universe to sort things out.

What am I going to do about Gino and Luna?

The answer was nothing for the time being, she decided. Theo was adamant they'd done nothing wrong and he'd said Luna had apologised to him. Tanya seemed sure that Gino was harmless. Maybe they'd be okay with her next time they met. Maybe they *would* settle down and gradually accept her. She decided she had to give them a chance and, in the meantime, see if the police found any evidence of a different culprit.

She got dressed and went downstairs to join Theo, desperate for a bit of peace and calm, determined to put everything out of her mind for the rest of the evening.

* * *

Three days later, she was back at her apartment to collect some clothes, pick up her post and take the bin bags of rubbish to the tip. Theo had bought her a new laptop and she'd sorted out an insurance claim, which had taken hours getting the right information together. Now she was ready to finish her clean-up operation and think about what she was going to do next.

Theo was still trying to persuade her to move in with him and let the apartment go. She would admit to being sorely tempted, but if she gave up her home and things didn't work out with Theo's kids, she would have lost her bolthole. Finding a place to rent was desperately hard at the moment, especially for people who were self-employed and if she gave up this apartment, there was no telling how long it would take to find another. She'd be homeless. The sensible thing was to hang on to it for now. But at least if she was staying at Theo's, it would give her a chance to redecorate, as her landlord had suggested, and give the place a proper clean. Then she might feel comfortable coming back.

The break-in had unnerved her so much, she found herself glancing around as she went backwards and forwards with the bin bags, loading them into her car. She thought she heard footsteps, but when she looked, nobody was there. Then she convinced herself she heard someone cough, but again, it was just her imagination.

Most people who lived on the row were out at work during the day, apart from the medical students in the end house. It was a quiet street and where she parked at the back was quieter still. It was no surprise that she should feel so jumpy after the break-in, but she was starting to get on her own nerves, telling herself to just get on with the job, then she could go.

Finally, she finished loading the car and was locking the back door when the hairs stood up on the back of her neck. She'd heard something, a voice she thought she recognised. *Was that Luna, or am I imagining it?* She was certain she'd heard someone say 'Anna'. Her body tensed, her hand poised, clasping the key in the lock, while she listened some more. But before she could turn, footsteps ran up behind her and something hard and heavy struck her on the back of the head.

Her world turned black.

23

Anna came round slumped on her back doorstep, struggling to remember what had happened. Her ribs hurt. And her legs. And her stomach. And her face. At the speed of a tortoise, she managed to get onto her hands and knees, and sat back on her heels, the world spinning around her, a weight seeming to sink to the back of her head. Her stomach heaved and she puked onto the steps, retching until there was nothing left but bile.

'Hey, are you okay?' She glanced over to see a man standing by the back gate. He walked towards her, a shopping bag in his hand, the back lane being a cut through to the supermarket.

She groaned, a wave of dizziness washing over her, feeling too ill to even speak.

He put his bag down. 'Have your hurt yourself? Oh my God, is that blood?' He grimaced when he got closer, pulled his phone from his pocket. 'Oh, your poor face. You're going to have a real shiner. Look, I'm calling for help, okay? Looks like you've had a nasty fall.'

She could feel herself tipping sideways and put out an arm to steady herself, but there was nothing there to connect with.

'Let me help,' he said, grabbing her before she smashed into the steps. 'Let's get you lying down.' He took off his jacket and folded it for a pillow, putting her in the recovery position before calling an ambulance.

He crouched beside her, gave her a reassuring smile and she couldn't quite place him. She thought she knew all her neighbours, but she was sure she hadn't seen him before. 'I'm Adam, by the way. End house.' Ah, that made sense, he was one of the medical students. No wonder he knew what to do. 'Look I'm going to go and get a blanket to keep you warm while we wait for the ambulance. Won't be a moment.'

She managed to murmur a 'thank you' before she drifted into blackness again.

* * *

The sound of the paramedic's voice brought her round and her eyes blinked open to see a dark-haired woman peering at her. 'Oh hello, you're back with us. I'm Jenny, we're just going to get you to the hospital for a check over. We've got the stretcher here and we're going to lift you on it, okay?'

She managed a nod, feeling hands lifting her before she blacked out again, only coming round when she was wheeled into the emergency department, hearing the bleeping of machines, the hum of conversations. She squinted against the glare of overhead lights, her body aching and sore. Slowly, she remembered what had happened. She'd been attacked. Someone had crept up behind her and whacked her on the back of the head and she was pretty sure she knew who that someone might be. She adjusted her position on the bed, trying to get more comfortable but there was a pounding in her head that wouldn't stop.

A nurse came to do observations, giving her a gentle smile as she wrapped the blood pressure cuff round her arm.

'Do you think I could have a painkiller? I've got a terrible headache. And my ribs hurt.' Just speaking made the pain worse.

'The doctor will be round in a minute, so you can ask him. But we don't normally give painkillers with head injuries. Not until we know what's going on.'

Anna groaned inside, her anger mounting that someone had done this to her. But she hadn't been able to tell anyone what had happened yet.

'I was attacked,' she said to the nurse, who stopped what she was doing.

'Oh... the paramedics said it was a fall.'

'That's what the man who found me assumed, and I was so nauseous and woozy.' She winced, every word spoken a hammer blow to her brain. 'I couldn't actually speak to him to tell him any different.'

The nurse was frowning. 'Okay, well I'll pass that on. I'll just finish up here, okay?' She put a monitor on Anna's finger, checked everything was working, pressed a few buttons on the screen.

'I need to speak to the police.'

The nurse nodded, preoccupied and Anna wondered if she'd actually heard what she'd said. 'Yes, I know,' she said, as she finished what she was doing with the screen. She gave her a quick smile. 'I'll go and sort that out for you now.'

They decided to keep her in for observation because she kept blacking out, although the x-rays showed no broken bones, no damage to her skull. In light of the new information that she'd been attacked, the doctor thought she'd had a bit of a kicking. She also had concussion, but nothing too serious. Everything would heal given time.

* * *

Sometime later, once she was settled in the ward, two police officers arrived to ask her about the attack, and she slowly answered their questions. Every word she spoke jarring through her and she hoped they wouldn't stay long.

'So, you're saying you think your fiancé's children attacked you?'

She nodded. 'That's right. I'm sure I heard Luna's voice seconds before I was hit. So, it couldn't have been Luna who hit me, but it could have been her brother. And maybe both of them put the boot in once I was down. I don't know.'

'And these are the same people you thought had broken into your home, but we then found had a solid alibi?'

Anna sighed. 'That's right. If they didn't break in, they organised for someone else to do it. I am 100 per cent sure they were behind it.'

'I take it you don't like them,' the officer said, carefully and she had the distinct feeling he thought she was accusing them out of spite rather than genuinely thinking they were responsible. That she had some sort of vendetta against them. Whereas the opposite was true.

She gritted her teeth, thinking they probably had another cast-iron alibi organised for this little episode too. They were going to make her look stupid again, discredit her in the eyes of the police and then they'd be able to do anything, and nobody would believe Anna's version of events. *They'll think I've got mental health problems or something.*

'It's not so much that they don't like me. I've only met them a few times, so I don't really know them. But they have strongly objected to my engagement to their father. That's what they don't like: the fact he wants to get married again and possibly sell the family home.'

Her headache was getting worse, the effort of talking becoming too much. She rubbed at her forehead. 'I don't think I can tell you any more today.' Her stomach lurched and she put a hand over her mouth convinced she was going to be sick. 'I'm not feeling too good.'

The officers looked at each other, the one taking notes closing his notebook before they both stood. 'That's enough to get us started. We'll begin the investigation and give you an update tomorrow. We might have some more questions by then.'

Anna could hear footsteps hurrying across the ward, then the curtain was pulled back to reveal Theo, looking anxious.

'I just found out you were here. Christ, what's happened? They said you'd been attacked?'

She closed her eyes, a wave of nausea flowing over her, too weak to re-tell her whole story. His hand clasped hers.

'Ah, you must be the fiancé,' one of the police officers said. 'I wonder if you have a few moments to answer some questions?'

'You go,' Anna murmured, her eyes closing as her stomach lurched again. 'I just need a bit of a rest.'

'Of course. Of course,' she heard him say, felt a kiss on her forehead. 'I'll be right back.'

* * *

The air was filled with the smell of cooking when she woke again, food being handed out to the patients on the ward. She looked at her plate of baked potato, beans and cheese and wasn't sure if she fancied it or not. On the one hand she was hungry, but on the other, the effort of sitting up and actually eating it felt like too much.

Her head was feeling clearer though and she stared at the ceiling thinking about the attack, wondering if she'd told the police everything they needed to know. Thank goodness her neighbour,

Adam, had shown up when he did. Otherwise, she could have been lying there for hours. When she was discharged, she'd definitely have to go and thank him.

In the back of her mind, she could almost decipher what Luna had said and she focused on that, trying desperately to catch it before it disappeared, teasing it out of the recesses of her mind. 'There's Anna. It's a warning,' she thought she'd heard her say. 'Nothing too brutal.'

That was it! But could she be sure the voice was Luna's?

'Anna, I need to speak to you.' Theo was back and she realised he must have been away for quite some time.

He adjusted her bed, so she was sitting up and sat next to her, a deep frown on his face, his voice hushed, no more than a fierce whisper.

'What on earth are you doing pointing the finger at my kids again? The attack on you has nothing to do with them and once again I've spent hours of my life talking to them and the police, trying to find out what is going on.' He bent towards her. 'I can tell you they are getting extremely upset about this.'

'Not as upset as I am about what they've done to me,' she snapped, then wished she hadn't as a vice seemed to tighten round her skull.

'They both have solid alibis. Again.' He gave a frustrated huff. 'You've got to stop this. Not only is it vindictive, but you are putting a wedge between you and them.'

More like a wedge between you three and me, she thought. And wasn't that exactly what they wanted? Their plan was working. 'I'm not saying they attacked me. I'm saying they *organised* an attack on me. I heard Luna talking, just before it happened. Then someone came up behind me.'

Theo shook his head, his lips so firmly pressed together they had all but disappeared. 'Sorry, I'm not buying it. I know my kids and they wouldn't do it. I think you're imagining things. How do you know it was Luna if you didn't see her?'

'You *think* you know your kids,' she murmured, aware that she'd never persuade him they were to blame. And that was a problem unless the police came up with something concrete. She didn't have the energy to fight her corner, but she knew Gino and Luna were winning. They were getting what they wanted. The question was how could she prove what they'd done?

A more worrying question was: *what might they do next?*

24

The next day, she was told she was being discharged from hospital and rang Theo, knowing he had a day off. He came to pick her up, his mood sombre and silent, answering with as few words as possible, his voice clipped and curt. Clearly, he was still in a mood with her about pointing the finger at his children and she hoped they could have a proper adult conversation about it when they got back to his house.

She was still feeling delicate and not up for a fight, but had decided that, for the sake of self-preservation, she would have to press pause on her relationship with Theo unless he agreed to see his children's terror campaign for what it was and make them stop. It was going to be a difficult conversation, but she knew it was the only way forward. He'd been so desperate for them to continue their relationship when she'd told him it was over a few days ago, perhaps the threat of leaving him would make him see things in a different light.

Her head felt better, and she'd been able to have some painkillers at last, but her body was stiff and sore, and she had trouble keeping up with him as he strode down the corridors ahead of her. Even when she asked him to slow down, he still marched ahead, unwilling to make allowances for her injuries. It was an uncaring side to him she'd never seen, and it was making her uneasy.

His behaviour struck her as strange, but not as strange as the fact he drove to her apartment, rather than to his house. He parked outside and just sat there, not speaking for a few moments. She could see his jaw muscles moving, like he wanted to say something but couldn't find the right words.

'Is everything okay?' she asked, a stupid question because she knew it wasn't.

He turned to her then, an expression on his face she couldn't work out. Was he angry? Sad? It was hard to say. Her body tensed as she waited for another telling off about implicating his children in criminal activities and how it could ruin their careers, their whole lives. Blah de blah de blah. What about *her* and her life and her career? Why wasn't he prioritising that?

But it turned out, that's not what he wanted to talk about.

'You know, my working life is full of surprises.' His voice was weary and he was staring through the windscreen, not looking at her. 'Good surprises and bad surprises. Sometimes people live, who you were sure wouldn't make it. And sometimes people die unexpectedly.'

Her body relaxed and she reached for his hand. This wasn't about her, and what had happened with his kids, it was about him having a hard time at work. It was easy to forget that his job pivoted on life and death decisions because he never spoke about that aspect of it. Easy to underestimate the sort of pressure that must put on a person.

'I'm sorry if you've been having a difficult time.'

He slapped her hand away, looking at her as if she'd tried to mortally wound him. 'In my job, every day is difficult. But you know that.'

Her hands found each other, and she clasped them tight, not sure where this conversation was going, or why he hadn't taken her back to his house.

'A couple of years ago, I had a really difficult situation. I was in the middle of an operation, and I got word there'd been a pile up on the A55. Several casualties with severe injuries. They needed me in theatre as soon as we'd finished.'

Her hands gripped each other tighter. There was a familiarity about this tale, and she didn't like where it was going.

'Long story short, we rushed the operation and left a clamp and a swab inside a patient. It shouldn't have happened, but we were needed in the next theatre to save a child's life.'

'The next day, we realised our mistake and set about correcting the situation. Unfortunately, I was distracted in the middle of that operation. Somebody said something that took my mind off what I was doing for a second and an artery was cut, it wasn't noticed in time, and the patient died.' He took a deep breath. 'I'd been working all night on the casualties from the pile up. I should have gone home, let somebody else do the operation, but I felt a responsibility to my patient and my team to put right the original oversight.'

She opened the car door, needing some fresh air. The patient he was talking about was Ollie. The story was his. But before she could get out, he pulled her back, locked the door.

'You will sit there while I finish,' he snapped, the tone of his voice so stern she knew she had no choice.

'Anyway, investigations were held. I was absolved of blame. It wasn't intentional and these things happen in surgery every now and again. No operation is without risk.'

He was silent and when she could bear it no longer, she glanced across at him, saw him staring at her, eyes blazing, his jaw working from side to side. Her palms were slick, her face burning.

'That was your husband, wasn't it?'

Anna chewed at her lip, nodded.

'And you are the wife who wrote me hate mail? Tried to get me disciplined for negligence? Insisted I was investigated?'

She couldn't respond, couldn't admit to it. The silence was unbearable and eventually she had to speak.

'That was before I knew you. Before I understood you'd always do your best to save a patient.' She reached for his hand again, but he snatched it away.

'And why, may I ask, would you then want to date me?' He gave her a stony glare. 'No, let's not fudge the issue. We've gone way past that, haven't we? Why would you want to *marry* me if you hate me so much?' He practically snarled at her, his gaze so intense it seemed to pierce her brain. 'It's all been a pretence, hasn't it?'

Panic fluttered in her chest. How could she possibly explain herself? There *was* no sensible explanation, except that she'd fallen in love with him. Despite her best efforts to deny it, that's what had happened.

'I don't hate you, Theo. Not any more. Honestly, I don't. I'll admit that I did at one time. But not now. That was grief talking. I love you, Theo. Honestly, that's the truth.'

He gave a derisive snort. 'You expect me to believe that? I have written proof that this is all a game to you. Someone very kindly sent me an anonymous message. An extract from your journal, I believe.' Her breath caught in her throat. *Oh God, no.* She squirmed in her seat. 'Your plan was to jilt me at the altar, wasn't it? Maximum emotional harm. I am Project Theo to you. Not a person, I'm a bloody mission.' He smacked the steering wheel with his hand and she jumped, startled by this show of anger.

Her heart stuttered. That was exactly what she'd written in her journal. The one she kept on her laptop. Writing down her thoughts was part of her therapy, and she realised that whoever had stolen her laptop must have sent that message to Theo, told him who she was. Didn't that confirm it must have been his children?

'You are a vindictive, deceitful witch,' he hissed, his eyes filled with hatred. 'I never want to see you again. Do you understand me?'

He got out of the car, opened the back door and threw a handful of carrier bags on the pavement before slamming the door shut. She could only imagine it must be her clothes and the bits and pieces she'd left at his house.

'Get out!' he bellowed, as he got back in the driver's seat, his anger boiling over. 'Get out of my sight.'

She scrambled out of the car, closing the door just as he screeched away from the kerb.

25

She gathered her bags and shuffled inside, so shocked that her brain was refusing to work, her mind locked on his final words. He was furious with her, his voice soaked with loathing, and it was hard to believe there could be any way back for them now. This really was the end. After just over five months of dating, he'd dumped her.

The apartment was barren and unwelcoming. She shivered, even though it was warm outside. Everything that had happened over the last week was her fault, she thought as she slumped on the sofa, letting her bags fall to the floor. If she hadn't started this crazy plan, Gino and Luna wouldn't have wanted to scare her away from their father and she would still be bobbing along, managing to earn an income and living a decent life.

But it hadn't been a decent life, she reminded herself, her teeth nipping at her lips as she tried to keep her sadness at bay. She'd been miserable. Lonely. Empty of joy and full of bitterness. An obsession with getting revenge had been eating her up, stopping her from moving forwards, changing her into someone she didn't recognise. Someone she didn't even like.

Ironically, once she'd got to know Theo and understood the pressures he worked under, she'd found herself questioning whether her mother was the one talking sense. Despite her anger towards him, she'd found she liked Theo's company, found they had the same sense of humour, enjoyed the same music, the same foods. And then, without realising it was happening, she'd stupidly fallen in love with him.

There, she'd admitted it. She loved the guy and now he hated her. She heaved a sigh. How the tables had turned, a full one-eighty, in the blink of an eye.

Only myself to blame.

How did she imagine he wouldn't find out who she was? Talk about blinkered thinking. At some point it would have come out, so this situation had been inevitable from the moment she'd started her pursuit of him. She bit her lip harder, trying to stop the tears from falling, searching for a positive she could cling on to.

It would have been worse if he'd discovered the truth further down the line, she reasoned, and they were already married. Because that's where she'd been heading in her mind. She wasn't going to jilt him, her emotions had taken her way past that point, to a place where she'd had happy daydreams about their future together, even a family of their own.

She puffed out her cheeks, telling herself there was no use moping. That wasn't going to get her anywhere. She needed to pick herself up and start again, but right now, what she needed was a hot drink to warm herself up. She struggled to her feet, wondering how long it would take her body to heal, because there wasn't much she could do while she felt so sore. Every time she moved, something ached, or a muscle objected, sending a stabbing pain through her body. Even blinking was uncomfortable with her black eye. If she'd had a duvet she would have gone to bed, but she didn't even have that.

She hobbled into the kitchen and filled the kettle, staring out of the back window as she waited for it to boil. The gate was still open, and she could see her car stuffed with bin bags, reminding her there was so much to do.

The kettle came to the boil, and she made a coffee, good and strong to keep her mind from going to sleep. Which was exactly what her body would like her to do. But she wasn't comfortable in the apartment on her own and needed to stay alert, not convinced that Luna and Gino had finished with her yet. There was a good chance they didn't know Theo had broken up with her, that their job was done. She shuddered to think what they might try next.

But... what if it really wasn't them? asked a voice in her head. What if they were telling the truth and were innocent and she'd been jumping to conclusions? Christ, she didn't even want to think what that might mean.

She got out her phone and rang the police, asking to have a word with the officers who came to see her in the hospital.

'I'm afraid we haven't made much progress,' the voice on the line told her. 'We did house-to-house on your terrace and spoke to all the neighbours who were around at the time of the attack, but nobody saw or heard anything.'

'Did you speak to Adam? He's one of the medical students at number twenty-four. He was the one who found me and called the ambulance.'

'Let me just check that for you.'

The line went quiet for a few moments, and she drummed her fingernails on the worktop while she waited. The officer came back on the line sounding puzzled. 'I don't have a record of anyone by that name and we did speak to the occupants of number twenty-four. Nobody called Adam though. Are you sure you've got the right house?'

'But he told me that's where he lived.'

'Do you think you may have misheard?'

'No, it was definitely Adam and he said that's where he lived and he seemed to know first aid.'

'With respect, lots of people know basic first aid without being medical students. And anyway, none of them were in at the time of the attack. They were all in a lecture. And we've confirmed that was the case. Plus... I can see now, just checking back on the people we spoke to on your row, there wasn't an Adam.'

'Oh... right.' She was thoroughly confused now. Why would Adam, if that even was his name, have given her a false address?

The officer told her they were following up a sighting of a vehicle of interest, that was illegally parked in the vicinity at around the time of the attack, and he'd get back to her when they had any news.

She thanked him and rang off, a horrible sinking feeling in the pit of her stomach. Was Adam her saviour, or could it be possible that he was the one who'd attacked her?

No, she shook her head. That was silly logic. Nobody would do that, would they? Attack someone and then help them while they called an ambulance. No, that would be weird. But then, if Theo was right and this vendetta against her was not his children, maybe it was a weirdo. Could it be someone who'd seen her at the gym, maybe?

Christ, she needed to talk this through with someone because her brain wasn't making sense.

She picked up her phone again, relieved when it was answered on the second ring. 'Tanya, thank God.'

'Hey, what's the matter? You sound all wound up.'

Anna took a deep breath, not sure where to begin. 'I don't suppose you could come round, could you? I was attacked outside the house yesterday and I've just got home from hospital and—' She burst into tears, unable to even finish her sentence.

'Oh no, that's terrible. Look, I can finish in about an hour. My last client just rang in to say they're not well. Do you need me to pick up anything for you on the way over?'

Anna hung her head, swiping at her cheeks with the sleeves of her hoodie, sniffing back her tears. 'That would be fabulous. Honestly, I don't know how to thank you. I need a duvet, that's the main thing, and pillows. The intruder last week ripped mine to shreds, and I haven't replaced them yet because I've been staying at Theo's. And if you could get me a couple of ready meals. That should keep me going for now.'

'No worries, I'll be there as soon as I can. And in the meantime, make sure the doors are locked, okay?'

They said their goodbyes and Anna took her drink back into the lounge. *Thank goodness for Tanya*, she thought, sipping her drink, wondering how she was going to get herself back on track this time. She'd had so many knocks in the space of a few days, she felt thoroughly defeated.

Her mind drifted back over the whole five months of her relationship with Theo. Those first, tentative dates, the thrill of having an attentive boyfriend. The first kiss, meeting Luna, the gentle lovemaking, a magical weekend in Paris, the pub lunch with his kids, then his romantic proposal. Followed by that disastrous announcement of their engagement to his children, which had led to carnage. Anna had been kidding herself if she'd thought she could drive a wedge between Theo and his kids. Luna had shown how to truly drive a wedge between two people. What a great job she'd done of breaking up Anna's relationship with Theo.

A tear tracked down her cheek and she wiped it away, something niggling at the back of her mind. Then she remembered what it was. When she'd been in the Boat House on the night she'd met Luna, she'd taken the top sheet of blotting paper from Emilia's desk, stuffed it in a side pocket of her handbag and had promptly forgotten about it. Something about it had attracted her attention and now she decided to take a closer look.

Her bag was on the floor, and she picked it up, found the folded paper and took it over to her desk, where she flattened it out. It was covered in doodles, scribbled numbers, and cryptic notes. But the most interesting thing was what she could feel rather than see. Indentations of words that had been written using the blotter to lean on. She grabbed a pencil and started to go over the page with it, shading lightly, like she'd seen in a detective drama years ago, smiling to herself as letters and words began to appear.

Once she'd finished the whole sheet, she leant in to study what had been revealed, surprised to find Emilia's signature written over and over again in a long column, evenly spaced, like someone was practising how to write it. Other words came to light, and she realised, with a start, that she was reading a suicide note. Not written once, but three times, slightly different versions, making her think that whoever had been writing had been trying to make it perfect.

Now who did that with a suicide note? And who would need to practice their own signature?

26

Tanya finally turned up a couple of hours later, waddling up the front path fully laden. She was carrying a new duvet under one arm, a bag of pillows under the other and had a bulging carrier bag in her hand. Anna hurried to let her in.

'Oh, my word, look at your poor face,' Tanya said as she stopped on the doorstep, holding out the carrier bag. 'Can you grab this before I drop it?'

'You are an angel,' Anna said, taking the bag and standing back to let her inside. 'I'm really not up to shopping today.'

Tanya took the duvet and pillows into her bedroom and Anna followed her in. 'I thought you would be staying at Theo's, but I can make up your bed if you like.' She gave her the side-eye, obviously fishing for information, but Anna wasn't sure she could tell her yet without bursting into tears.

'That would be brilliant, thank you. The doctors think I had a bit of a kicking, but I can't remember anything.' She winced as she bent to pull open the drawer where she kept her clean bedding.

'Hey, stop it,' Tanya said, coming over and sorting out a bedding set. 'I can see you're hurting.'

Anna straightened up and got out of her way. 'Whoever it was sneaked up behind me and whacked me over the head.'

Her hand instinctively went to the back of her skull where she had a neat row of stitches. Thankfully, the lump had gone down now, but they'd warned her it would take a little while for her bruises to heal and the head injury meant she needed to take it easy.

Tanya got to work while Anna picked up the bag of food and took it into the kitchen, slowly unloading it onto the worktop, each movement making her grit her teeth against the pain. Her friend reappeared in the kitchen doorway and gently moved her out of the way. 'Let me do that. You put the kettle on.'

Anna made their drinks while she watched Tanya stacking the pile of ready meals in the fridge, her mind busy with mental arithmetic, trying to work out if she had enough money in her account to pay her back. 'I hope the shopping's okay,' Tanya said, closing the fridge door. 'I wasn't sure what you had in, but I bought enough for a few days.' She pulled a slip of paper out of her back pocket. 'I'll leave the receipt here.' She tucked it under a tin of baked beans she'd left on the worktop. 'You can do me a bank transfer when you've got a moment.' She smiled. 'No rush. I've just been paid.'

'I don't know how to thank you,' Anna said with a grateful smile, passing her a mug of coffee. 'You're a real lifesaver.'

Tanya took the drink, held it to her chest. 'So, I'm dying of curiosity here. Why aren't you staying at Theo's?'

'He...' Anna swallowed, not sure if she could even say it. 'He broke up with me.'

She looked at the floor, an emotional whirlpool gathering in her chest, and she knew there was nothing more she could say on the matter without collapsing into a sobbing mess. Even though she now had questions about the man and how his wife had died, she still hadn't been able to sever the emotional tie, not just to him, but what he represented. A future she could have been excited about. A dream she thought she'd lost when Ollie had died. And now she'd lost it again.

Tanya's eyes went round, her jaw dropping. 'Oh. My. God. I was not expecting that. You only just got engaged.' She frowned, took a sip of her drink. 'What on earth happened?'

Anna couldn't speak without having a complete meltdown and after a few moments of silence, Tanya seemed to sense her discomfort, rolled her eyes. 'I'm sorry. It's none of my business. I'm so bad at just blurting things out.' She reached out to Anna, put a hand on her shoulder. 'That's bad timing with everything else that's going on. Do you think it was too much drama for him to deal with?'

'No, that wasn't it.' Anna walked towards the living room. 'Come on, I need to sit down. Let me tell you what happened.'

It was a hard story to relate, and she kept having to stop to push back her emotions, but she finally managed to get to the end.

'He practically pushed me out of the car. Told me he never wanted to see me again.'

Tanya pulled a face. 'Ooh, that's harsh, isn't it? He could at least have talked to you about it.'

Anna shook her head. 'No, his mind was made up.'

'The guy's an idiot, his daughter's a bitch and his son has... issues. You're better off out of that family. Honestly, hun, you'll look back and see this as a great escape.'

Anna nodded, but the hurt was too fresh for her to feel anything apart from heartache, however well-meaning her friend's comments might be. 'Even if this is the end, I want the chance to explain myself. To talk things through with him.'

'Have you tried ringing?'

She shook her head and instantly regretted it, her poor brain objecting to any sudden movement. 'Not yet.'

'Well, if that's too much, message him. Perhaps that will start the conversation you need to get closure on it all.'

'This is why we're friends,' Anna said, wondering why she hadn't thought of it herself.

She scrolled through Instagram. 'I can't see his profile any more.' She looked up, caught Tanya's eye.

'He's not blocked you, has he?'

'You know, you could be right.'

'I'll look on my phone,' Tanya said. She scrolled for a moment. 'Yep, I can see him, his profile's still up. He's definitely blocked you.'

Anna sniffed, told herself not to start crying again.

'You could go old school and try a text?'

Quickly, Anna tapped out her message and pressed send:

> I can't tell you how sorry I am that you had to see that journal entry. It was written in anger weeks ago and is in no way a reflection of how I feel about you. I love you, Theo, and I want to be your wife, for us to have a future together if your children will allow that to happen. Please can we talk? Xxx

She frowned. 'Why won't it send?' She tried again. And again, before realising what that meant. 'Looks like he's blocked my phone number as well.'

Tanya put her empty mug on the coffee table and gave Anna a gentle hug. 'Look, I know you're hurting now, but you might feel better about this tomorrow. You've got to remember where this started. Theo killed your husband and, at the end of the day, if your objective was to hurt him, it looks like you succeeded.' She rested her head against Anna's. 'You were going to jilt him at the altar anyway. It's just happened a little earlier. You know, the guy wanted to marry you, which means he was totally in love with you and although your heart is feeling bruised, *his* heart is broken. That's why he's so angry with you.' She gave Anna a squeeze, which made her wince. 'You did it. Mission accomplished. Now you can put it all behind you and move on.'

She considered Tanya's words, and realised she was right. She *had* accomplished what she'd set out to achieve. She just hadn't expected to get hurt along the way. That's what had thrown her. 'If only it was that easy,' she murmured.

'It really is though.'

'I just have bad vibes about the whole thing. You know that awful sinking feeling in the pit of your stomach when you know something terrible is about to happen?'

Tanya pulled away, frowning. 'Why's that, do you think?'

She wrinkled her nose as she tried to put her thoughts in order, deciding to keep them to herself for the time being. She wanted to go over her research, re-read the news reports on Emilia's death before she started making accusations. But she was sure there was something distinctly suspicious about her apparent suicide. And if Emilia hadn't ended her own life, then who had? She had the names of three people in mind. One of whom she might be in love with.

'I suppose I'm just shaken up after everything. It's been a lot in a matter of days. Like my life has been hit by a hurricane.' She sighed. 'I'm still mentally clearing up.'

'Aw, it's been tough, hasn't it?' Tanya dropped her arm from Anna's shoulder, shifting in her seat so she could see her face. 'But after what's happened, the best thing you can do is draw a line under all of this.' She gave an emphatic nod. 'Walk away, my lovely. Just walk away.'

'I know. You're right.' She swilled her now-cold drink round in her mug. 'I'm just hoping everyone else who's been involved feels the same.'

Silence descended for a moment, both of them lost in their thoughts.

'At least it's all been reported to the police.' Tanya gently prised the mug from Anna's hand, put it on the coffee table. 'So... what have they said?'

'Very little. I asked for an update earlier and they don't seem to have got very far. Although... they did say they were investigating a car that was parked illegally nearby at the time of the attack. So that might be a lead. And the guy who helped me seems to have told me a false name and address, which is weird.' She sighed. 'I've just got to wait, I suppose, let them do their stuff.'

'Here's another positive to cheer you up.' Tanya pointed to Anna's left hand. 'If he's dumped you, he's broken the contract and that ring is yours. I bet it's worth a bit of money. You could always sell it to keep you going while you get your business up and running again. That might make up for some of the damage his kids have done.' She got to her feet and stretched like a cat. 'Look, I'm going to head off now. I told my mum I'd go over there this evening. She's still feeling a bit low after her old dog passed away.' She pulled her car keys out of her pocket, pointed them at Anna. 'Any problems, you give me a call, okay?'

'Thanks for everything,' Anna said, watching her friend let herself out.

* * *

Anna stared at her engagement ring, thinking about Tanya's suggestion. Now Theo had blocked her from contacting him, it was obvious he wasn't going to let her explain. Their relationship was over, and she had to try and accept the situation. In which case... it wouldn't do any harm to have the ring valued, would it?

There was a little jewellery shop just down the road. They

would be able to tell her what it was worth, and she was curious now. She'd spent all her accessible savings on Project Theo – the clothes and the beauty treatments – and she would be struggling for cash while the insurance claim was sorted out. Realistically, it would take a couple of weeks to get any sort of cashflow coming in again. Selling the ring wasn't a bad idea as a contingency fund. Even if she just pawned it for a short while, the money would help.

Talking things through with Tanya had changed the way she was feeling. Her sadness had morphed into anger at the way Theo had treated her, not allowing her a moment to explain herself. The callous way he'd let her struggle after him at the hospital. His blank refusal to believe his children would ever do anything wrong. Tanya was right. Again.

The ring sparkled in the light. It was a big stone. The money would definitely come in handy. *Think of it as compensation*, she told herself, liking the idea more and more. *I'll go now*, she decided, before she could talk herself out of it.

It was raining. Of course it was, it had been that sort of a day. But it meant she had to struggle into her jacket before she could shuffle down the road, each step sending a stab of pain through her bruised body, a stinking headache jarring her brain. But she was on a mission and determination drove her on.

The bell tinkled as she opened the shop door and a middle-aged man looked up from the glass counter where he was putting watches out on a display tray.

'How can I help you, love?' He stopped what he was doing and gave her a warm smile.

She slipped the ring off her finger. 'I'm thinking about selling this and I just wanted an idea of what it might be worth.' She swallowed, embarrassed because it was probably clear to him there was a story of rejection behind her actions.

He took it from her and turned it over in his hand, peering at it from different angles, held it up to the light and frowned. Shrugged. 'Twenty quid, maybe.'

She gasped and snatched it back, putting it in her pocket rather than back on her finger. 'I don't think so,' she snapped. The guy must believe she was stupid. 'It must be worth hundreds, or even thousands.'

He shook his head. 'Nah, sorry love, it's not a real diamond and it's not real gold. It's a fake.'

Her mouth dropped open. 'I don't believe you.'

He shrugged. 'You don't have to believe me. Take it somewhere else and they'll tell you the same thing. There's no hallmark, which you would have if it was genuine gold. And the stone is the wrong colour and doesn't refract the right properly for it to be a diamond.' He returned to his task of putting watches on the stand. 'I've been working in the industry all my life and I am 100 per cent certain I'm right.'

He sounded so sure, she believed he was telling the truth. She turned to go.

'Ditch the guy who gave you that,' he said as she opened the door.

Too late for that, she thought as she walked home, her mind picking over this shock discovery. If Theo had given her a fake ring, it meant she'd read the situation wrong. It meant that he'd never genuinely meant to marry her. And that must mean... he knew who she was before he'd proposed.

27

Ten days later, Anna had heard nothing from Theo. Neither had she seen his children loitering about and her bruising had subsided. The insurance claim had been paid, so she'd been able to order more stock and had started to work on her Etsy shop again.

With plenty of time on her own to think about things, she understood that Tanya was right about walking away from Theo and his family. But if they did start their nasty tricks again, at least she now had some information she could use against them. The police would be very interested in the piece of blotting paper she'd found and the hidden writing she'd uncovered. To keep it safe, she'd put it in a plastic Ziplock bag and hidden it underneath her wardrobe. It was an insurance policy against future problems with the Heaton clan and that, at least, gave her some peace of mind.

Her research had led her to believe that Emilia's death could still be questioned given her new bit of evidence. She'd read through the news reports on the inquest and seen that she'd died of drowning, but before death, she'd suffered a head injury. The coroner ruled death by suicide because there was a note, and the police had concluded the injury had been caused when she'd hit her head on a rock after jumping off the jetty. They had investigated, of course, but could find no evidence of foul play. There was, however, plenty of evidence that Emilia was in poor mental health and had just been given the news that her husband planned to leave her, and she was going to lose her home. Her suicide note had suggested it was the break-up of her family that had led her to take her own life. It was too much heartbreak for her to bear.

Anna believed a different conclusion could be drawn. Luna would hate the family being broken up. If her mother died, then the house would stay in the family. Not only that, her mother's death would scupper Theo's plans to leave. He was a devoted father and as Anna had seen, he would do anything for his children. Could Luna have killed her mother – either intentionally or by accident and covered it up as suicide?

She didn't have the answers, but she thought her evidence would be ample cause for the police to reopen their investigations. Theo and his family wouldn't want that, would they? So that was the ace she had up her sleeve, ready to play if there was any more trouble and it made her feel confident that she was a match for them whatever stunt they might decide to pull.

However, given the lull in malicious activity, she was starting to believe it really was all over and for that she was grateful.

On another positive note, she realised Project Theo had stopped her obsession with the unfairness of Ollie's death and all in all, she believed there was a chance for her to be happy again in the future. *Every cloud has a silver lining*, she kept telling herself. Even finding out the ring Theo had given her was a fake had helped, especially when Tanya called round on her way home from work and she finally felt ready to talk to her about it.

'What a loser,' Tanya said, starting to giggle. 'Imagine thinking he could get away with buying you a fake. If he thinks it's okay not buying you a proper ring, then you're definitely better off without him.' She was convulsed by a proper laughing fit and, after seeing there could be a funny side to the story, Anna joined in. 'Plenty more fish in the sea,' Tanya said, when her laughter died down. She gathered Anna to her in a hug. 'Get yourself down the gym a bit more and you never know who you might meet.'

Anna rolled her eyes at that. 'Yeah, maybe that's not the best place to meet people. Look what happened with Theo.'

'He'll be the right person for somebody.' Tanya replied with a grin. 'Just not you. I mean, there was way too much emotional baggage from the start. Even if he hadn't found out what you were planning, you were together for all the wrong reasons.'

Anna thought Tanya was probably right. Again. Her friend's reaction made her realise she could make a different choice in how to process the revelation. Perhaps he hadn't known who she was before he proposed after all. Secretly, his deception still rankled, but on the whole, she was starting to fade out the memories of the good times they'd had together and focus on all the bad things that would have made their relationship impossible in the long run.

* * *

The next morning, Anna decided to go back to the gym, her membership being another bonus of her failed Project Theo. And there was her friendship with Tanya as well, something she wouldn't have had before either. In fact, her whole health and beauty regime had been down to Project Theo. So, lots of good things had happened that could help her bounce into a better life.

The only thing she was a bit nervous about was bumping into him, but she was hoping if that happened, they could just ignore each other. Or at the very least, be civil. Anyway, she was pretty sure she'd picked a time of day when he wouldn't normally be there and was humming to herself as she entered reception.

Jen, the receptionist, glanced up as she walked in, a look of surprise flashing across her face. 'You're a dark horse, aren't you, Anna?' she said, giving her a weird smirk. Anna couldn't work out what she was talking about. Had Tanya told her about the failed engagement, the fake ring? She hoped not because all of it was pretty embarrassing.

Confused, Anna hurried out of reception and made her way to the workout room. Tanya wasn't in that morning, but they were meeting for lunch in town afterwards. Gethin was in charge and when he saw her come through the door, he stopped putting the weights back on the rack, and gave her a wolf whistle. 'Go Anna,' he called, which made a few heads turn her way.

People were sniggering, trying not to laugh, flashing coded looks at each other. She could feel her cheeks burning and checked herself in one of the floor-length mirrors, wondering what was so funny. Her black eye had faded to almost nothing. Most of her other bruising was barely visible. The joke was a mystery.

Deciding to ignore them, she did a short routine, not wanting to over-exert herself on her first session back, then made her way to the changing rooms for a quick shower.

She was getting dry when her phone beeped. Then another beep and another. She could tell by the sound they were notifications, but it was rare for her to get so many. *How odd,* she thought, as she checked what was going on, dropping her phone in horror when she saw what everyone had been reacting to. It was a short video, posted on the gym's Facebook page, that she'd been tagged in, and she was star of the show.

Her hand covered her mouth as she made herself watch the video, her heart hammering in her chest as she tried to work out how this could have happened. The poster was an account called 'Annalikesboys'. Clearly fake because she had nothing to do with it. The clip was from a porno movie, and somebody had put Anna's face on the woman's body. It looked very real, and a casual observer wouldn't know it was a fake. It had been posted with a caption that read:

Anna's warm-down routine after her gym session.

It had hundreds of likes and a whole list of crude comments she couldn't bear to read. The account of Annalikesboys had tagged her to make sure she was aware of their handiwork.

Mortified didn't begin to explain how she felt. People would think it was real. Christ, how was she going to be able to show her face in here again? How was she even going to get out of here without dying of embarrassment? She stood with her eyes closed, not moving, not knowing what to do for the best. There wasn't an easy option.

Finally, she got dressed and hurried to reception, her eyes on the floor the whole way, not looking at anyone she met in the corridor. It was a relief to see that Jen wasn't busy with any clients and for the moment, the reception area was empty.

'I need to talk to you,' she whispered, as she approached the reception desk. *Oh God, this is unbearable.* 'Something has been posted on the gym's page of me doing— stuff, and it's a fake. I need you to take it down.'

Jen raised her eyebrows. 'Oh, it's fake, is it?' She clearly didn't believe her.

'Yes, it is,' Anna hissed, looking around to make sure they couldn't be overheard. 'I'd never post anything like that.'

Jen's expression changed then, became serious. 'I was going to catch you on your way out. The manager isn't happy and you're lucky he's on his break at the moment. He asked me to have a word and give you a warning that your membership will be revoked if anything like this happens again. He said there have been a few calls from our female clients this morning complaining about it.'

Anna's heart sank. 'I can't promise it won't happen again because it's not me who posted it!' Jen's expression said she still didn't believe her and tears pricked at Anna's eyes. 'Do you seriously think I'd want to humiliate myself like that.'

Jen's voice softened. 'Okay, if you say so.'

Anna blinked back her tears, desperate not to start crying in reception. 'I want you to delete it and block the account Annalikesboys. Then hopefully it won't happen again.' She dropped her eyes to the floor. 'I can't tell you how embarrassed I am. This is me being humiliated by someone. It's malicious.'

Jen seemed to understand then how devastated Anna was feeling. 'It's okay, I've already done that. The manager told me to just before you came through.' She tapped a few keys on the computer, went onto the gym's Facebook page and showed Anna that the post was gone. Then she blocked Annalikesboys from posting again. 'That make you feel better?'

'Yes, thank you,' Anna sniffed, her eyes stinging. 'I want to know who was responsible for posting it though? The username Annalikesboys is not my account.'

Jen shrugged. 'It's a public page. Anyone can post on there, I'm afraid, so we'll probably never know.'

Anna's jaw tightened and she thanked Jen again before heading out of the door, feeling several pairs of eyes on her back as she walked away. She messaged Tanya and told her what had happened, said she couldn't face being in town in case she met someone who'd seen the video. Instead, she trudged home, her hood up, head down, horrified that someone had done this to her, knowing she could never set foot in the gym again.

Not long after she'd got back, there was a knock on the door and

Tanya was standing on the doorstep with takeaway pizza and a couple of coffees.

'I'm so sorry this has happened to you,' she said as she walked in. 'I had a look when you messaged me, but the post had gone, so I didn't see it.'

'Well, I'm glad about that. I wasn't convinced it had really been deleted. But I felt like everyone else in the gym had seen it. It was awful. Mortifying. I didn't realise what they were all sniggering about until I'd done my session and had a shower.' She blew out a long breath, still shocked that it had happened. 'You wouldn't believe it. My face on a porn star's body. And if you didn't know me well, you wouldn't be able to tell it was fake.'

Tanya flopped onto the sofa, Anna sitting at the other end, the pizza box in between them. 'So, who do you think did it?' Tanya took a slice of pizza, but Anna wasn't hungry. In fact, she felt sick and had done ever since she'd seen the video.

'I'll probably never know. It was a fake account, of course. Annalikesboys.'

Tanya giggled. Then flapped a hand. 'Sorry, I'm sorry, I know I shouldn't laugh but you must see the funny side.'

Anna bristled. 'Surprisingly, I can't.' She watched Tanya take another bite of her pizza, and she could tell by the twitch of her lips she still thought it was funny.

Tanya sipped her coffee. 'Are we looking at Luna and Gino again as chief suspects?'

'I'm actually thinking Theo might have had a hand in this one. He's the one with a connection to the gym. I'm not even sure his kids know I go there.'

Tanya whistled through her teeth. 'Jeez, you think so? But I suppose with the sexual element to it, you could be right. He wants to humiliate you, the same way he feels you humiliated him. Is that what you're thinking?'

'That's exactly what I'm thinking.'

She took a sip of her coffee. 'Are you going to tell the police?'

Anna huffed. 'Is there any point? They haven't made progress with the break-in or the attack on me, so I can't see them doing anything with this. I mean there's no physical harm done this time, people seem to see it as a joke.' She gave Tanya a pointed look. 'It's only me who doesn't find it funny. And I suppose it's been deleted now, the account is a fake, so whether it's possible to find out who set it up I don't know.'

Tanya popped the last of her pizza into her mouth and licked the tomato from her fingers. She gave Anna a sheepish look. 'I'm sorry I laughed. Honestly, I can see it's really upset you and that was wrong of me. I mean if I was in your shoes, I wouldn't be happy about it either.' She took a sip of her drink. 'I feel for you, I really do. Let's hope that's the end of it. It's ridiculous what that family has put you through.'

'I know,' Anna said, wearily. 'I'm dreading what they're going to do next.'

Tanya changed the subject then, obviously bored with the latest of Anna's tribulations. She suggested a movie at the weekend, but Anna declined, not sure about her friendship when Tanya had found the whole episode so hilarious. *What is wrong with people?* She'd rather be alone than spend her time with pseudo-friends who might be laughing at her behind her back. She didn't even believe Tanya when she said she hadn't seen the video, because she knew she was an admin for the gym's page. Of course she would have seen it.

A little while later, they said their goodbyes and she watched Tanya pull her phone out of her pocket to make a call the minute she left, laughing as she walked down the street.

Hmm. Although Tanya had been kind and helpful, this latest episode had shown a different side to her personality and made

Anna have a re-think. She wasn't sure she trusted Tanya. Not one little bit.

When she let her mind run back over their recent conversations, she realised they could be seen as information gathering exercises as much as anything else. Wanting to know what she was going to do. And did she see a flicker of relief on Tanya's face when she'd said she wasn't going to go to the police with this latest act of harassment? She thought she had.

Now she considered it, Tanya was ideally placed to put up that fake post, wasn't she?

28

Later that afternoon, after ruminating on the whole fake porn episode, Anna decided she was jumping to conclusions. The fact that Tanya had laughed at something a lot of other people had found funny too didn't make her less of a friend. Or untrustworthy. She'd been there for Anna ever since they'd first met. It was human nature, and she was the type of girl who was forthright with her emotional responses; something Anna liked about her. She didn't pretend, she was real, and you couldn't have it both ways.

Feeling thoroughly disheartened, Anna rang the police for an update, but the officer had nothing new to tell her. She mentioned the fake video, but he didn't seem to think there was much they could do about that apart from make sure it had been taken down. Yes, he understood it was harassment, but new technology had an unfortunate way of making it easy for people to do stuff like that and they really didn't have the manpower to chase up every incident. They were prioritising the personal attack and the break-in, but he'd add a report to the file.

The conversation left her feeling she had been firmly put in her place. She sensed a lack of urgency and although she knew the police were under-staffed and had more serious crimes to deal with, she had hoped for some concrete evidence to be found that might lead to an arrest. Only then would she believe there could be an end to her torment.

Deciding she couldn't rely on the official route to find the perpetrator, she realised that it was going to be up to her to do it for them. She would have to gather evidence to prove Luna and Gino, and maybe Theo as well, were trying to destroy her. Because she couldn't just let them ruin her life. They couldn't be allowed to get away with it.

Okay, so she was aware that she'd started it, with her play for Theo and her stupid plan. The family had written evidence of that now Theo had a copy of her private journal. But that was harmless compared to what had been done to her. Disproportionate revenge. They'd made her suspicious of everyone, nervous in her own home, jumping at every sound. And this latest episode had taken away her social life, just when she'd started to enjoy getting to know new people again and being part of the gym community. It was no way to live her life and even if she couldn't bring them to justice, at the very least, she had to work out how to make the harassment stop.

After mulling it over for the evening, she lay in bed, unable to sleep. Her bedroom was at the front of the property, and she thought she heard scuffling. Straining to hear, she was immediately alert and sat up in bed, swinging her feet onto the floor.

Is that somebody outside the front door?

She crept to the window, peeped round the curtain. The streetlight that illuminated this part of the road wasn't working, and it was pitch-black outside, but she'd been lying in the dark for hours, so her night vision wasn't too bad and at least there was a moon tonight. Hardly daring to breathe, she scanned the area but decided there was nothing to see, no unusual shadows, no movements.

The mewl of a cat made her jump, followed by a low growling

sound and she let the curtain drop back into place. Just cats, she told herself, as she climbed back into bed, satisfied there was nothing amiss.

The next morning, she woke late and was making herself a coffee when there was a loud rap on the front door. It was the postman, who handed her a couple of parcels and a letter.

'I wasn't sure if you'd seen,' he said, looking slightly embarrassed. 'But you might want to get that wiped off.'

She frowned, puzzled, not sure what he was talking about, her mind not really woken up yet. He pointed to the door and her brain froze, her mouth dropping open in disbelief. In big white letters, spray-painted across the dark blue gloss of the door was the word:

whore

'Christ!' she gasped. 'How the hell am I going to get that off?'

'Probably need a repaint, love.' The postman shook his head. 'Sorry to be the bearer of bad news.'

'No, it's okay. Thank you for telling me. I might not have seen that for a couple of days because I tend to use the back door.'

'Yeah, that's what I thought.' He gave her a wave and carried on with his round while she stared at the door. Now all her neighbours would be wondering why someone would be painting derogatory insults on her door, trying to guess what she'd done. She could almost see the curtains twitching, could feel herself shrivelling inside.

She sighed and slammed the door shut, angry and frustrated and thoroughly awake now. This was the final straw. She had to make it stop, and quick. Her heart sank when she thought about ringing the police again, but she had to add this latest episode to the list of harassments on file. After a brief conversation with the officer, she took a photo and sent that through to him, thinking it was probably the last she'd hear of it.

Her next job was to go and get some paint and get rid of the graffiti. That took her all morning because it needed two coats, but she was satisfied once she'd finished that the words were no longer visible. This constant firefighting was completely draining, and she couldn't help thinking there would be yet another fire to put out tomorrow. But how could she get it to stop?

She thought about her evidence stashed under the wardrobe. *Should I use it now?* But if she presented it to the police, the family would counter with her Project Theo admission. They'd say it was a vendetta and the police already sounded a bit tired of her constant enquiries. Her evidence was there as a last resort, but she decided there was something else she could do first.

Go and talk to Luna.

29

The very idea of confronting Luna brought her out in a cold sweat, but she had to be brave to sort out this mess. She was 100 per cent convinced Luna was behind everything, orchestrating things even if she hadn't done them herself. And if that was the case, persuading her to stop was the only solution. Her jaw tightened as she pictured an angry Luna. She was taller than Anna, more ferocious and definitely more cunning. However, Anna would have the element of surprise.

Without letting herself dwell on things too much, she set off for the Boat House. But there was nobody home, no cars on the driveway. She waited for an hour, wandering around the grounds, wondering how it had come to this. She walked along the stone jetty that jutted out into the Straits, peering into the dark water. Could you really drown by falling off here? It didn't seem deep enough, but the tide was out, and she could see the dark line on the stone where the water level reached at high tide. Plenty deep enough at that point. Especially if you hit your head on one of the rocks lurking under the water, or on the edge of the jetty itself.

She shivered in the dusk, unnerved by the solitude of the place, the way nobody would know you were here. *Time to go,* she thought, as she lost her nerve and headed home.

* * *

Her journey took her past Theo's estate and she found herself turning into his road, driving past his house. The curtains were drawn but the lights were on. His car was in the drive. Luna's car too. Her heart did a peculiar skip and she pulled to the side of the road. This was it. This was her opportunity to bring this horrible episode to a close because she could speak to both of them at the same time. Have a reasonable, measured conversation. She would be contrite and apologise, ask for their forgiveness, beg them to draw a line under the whole thing.

With her heart hammering in her chest, she walked up the driveway and rang the doorbell. Her palms were slick with sweat, and she was nervous to see Theo again after the way they'd parted.

The door opened and there he was in a white shirt and grey chinos, looking handsome and calm until he realised who was standing on his doorstep. His eyes met hers and narrowed, his eyebrows pinched together. The sight of him made her gulp, her mouth so devoid of saliva she wasn't sure if she'd be able to speak, her carefully practised apology stuck in her throat.

'What are you doing here?' he snarled. 'I told you I never wanted to see you again.'

He went to close the door, but she stuck her foot in the gap, wincing as he tried to make her move it by banging the door again and again. He looked feral, his teeth bared in frustration and she started to gabble, desperate to get this excruciating encounter over with.

'Theo, I'm sorry, I'm really, really sorry. I've been so stupid, and I promise I have absolutely learnt my lesson. But please can you and your family stop harassing me now?'

His frown deepened. 'Harassing *you*?' His voice was indignant. 'You're the one standing on my doorstep. It looks very much like you're the one doing the harassing.'

'Well, if it's not you, then it must be Luna. I can't go on like this, I need it to stop. Can I talk to her please?'

He leant towards her, his eyes flinty with anger. 'I have no idea what you're talking about and if you don't get off my property, I'll be calling the police.'

'What's happening, Dad?' Luna's voice drifted from the lounge. Then she was standing behind him in the doorway. 'Oh God, it's you.' She screwed up her face like she'd smelt something terrible. 'What on earth do you want?'

'I want you to stop it, Luna. I've apologised to your father and I'm happy to apologise to you. But I want us to go our separate ways and leave it at that. Please. No more dirty tricks.'

'Dirty tricks?' Luna sneered. 'I have no idea what you're talking about.' But there was a satisfied gleam in her eyes, her face not giving the same message as her words. 'You're the one who keeps getting me hauled in front of the police on the basis of no evidence whatsoever. You're the one who's been playing tricks on *us*.' She looked at Theo. 'That's right, Dad, isn't it?'

He put a protective arm round Luna's shoulder. 'Absolutely. You must think we were born yesterday. Did you really believe we wouldn't work out who you are? Luna warned me about you, but I didn't want to believe anyone would be that malicious. Then in Paris, once you were relaxed, you gave me plenty of clues. Luna confirmed it once I got home.' He must have seen the shocked look on her face because his lips curled into a satisfied smirk. 'You thought you were so clever, didn't you? I decided to see how far you would go, play you at your own game. But this last episode with the police was the final straw. Now piss off, Anna, before I call the police again and we see who they think is harassing who.'

Anna was dumfounded. 'You knew when we were in Paris?' That lovely romantic holiday had been a mirage. She could hear her teeth grinding together, her soft centre starting to harden, like cooling lava turning to stone. 'Then you bought me a fake ring. Hah, that figures.'

He sneered at her. 'It didn't take you long to try and cash that in, did it?'

How did he know that? She glanced at her bare ring finger and took a deep breath. She would have to think about that later but here and now, trading insults was not going to get her anywhere. What she needed was a truce. Having exhausted all other avenues, it was time for Anna to pull out her trump card. 'Okay, so you're all very clever. And I'm stupid. Let's agree on that. But if you don't stop harassing me, then I will have to take my evidence to the police.'

Theo and Luna glanced at each other, a flicker of unease in their eyes. 'What evidence? What are you talking about?'

'I have evidence that Emilia's death wasn't suicide. Written evidence. And if you don't stop harassing me, then I will take it to the police.' She noted the horror on their faces, gave a satisfied nod. She was right. They *were* hiding something.

They glared at her. She glared back, the silence as good as an admission of guilt.

'You're lying,' Theo snarled before he slammed the door on her foot again, so hard this time she screamed and snatched it away for fear he was going to break bones.

The door closed and she hobbled back to the car, her spirits at an all-time low. She'd played her trump card but wasn't sure if it had worked. Yes, they'd been horrified at the idea there might be evidence, but did they believe her?

She drove home, feeling shaken by the encounter, replaying the conversation in her mind. Theo sounded so certain they hadn't been involved in the dirty tricks on her. Of course, the fact he said they didn't do it, didn't mean it was the truth, but she had to at least consider the alternative. If he was right and it wasn't them who'd been causing her trouble, then who could it be?

The only name she could come up with was Tanya.

And the more she thought about it, the more it started to make sense. She'd made herself into Anna's confidante, knew more about her than anyone else. She knew what would hurt her, what might destroy her. She'd known about her plan with Theo. She was the only person who knew everything. Was it possible she had her own agenda and had been playing her own game with Anna while pushing the blame onto Theo's children?

But why would she do that?

30

All fired up, she drove to the gym, knowing that Tanya would be working. She parked up and gave her a call, but it went to voicemail. It was likely she was with a client and, looking at the gym now, Anna felt sick at the thought of going in there. She told herself to be brave, she could cope with the sniggers, but her body refused to move.

She sat there for a while before deciding her inability to get out of the car was the universe telling her to go home and calm down. Gratefully, she started the engine and drove back to her apartment, still unable to summon the energy to get out of the car. The events of the last few days had really taken a toll on her, and she hardly dared go inside in case there was another nasty surprise. Dog poo through the letterbox. Or the windows broken, or—

The ringing of her phone broke into her thoughts.

'Hiya, I missed your call.' Tanya sounded out of breath. 'I was just fitting in a workout before my next client. Is everything okay?'

'No, it's not,' Anna snapped, before she realised her tone was all wrong. She sighed. 'There's been more trouble. I don't suppose you fancy coming round when you've finished, do you? I'll make something to eat, if you like?'

'Yeah, okay, that would be great.' There was a smile in Tanya's voice, as usual. She was one of life's cheerful people and it made Anna question her latest theory. 'It'll be about eight, I think.'

'Perfect, see you later.'

There, the universe was helping her again, making her believe this was the right thing to be doing. Tonight, she would get her chance to have a proper chat with Tanya. In the meantime, she could do a bit of online investigating. Finally, she managed to get herself out of the car.

She set up a new Instagram account under a false name and started browsing. She could access Theo's account now, but he hadn't posted anything since they'd broken up and she noticed that he'd deleted every picture he'd taken of her or the two of them together.

Then she looked at Luna's account. It was all house stuff and the work she'd been doing on the renovations, like she was lining herself up to be an interior designer or something. Definitely all business, nothing personal at all. Gino wasn't on Insta. But Tanya was.

She pulled up Tanya's account, finding it was all gym related and not what she was looking for at all. Anna remembered Tanya had said she had another account, a personal one, but it could be called anything, so she couldn't think how to find it and anyway, it sounded like she no longer used it much. She chewed at her lip, thinking she'd learnt absolutely nothing new.

The final place she looked was the gym page. She knew the video of her had been removed from the Facebook page, but she'd forgotten they had an Instagram page too. She had a quick browse through the pictures and reels, feeling a pang of regret that she wouldn't be part of that community any more. It was a place where she'd felt at home, and she was starting to get to know some of the other clients who had a similar timetable to her.

Something caught her eye, and she scrolled back, enlarged the picture, her heart giving a startled leap. Gethin had posted a video of him teaching a client how to do squats correctly, and in the background were two people reflected in the mirror.

Tanya and Theo. Not unusual for them to be in the gym at the same time. What was unusual was the fact he was very clearly kissing her. She checked the date. Two days ago. Before Theo had broken up with her. *Hmm... so what is Tanya's game?*

31

Anna made the evening meal with a lot of thumping of pans and ferocious chopping of vegetables. But she found it was a cathartic way to get rid of her anger, while her mind sorted through the questions Tanya needed to answer. If that picture of them had been taken only two days ago, how long had their little romance been going on? When she thought about it, there'd been a marked change in Tanya's behaviour towards her, evolving from sympathy to making fun of her. How she'd laughed at the fake porn video, which suggested it was likely to be her doing. And the fake engagement ring. She'd found that hilarious and it had been her idea to get it valued.

There was no doubt she'd enjoyed Anna's downfall but there were questions about timing and what happened when. Theo had told her earlier that he'd known she was faking their relationship during their trip to Paris, when he'd managed to piece a few things together and confirm what Luna had told him. She remembered a few deep conversations they'd shared. Theo talking about Emilia, and she'd opened up about Ollie. Not a lot, just snippets. It was a bit of a breakthrough, she'd felt, at the time. A sign that he trusted her enough to share what had happened. It encouraged her to do the same, although up to that point, she'd shared very little about herself. Of course she was careful, or at least had tried to be, but she'd been pleasantly drunk, and couldn't quite recall the whole conversation. What had she let slip?

Up to that point, Theo had never asked about her past. He didn't seem interested, happy to leave it be and live in the present, their conversations focused on whatever activity they were doing together or plans for the future. Now she could see that was a bit odd. Did he not want to talk about the past because he had things to hide – just like she had? Wouldn't he want to know her better, know what had shaped her into the person she was today? At the beginning, she'd put it down to ego and him only being interested in himself. He'd certainly dominated their early conversations, but she'd been happy to listen and learn how to be the partner he wanted.

It seemed they had been involved in an elaborate dance, neither of them genuine, pushing each other to see how far they would go with the pretence without the other realising. It made her feel sick to realise she'd been played so comprehensively. She decapitated a carrot with such force, the top flew across the worktop and bounced on the kitchen floor.

She went to retrieve it, telling herself to calm the heck down. *You'll be chopping a finger off next and they're not worth that. None of them are.*

She was making a lamb casserole and once all the vegetables were chopped, she layered everything in a casserole dish, with thinly sliced potatoes on the top and slid it into the oven. It was the sort of dish she could leave on low if Tanya was running late, something that seemed to happen regularly.

A bottle of wine stood on the worktop, and she opened it, poured herself a glass and leant against the fridge while she took a big glug, then another... Before she knew it the glass was empty, but her mood had mellowed a little. Enough to make her not want to kill anyone at any rate.

She sat on the sofa, nursing a second glass of wine, her mind drifting as she listened to some calming music. She frowned as she thought back to all the times Tanya had kept her waiting. Was that a control thing? A way of exerting her power. Christ, she'd been so gullible she was furious with herself. *How did I not see through her?* Conniving, scheming little—

The doorbell rang, stopping Anna from finishing the sentence in her head. She steadied herself, took a deep breath and pinned a smile on her face before answering.

Tanya bounced inside, grinning as usual, because after all, Anna's situation was hilarious, wasn't it? Anna could hear her teeth grinding and loosened her jaw, not ready for a fight just yet. They could have a chat, she would mellow Tanya with wine, then they could eat. Once her guest had been lulled into a false sense of security, then she'd go on the attack. Ambush her when she was nice and relaxed and her guard was down.

It was hard to keep the conversation light, but Anna managed to witter on about the insurance money coming through and her business, asking Tanya about her day and what she'd been up to in the time since they'd last seen each other. Thankfully, once they'd finished eating, Tanya reverted to type and started quizzing Anna on the latest thing that had gone wrong.

Okay, she thought, mentally shifting into a different gear. *Time to get the party started.*

She pulled out her phone and showed her the pictures of the front door.

Tanya gasped, but now, to Anna, it didn't sound like genuine shock. Now it sounded like it was for show. She kept glancing at her and sure enough, she saw the flash of a grin. Evidence, she felt, to prove her case. Tanya was in on this latest episode of harassment.

'That's dreadful,' Tanya said, handing back the phone. 'Did you report it?'

'Yes, but they didn't seem very interested.' She sighed. 'If they can't find out who attacked me, or who broke in, I'm not expecting them to be worried about a bit of graffiti.'

'But it's harassment.' Tanya looked at her, wide-eyed, seeming to want a greater response, a higher level of dismay and hurt.

Anna had to stop herself from leaning across the table and slapping her across the face. 'Anyway,' she said, as if unconcerned. 'I've sorted it out. I painted over it. And I know who did it.'

'You do?'

'Yes,' she said, staring Tanya in the eye. 'It was you.'

Tanya looked surprised for a second before she threw her head back and laughed. 'God, you're funny.'

Silence. Tanya shifted in her seat. Looked a little uncomfortable, the grin dropping from her face.

Anna kept her composure, determined that her hurt would not show. But inside, her anger was boiling at a volcanic heat. 'I know it was you. And the sex video. That was you too.' She watched Tanya squirm, a range of expressions flitting across her face, like she didn't know how to respond to this direct confrontation. She finally settled on an outraged frown.

'Don't be ridiculous,' she snapped.

Anna pushed her chair back and stood up, leaning across the table, eyes narrowed. 'I am not ridiculous!' she shouted, her temper exploding in an outburst that surprised her as much as her guest. It was too hard to keep her anger in check now Tanya's guilt was so obvious. 'I know you think I'm stupid, but I'm really not.' She picked up her phone and found the video at the gym, passed it to Tanya. 'Tell me, who can you see in the picture?'

Tanya's frown deepened and she glanced up at Anna, clearly confused. 'It's Gethin.'

Anna grabbed the phone back and enlarged the picture, zooming in on the incriminating evidence. She handed it back. 'In the mirror. Who are those two people?'

Tanya gasped, her hand covering her mouth. She dropped the phone on the table like it had burnt her hand.

Anna felt a warm glow of satisfaction. That was the face of a guilty person, and momentum was on her side. 'You and Theo. Kissing. And that was posted two days ago. So maybe you'd like to tell me what's going on?'

'We were larking around, having a bit of fun at the end of the day. He just grabbed hold of me,' Tanya blustered, her cheeks suffused with colour. She looked down at her hands, sounding more contrite now. '"One little kiss", he said. You can see he's got me pinned against the wall. He wouldn't let me go until I said yes. I didn't want to but he's so persuasive. You know that.'

'No, I don't think I do know that. He never persuaded me to do anything.'

Tanya gave a derisive laugh. 'Oh, I think he did. I think he persuaded you to fall in love with him, without you even realising what was happening.' Now Anna felt she was on the back foot because that was painfully true.

She backed away, leant against the worktop, her arms folded across her chest. 'So, you and Theo... are you an item?'

Tanya gave a bark of a laugh. 'Don't be daft. I told you, it was a one-off. He made me do it. I didn't know why at the time, but now I've seen that video I can understand what his game was.' She gave a dismissive snort. 'Me and Theo. Nope. That's never going to happen.' She gave an emphatic shudder.

This was confusing. How could Theo make Tanya do anything? Did he have some sort of a hold over her? She decided not to ask the question, not wanting to distance Tanya if she was telling the truth and she'd jumped to the wrong conclusion.

'I need him to promise me that we're done with stupid games. I need him to come and talk to me and tell me to my face.' She caught Tanya's eye. 'He's not speaking to me, so you're my only hope. Do you think you could ask him to stop?'

Tanya looked dubious. 'Well, I could try. But I can tell you, he's pretty mad with you at the moment.'

Anna paced across the kitchen floor, more questions buzzing round her head. 'What about the break-in. Was that you too? And the attack?'

Tanya held her hands up. 'No, of course not. I wouldn't do anything that awful. Look I'm really sorry about the pranks, but they weren't my idea. Theo organised it all and then made me do it.'

Anna snorted. 'Yeah, right. Like why am I going to believe you?'

'Look, I didn't do it because I wanted to hurt you. I did it because I was stuck between a rock and a hard place. I had to save —' Tanya swallowed the rest of her sentence, got to her feet and edged towards the living room, her eyes flicking towards the front door. 'I'm sorry I've upset you. I know it's been hard on you, and they were stupid pranks, but I promise nothing like that will happen again.'

Anna glared at her. 'You think I'm ever going to believe a word you say? And what did you have to save?' She huffed when she got no reply. 'If anything else happens, I will be going to your manager and telling them exactly what you've done. I have a recording of this conversation and I have the pictures and don't think I won't do it, because you are ruining my life and I won't have it. Understand?'

Anna hadn't actually thought to record their conversation, but Tanya wasn't to know that, and she did have the pictures. Hopefully the threat in itself would be enough because she knew her ex-friend couldn't afford to lose her job. She intensified her glare, letting all her anger filter into a look that would have forged steel.

Tanya pressed her lips together, nodding vigorously as she backed into the living room. She looked like she wanted to say something but wasn't sure. Anna watched as she edged closer to the front door, her hand grasping the door handle as she finally spoke. 'All I can tell you, is... I'm the least of your worries.'

Then she was gone, and Anna was left wondering what she could have meant.

32

A week later, Anna was starting to believe her conversations with Theo, Luna and Tanya had done the trick. Nothing untoward had happened for the last seven days and she was beginning to relax and piece her life back together. She'd been working hard on new items for her Etsy shop, money had started to come in and she'd been sending a steady stream of orders out.

Financially, she was still having to tread carefully, but it looked like she could pull through this bad patch. She'd invested in a video doorbell as a precaution at the front of the property, but couldn't yet afford a camera at the back, so she wasn't using that entrance as much, especially when it was dark. She'd even cancelled her membership at the gym and signed up for a different one on the other side of town.

She hadn't had any contact with Tanya, but neither had she heard from Theo, and she still needed his personal assurances that he and his children were done with their vendetta. If she didn't have that, she would always be anxious, looking over her shoulder, wondering if they were going to turn up again. It meant she was living on her nerves, adrenaline constantly firing through her veins, disrupting her digestive system and ruining her sleep.

For all she knew, Tanya had asked him to stop, and he'd agreed, but nobody had thought to tell her. She messaged Tanya, suggesting the threat of telling her manager what she'd been up to was still on the table.

An immediate reply pinged back:

> I have asked Theo to stop, but he hasn't said yes or no. Said he doesn't want to talk about it, so I'm not sure there's much else I can do. Please don't tell my boss. Please!

Anna didn't think there was much Tanya could do either. In reality, this was between her and Theo. After a half-hour debate with herself, she decided to go and see him again and hope, now that a bit of time had passed, he might have calmed down.

Not today though. She needed to think about what she wanted to say. She also needed to decide on the best place to confront him. Going to his house didn't work because he could just slam the door on her. She decided it might be better to accost him coming out of work, where he'd have to be on his best behaviour and things shouldn't get too heated. The hospital would be as safe a place as any.

The next morning, she woke up early, feeling more energised after a better night's sleep and decided to head up to the new gym for an early workout before she started packing up orders. It was a lovely warm morning, the sky was clear and she swung her gym bag as she hurried up the back path to her parking space.

When she opened the back gate, a weight landed in the pit of her stomach, her good mood shattering into a thousand pieces. Someone had tipped a can of red paint all over her car. And by the looks of it, the paint was gloss and it had dried, set hard. The windows were covered, the car not fit to be driven.

Gritting her teeth, she took out her phone and snapped some pictures, tears stinging at her eyes. Just when she'd thought it was all over, they'd struck again. Whoever 'they' might be. She'd never get this paint off. Her car was ruined, and she'd have to put in an insurance claim for that now to get it sorted out. Which meant she'd be without her car for a while. Her mind raced on, listing all the inconveniences until she was positively hopping up and down, incandescent with rage.

This is going to stop, right now.

She decided it was a waste of time trying to speak to the police on the phone and they might take her more seriously if she went to the station.

* * *

After a bit of a wait, she was called into one of the station's meeting rooms and she went through all the details and showed the officer the pictures.

'This is a continuation of the previous harassment,' she said, her anger threaded through every word she spoke. 'It's all connected, and I don't know what's happening with the previous incidents, but as I have told your officers several times, the perpetrators are Luna and Gino Heaton and their father, Theo. One of them did this. But all three of them are in this together. It's an ongoing vendetta.' She hesitated, having to let a flush of emotion subside before she could speak, but still her voice cracked. 'They're trying to break me.'

The officer frowned. 'And why would they be doing that?'

Unfortunately, that was the question she couldn't definitively answer. She opened her mouth to speak, then shut it again. 'I don't know' wasn't going to get the police excited to help her. Neither was 'they don't like me'.

She sighed and looked down at her hands, tugged at a hangnail while she decided how much of the truth she should tell. 'I was briefly engaged to Theo. His children took an instant dislike to me because he suggested we might sell the family home, which his daughter has been renovating, and buy a new place. They went mental about that. Absolutely off-the-scale mental. Then Theo found out I was the wife of a patient of his who died, and at that point he decided I was trying to scam him or something and he called the relationship off.'

The officer raised his eyebrows, pursed his lips. 'Right. A bit of a domestic situation. And you think there's still bad feeling, even though you're no longer engaged and therefore there's no threat of the house being sold?'

The way the police officer said it made her wince. It sounded very improbable when it was put like that. She nodded. 'That's right. Theo feels wronged. This is revenge.'

'And you say he's a surgeon up at the hospital?'

'That's right,' she said, blushing. Oh God, she knew exactly what he was getting at. Would a surgeon really resort to pouring paint over somebody's car? It sounded so childish and petulant, an unlikely action for someone in such a responsible position. She sighed, her body heavy with defeat, knowing without a shadow of a doubt that the police wouldn't be chasing this up anytime soon.

The officer gave her a reassuring smile. 'It's not acceptable, what's happening to you, but we need to keep an open mind. Looking at the file, it appears the Heatons all have alibis for previous incidents, but this is the fifth attack on you or your property, so obviously somebody has an axe to grind. Can you think of anyone outside Mr Heaton and his family who might have a grudge?'

She shook her head. 'No, I really can't, and it seems a strange coincidence that all this trouble started after we got engaged and his kids had a major tantrum about it. I've never had any trouble before.'

The officer collected up the paperwork, a clear sign the interview was coming to an end. 'Leave it with us and I'll add this to the case files, speak to the officers who have been working on the investigation. Hopefully we'll have some answers for you soon.'

Not soon enough, she thought as she left the station.

She called an Uber and headed up to the hospital, determined she would wait for Theo to finish his shift. At some point today, she would sort this situation out. Then they could all go their separate ways and live happily ever after. *Ha! Yeah, right.* She wasn't convinced that was possible but at least she had to try.

The hospital receptionist was a bit cagey about giving information regarding Theo's working hours, but Anna told her she was his fiancée and she'd been away and lost her keys and couldn't get in the house. It was a convincing sob story, she felt, and sure enough, it worked. Theo would be finishing at one.

She checked her watch, an hour and twenty minutes to wait. The best place to catch him would be by his car and she knew where he parked so she grabbed herself a sandwich from the cafe and headed over there to wait.

His car was parked in a corner, bordered by shrubs on two sides. A long van in the next parking spot sheltered her from the breeze and she leant on the bonnet of his car as she ate her sandwich, working through the imaginary conversation she was going to have with him. Her mind drifted off as the time went by, taking her on a cringeworthy journey of her recent past and the things she should never have done.

She checked her watch. It was twenty-five past one and she'd expected Theo to be here by now. He must have been delayed, and all she could do was wait some more, making notes on her phone of things she needed to do for work.

'Anna!' She heard someone calling her name and looked up to see a tall figure striding towards her, but it wasn't Theo. It was Luna. And from the look on her face, she was not happy. Not happy at all.

33

As Luna got closer, her scowl turned into a smile.

'Anna, I'm so glad to see you,' she said, all breathy, like she'd been running, car keys clutched in her hand. 'I've been meaning to come and see you but honestly, I was too embarrassed by my behaviour.' She slowed to a stop. 'I've been so out of order; I know I have and I'm really sorry. It's just that Dad's such a softie at heart, and he's been taken advantage of before, so me and Gino, well, we're a bit protective.' She gave a burst of a laugh, like the rattle of an automatic weapon. 'Maybe a bit much at times.'

Anna eased herself away from the car, surprised to see that it was now two thirty and still no sign of Theo. She looked around, but the car park was deserted, not a soul in sight and the van in the space next to Theo shielded them from view.

Nobody could see them, and Anna wondered how Luna knew she was waiting there.

Hairs raised on the back of her neck as Luna came even closer, to a point where she was invading her space. Anna took a step back, felt the sharp prickle of shrubs stabbing at her, piercing her clothing. She couldn't go any further and Luna was blocking any escape route. For now, she felt trapped. Uneasy.

Luna was still smiling and although Anna tried to tell herself everything was fine, someone would come along in a minute, her heart was racing, adrenaline firing through her veins as the urge to run grew stronger.

'That night you got engaged...' Luna continued. She nipped at her bottom lip with her teeth, looking up from under her lashes, like she was ashamed. 'My only excuse is we'd been drinking.' She grimaced and held up her hands in surrender. 'I know that's no excuse. I know it isn't, but Gino's not good when he's had a drink and it all got so out of hand.' She sighed. 'I'm so sorry you had to see us like that. The thing is, I've poured my heart and soul into renovating the house. I was doing it for Dad and then for him to waltz in and say he might sell it. Well, it pushed all the wrong buttons, I can tell you.'

Anna swallowed, nodded. 'I can see that would have been a shock.' She was sure this was all a performance, Luna's acting skills being hammy at best, all exaggerated and blatantly false. Also, there had been no mention of her encounter at Theo's house the other night. She hadn't exactly been pleasant then, had she? Add to that the fact she knew the engagement ring was fake, that his proposal was never genuine, and it struck her for the first time, that the fighting at the Boat House must have been a performance for her benefit. A test to see if she'd stick with Theo if his children were that awful. They'd tried hard to scare her off, but she'd been too blinkered by her stupid project to quit while she was ahead.

Anna surreptitiously glanced around, but all the parking spaces were full, no cars driving up this way because it was a dead-end. It was an area designated for staff parking and now lunch was over, it was unlikely anyone would be coming this way. With that van blocking the view on one side and the hedge on the other, anything could happen and nobody would be the wiser.

Luna seemed oblivious to Anna's unease and carried on talking. 'The main thing I wanted to speak to you about, though, is these police reports.' Her smile faded. Anna's heart rate speeded up. 'You've got to stop blaming us for things we didn't do.' She pouted, like she was taking a selfie for her Insta feed. 'Look, I know Gino followed you home and he's admitted to that. But he was angry, and it was harmless. He didn't actually do anything. Now I've had the police on the phone again this morning about some paint on your car.' She gave an exasperated sigh. 'I know it's easy to blame us, but why would we do that? How would we benefit? I just don't understand your thinking.'

Luna seemed to have inched a little closer and Anna couldn't press herself any further into the shrubbery. Her chest felt tight, her palms sweaty. *The best form of defence is attack.* Shrinking into the hedge was not going to help her.

She whipped her hands up and grabbed Luna's shoulders, pushing her back, something she obviously wasn't expecting, because she lost her balance and had to clutch at the car to stop herself from falling.

'You are in my space, Luna. Just back off, will you?' Anna stepped away from her, to what felt like a safe distance. Now Luna was up against the car and Anna was out of the hedge with space behind her to run if she wanted and that gave her the confidence to say what Luna needed to hear. 'I know it's *your* doing,' she snarled. Anger permeated every word she spoke, and it felt good, at last, to be having this conversation. To get her feelings and her wishes out in the open. 'All these horrible things that have been happening to me are down to you. But I know you've had accomplices because when I was attacked, I heard you talking to somebody seconds before it happened. And I have evidence that your dad coerced someone to help him with some spiteful stuff too.'

She was getting into her stride now, happy to see the shocked expression on Luna's face. An expression she was sure was genuine. 'Even if you've managed to engineer perfect alibis, I know you three are behind it. And sooner or later the police will come to the same conclusion because I'm not going to let it drop.' She was seething, spitting her words from between clenched teeth. 'I don't understand why you ruined my car now I'm not with your dad any more, but I'll work it out.'

She took another step back, getting ready to run away, but couldn't resist a parting shot. 'You think you're so clever. I know you look down on me, don't think I'm good enough for your dad. But let me tell you, beneath the surface, he is not a good person. He is malicious and deceitful and downright mean.' She was thinking about the sex video, the graffiti on her door, kissing Tanya, knowing he was the one who had orchestrated those things. 'I know you're all trying to destroy me. Make me go away. But I'm not going anywhere. It's you three who will be going somewhere,' she jabbed the air with a finger. 'And that will be prison. Especially when I give the police my evidence about your mum, which will make them question what really happened to her.' Luna's eyes widened and Anna felt a glow of satisfaction, knowing that particular barb had found its mark. 'I am a whisker away from doing that. So, you need to promise to stop this nonsense now or that will be my next move.'

Luna sat on the car bonnet and clapped her hands, an ironic round of applause, a sardonic smile on her face. 'Very good,' she said in a condescending tone. 'I hope you feel better now?'

Anna was conflicted between the desire to hit her and the need to get away from her. But she'd come here to get a promise and she needed to stay until she'd achieved that goal. The sound of heavy footsteps made her turn, just in time to see Gino hurrying towards them, but she was too slow to run, his hand catching her arm before she could move more than a step.

'Nice to see you again, Anna,' he said, his voice friendly, his grasp on her arm so tight she yelped.

'You took your time,' Luna said, scowling at her brother. 'I've just had a load of abuse from this one. She says she not backing down. And she thinks she's got evidence. Not just relating to these events the police have been harassing us about.' She lowered her voice, her tone more urgent, emphasising the last sentence as she locked eyes with her brother. 'But Mum's death too.'

Gino's hand tightened on Anna's arm. 'I came as quickly as I could,' he panted. 'You woke me up.' Luna pursed her lips, clearly annoyed with her brother. 'Did you get the keys off Dad?' he asked and Luna held them up, shaking them in the air.

'It's a good job he spotted her and rang,' she said. 'Now we can nip this in the bud.'

He swallowed, gave a sharp nod of the head. 'Okay, let's do it.'

He pushed Anna towards the car, the lights flickering as Luna unlocked it.

'We thought we'd take you out for a drive,' Luna said, as Gino shoved her towards the passenger door.

'I don't want to go out for a drive,' Anna snarled, trying to pull her arm away from Gino. 'I'm not going anywhere with you.'

Luna smiled as she came round the car, standing behind Gino while he pushed Anna forwards, towards the car door. 'I'm not sure you have much choice in the matter.'

There wasn't much of a gap between the door and the shrubbery and branches scraped against her face as she fought against him like a wildcat, twisting and writhing with all the strength she could muster. After a monumental struggle, he managed to wrap his arms around her, pinning her arms against her body. He shoved her along like an unwieldy parcel, while she tried to brace her feet on the ground, pushing herself backwards to make it harder for him to make her move.

He got her past the passenger door, which Luna opened. It now formed a barrier, her only escape route blocked.

'Help!' she shouted, suddenly frantic. Her voice was so loud it hurt the back of her throat, but it was her only weapon and she had to use it. She took a deep breath, ready to shout again, but Gino slapped his meaty hand over her mouth, partly covering her nose as well. Now she was struggling to breathe. He kicked her behind the knees, making her legs buckle, allowing him to manoeuvre her towards the passenger seat, not caring that she banged her head on the way.

He was much bigger than she was, and it was always going to be no contest, however hard she fought. She tried to bite his hand as he pushed her into the seat, but it was clamped so tight over her face, her jaw wouldn't move. Before she could think of anything else to do, he let her go, slamming the door shut, and leaning on it so she couldn't get out.

She was gasping for breath, scooping great mouthfuls of air into her lungs while her brain worked at warp speed. Her body was operating in full on fight or flight mode now, her mind working twice as fast as normal, her senses on high alert.

The driver's door, I can get out of there before Luna gets in.

She scrambled over the central console, but Luna was too quick, leaning into the car and slapping her across the face. The shock of it slowed Anna for a second or two, enough time for Luna to shove her back into the passenger seat as she climbed inside, closing the driver's door behind her. Anna couldn't imagine what their plans for her were, but she didn't want to find out.

With no means of escape from the car, the only thing she could do was try and alert people to the situation. She leant across and pressed the horn, trying to attract attention and stop what was effectively a kidnap.

'Gino, do something!' Luna shouted, agitated now. 'Grab her arms while I get this sorted.'

The passenger door opened and before Anna could lash out at him, Gino leant in, pinning her arms to her sides again, the whole weight of him pressing on her wrists. There was no way she could move, although she did her best to bite any bit of Gino she could reach. She did manage to sink her teeth into his ear, which made him howl but he didn't loosen his grip. Instead, he leant more of his bodyweight on her, crushing her beneath him. Meanwhile, Luna had her bag on her lap, looking for something.

'Hurry up, will you,' Gino gasped as Anna wriggled and writhed and tried to headbutt him, all to no avail. Try as she might, she couldn't get him off her. Gino's weight was across her chest now, squeezing the air from her lungs. She couldn't breathe, and frantically tried to knee him, but there was no part of him she could reach.

She felt a sharp jab in her neck.

Within seconds her vision began to blur, a weird floating sensation taking over her body, her limbs refusing to move. The light faded and darkness came.

34

Anna blinked awake, the light feeling too bright, hurting her eyes. She squinted, trying to work out where she was, her mind fuzzy and sluggish. She was flat on her back on what she thought might be a narrow examination bench, the kind used by the massage therapists at the gym. A floor lamp was angled above her, shining down on her face, hiding everything else in the room in a veil of gloom. She blinked again, her vision still blurry as she tried to roll over, get herself sitting up, but she couldn't. Her body was secured somehow. She was fastened in place.

Fear made her heart flutter, her breath coming out in shallow gasps. Her arms were pulled downwards at an awkward angle on either side of her body, and she could feel pressure round her wrists and ankles. Panic made her writhe and pull at her bindings, thrashing like a landed fish, all to no avail. Her mouth was dry and she desperately needed a drink, but she didn't want to alert anyone to the fact she was awake until she'd had a chance to assess her situation. Work out her options.

If I have any options.

Slowly, her vision started to clear, and she was able to study her surroundings, familiar objects now recognisable in the gloom. The desk in the corner, the little chairs, the play area. It was the back office at the Boat House. The one she'd thought might have been Emilia's consulting room.

Nobody would have a clue where she was. Nobody. Her fear ramped up another notch.

Oh God, what are they going to do to me?

A new flash of panic made her pull at her bindings again, testing each one to see if there was any chance of getting free. She realised that although her ankles were bound together, they were not attached to the bench, and she could move her legs up and down, raise her knees to her chest. Not that it was going to be much use to her. But you never knew. She had to stay positive, had to believe she could create an opportunity to escape. Also, she could lift her head and shoulders a little. Her wrists were tied to the legs of the bench with cable ties, she thought, judging by the way sharp edges were digging into her skin. But she could slide them up and down if she shifted the angle of her body.

Not totally helpless after all. The trick was to work out how these small movements might help, which parts of her body she could use as a weapon should one of her assailants come close.

A flower of hope blossomed in her chest, easing her breathing, clearing her mind. The sound of her pulse whooshing in her ears began to fade and now she could hear the murmur of voices coming from the kitchen area on the other side of the door.

'Well... I don't know,' Theo's voice snapped, suddenly louder, clearly frustrated. 'I don't know what the answer is, but I don't like your idea. It's not going to work. And if it goes wrong, we are all in prison for a very long time.' Silence for a couple of seconds. 'It's too drastic and I want no part of it. This has already gone too far because of you. Carrying on with your vendetta when we'd both told you to stop.'

'Look Dad...' Luna's voice, equally loud. 'We can't let her go, can we? Think about it. She told us she has evidence that Mum's death wasn't a suicide. That it was suspicious. Just have a think what could happen to us if the truth comes to light?'

'No.' Theo's voice again, loud and firm. 'I'm not doing it. We'll have to think of something else.'

'You're not listening!' Luna yelled, even louder, so loud even Anna flinched. 'She's out for revenge. Haven't you learnt that about her? And if she gives the cops her evidence, whatever that might be, they will be taking a proper look at us and then you never know where that might lead.' There was a bang, like she'd slammed something on the worktop.

Theo mumbled something inaudible, then Luna was off again, trying to bully her father to do things her way.

'We're into a completely different scenario now. If she hadn't mentioned the evidence about Mum's death, I would have been happy to call it a day. I mean, I was running out of ideas on how to torment her anyway. And, to be honest, it was getting a bit old. Especially with all the chats with the police taking up so much time and making us all jumpy however well we sorted out our alibis.' Silence for a few seconds. 'It was fun for a while, but the fact she has evidence has changed the paradigm, hasn't it? I know we're not sure what she's got, but she seems confident it's damaging and would raise questions. Think about it, Dad. We can't risk it, can we? I mean as soon as we let her go, she'll be straight back to the police station. I'm sorry if I overstepped the mark. Really, I am. But there's no going back now. You've got to see that?'

'Bloody hell, Luna.' Theo was furious, she could tell by the way he was snarling at his daughter. 'Why does it always have to be your way? I can't believe you kidnapped her. What the hell were you thinking?'

More mumbling. Then Luna's raised voice again. 'Yes, in theory you're right, but I don't trust Gino not to talk if he's put under pressure. You know what he's like. He'll tell them everything and then all of our lives will be ruined. We're not going to let that happen, are we?'

'Oi, you don't need to talk about me like I'm not here.' Gino's indignant voice snapped at his sister. So, he was here as well; all three of them, working out what to do with her. Perhaps she could convince them to let her go. Tell them she'd stop complaining to the police, give them her evidence, move away, do whatever she needed to do to get out of this alive. But something told her Luna was on a mission to make her silence permanent. Promises wouldn't cut it because Luna wouldn't trust her to keep them.

To Anna, it was very clear that her life was in danger, the conversation about how and when to get rid of her made that obvious. Her heart raced even faster and she strained to hear more.

'You need to stop shouting!' Gino yelled. 'She's only through there.'

Their voices dropped to a murmur, and she stopped listening, unable to make out anything they said. Anyway, it was more important to try and free herself, her efforts more frantic now she'd heard their conversation. After a few minutes of hopeless writhing, she was out of breath and exhausted. It dawned on her that panic was not her friend. She was using up energy and hurting herself by tugging at her bindings. Patience would bring her rewards if only she could keep herself in the realms of calm. Use her brain instead of mindlessly thrashing about.

Taking a few deep breaths, she tried a more methodical approach. Starting with her right hand, she gently teased and pulled, but the cable tie was too tight for her to get much movement up and down the bench leg, let alone wriggle her hand free. After a few minutes, she stopped trying and moved on. Her left hand, it turned out, was a different matter. She supposed it was harder to reach over her body to tighten it on that side, as the bench was pushed close to the wall. Slowly and systematically, she tried to wriggle her hand free, hope beginning to bloom as she felt her progress.

Unfortunately, she had only managed to get her hand part of the way out when the door opened and Theo came in, closing it behind him.

35

Anna watched him come closer, her heart beating so fast it was almost jumping out of her chest. He had nothing in his hands, she noted. No garotte to strangle her with, no knives, or hammers or any other weapon. Just his hands, she thought, nervously as she continued to work at freeing her left hand, making progress millimetre by painful millimetre. Her eyes fixed on him, hoping he couldn't tell what she was doing.

He pulled up a chair and sat next to her, a grim expression on his face. Like he was at a funeral, about to read a eulogy. It appeared he was here to talk, nothing more at this stage, and she told herself to calm the heck down, even though her heart continued to race, the mere proximity of him making her panic.

'I'm having a bit of a hard time trying to persuade my children that we should let you go,' he said, as calm as if he was telling her he'd have to cancel an appointment.

'Please,' she croaked, her mouth so dry it was a struggle to speak. 'I won't cause any trouble.'

'But it seems you can't help yourself, can you?' His voice hardened, a steely glint in his eyes as he glared at her. 'How dare you come to my workplace? Thankfully, I saw you loitering by my car and was able to go back inside without you seeing me. I knew you were there for an argument because I'd also had a delightful call from the police. Which was taken by my secretary because I was in surgery.' His glare intensified. 'Now my secretary is giving me funny looks wondering why the police would be calling. So, imagine if you'd started having a go at me in the car park. How do you think that would go down with my superiors?'

She swallowed, her mind blank, unable to think of a single thing to say that might appease him.

'I managed to hang onto my job by the slenderest of threads after your husband died,' he continued. 'You were so persistent with your objections and accusations, I was a whisker away from being transferred to another hospital.' The anger was building in his voice as he spat the words at her. 'But why should I go? I was grieving as well, that's what people seemed to forget. Why should I have to uproot my life when I had just lost my wife and my children needed stability?'

His eyes locked onto hers, waiting for an answer. But she still couldn't speak, not sure what he wanted her to say and frightened to cause him more upset. The last thing she needed was for him to go off into a rage and do something on the spur of the moment.

Like kill me.

The idea that she was going to die was becoming more real now, because she couldn't see another way out of this. He didn't want her to speak. These questions were rhetorical, this was him saying what he wanted her to hear before... She gulped as the fear hit her like a physical blow, turning her insides to liquid, making her body shake.

His eyes dropped from hers and he sighed, waved a dismissive hand, like he couldn't be bothered with her any more. 'Thankfully, my team rallied round me and there was a block denial that anything had gone wrong. I mean, if my bosses knew what really happened, they would have had my guts for garters.'

She was consumed with such a surge of rage, now that she finally had his confirmation of wrongdoing, she was certain she would have killed him if she'd been free to attack.

He pointed at her, a burst of laughter erupting from him, so out of place it felt sinister. 'Oh, your face.' As quickly as it had started, his laughter subsided and his face became serious again. 'Anyway, I can tell you the truth now, because it doesn't really matter.' He shrugged. 'I mean some of what you know already is the truth. The first operation really did go wrong because of that pile up on the A55. It was all done in too much of a rush. We were all to blame for that, we didn't do all the checks we should have done, so of course we covered each other's backs. That's the behaviour I expect from my team, they all know it, and if anyone shows a shred of disloyalty, they're gone. That's how it is. That's the sort of team I run.' He gave a satisfied nod, and she wondered what she'd ever found attractive about this man. 'They know I can ruin their careers with a few chosen words to the right people, so I have trained them to toe the line. And they did an admirable job.'

This was not news to Anna; she'd suspected this was how the hierarchy worked. The local health board had been in special measures because of a toxic working environment and a lot of things going wrong. Especially in the emergency department. Her blood was at boiling point now, but she knew she had to keep her anger in check. At this moment in time, her life depended on it.

He bent his head towards her. 'The second operation...' He leant closer, his elbows resting on his knees, his hands steepled together, fingers tapping his lips. He sighed. 'The truth is...' He stopped and stared at her, but she could tell he wasn't actually seeing her, he was seeing what had happened two years ago on the operating table. 'It pains me to admit this, because I pride myself on my professionalism and attention to detail, but as I said, I wasn't concentrating.' His eyes met hers. 'In fact, I was chatting to my rather lovely anaesthetist about the new models of Porsche and which one I was going to go for next when my hand slipped and I severed an artery. Your husband shouldn't have died. I was negligent. You were right. It was my fault.'

He sat back in his chair. 'There, you know the truth now. Does that make you feel better?' He smiled. 'It actually makes me feel better to admit it to someone after two years of denials.'

Anna was finding it hard to process what he'd just told her. He *had* done wrong. It *was* negligence. Just like she'd tried to tell everyone, but nobody had wanted to hear. They'd jumped to his defence when he should have been punished in some way. Disbarred or something. But there had been no consequences for him. Nothing at all. He got to carry on with his life, while Ollie was dead and she'd been left a widow, living in the wreckage of her life.

Rage bubbled up inside her, filling her chest, then her throat until it forced its way out in a blood curdling scream that made it sound like she was about to tear the flesh from his bones. 'You bastard!' she yelled. 'You absolute bastard.'

He reared back in alarm. She heard the door open, and Gino stuck his head round. 'Everything all right, Dad?'

Theo waved a hand, a signal that said his son was dismissed, he should leave. 'Yep, all good. We're just having a little chat.'

Gino went back out again, closed the door behind him and she could hear him talking to Luna, the words too indistinct to decipher. Were they listening outside the door? Waiting for their father to finish her off, once he'd ended this torment with his self-satisfied confessional?

'I think the natives are getting restless,' he said, running a hand down his face, like he was wiping something away. 'I better get on with it.' He held up a finger. 'Here's something that might surprise you... I knew you were Oliver Betts' widow way before Paris.'

He looked sad rather than delighted by his deception. 'Luna did some research after she first met you. She does it with everyone I date. It didn't take her long to guess what your endgame was. She's intuitive like that, always suspicious of people until they prove themselves trustworthy.' He sighed. 'If I'd listened to her at the time — well we wouldn't be in this situation. But, I'll admit it, I didn't want to believe her, brushed away her concerns because I wanted to be right. I wanted to be with you.' He gave a harsh bark of a laugh. 'Obviously it was the hormones overriding my common sense because all I could focus on was getting you in bed. Yes, it was all about the sex. But until Paris, I'd convinced myself we had something going for us. The past was the past and we'd both moved on.' His eyes clouded with sadness. 'On our last night there, you were quite drunk and you said something to me that made me change my mind. You said, "you're not the bastard I imagined you'd be. You're making this much harder than I thought." And that told me Luna was right. You did have an agenda. You weren't being genuine.

'Once I got back, Luna had all the evidence I needed to know that you were playing games. I'll admit my pride was hurt. Who likes to be proved wrong? And we decided to play you at your own game, see how far we could push you. Obviously your intentions were *evil* so I had no compunction about Luna implementing her plan.'

There was fire in his eyes and she could tell that whatever he said, she'd really got to him. That was a win. Even if it was the only positive she could hold on to before she died. She'd done it. She'd truly hurt him and hadn't that been her goal? She'd taken his pride, humiliated him, bruised his ego and possibly broken his heart a little. That was the best she could hope to do. She smiled at him, making sure she kept eye contact, not wanting to give him the gift of her fear.

'Oh, we're smiling now, are we? Yes, well it's good you're enjoying your last moments.' He leant closer. 'Here's something that will make you laugh. I took advantage of your ego. The bit of you that believed I might fall for a loser like you.' He laughed. 'You were an okay lay though, I'll give you that. And each time I slept with you after Paris, it was all the sweeter knowing that I knew who you were. I knew what I'd done and I knew what was in store for you but you were oblivious.' He chuckled to himself. 'You thought you were being so clever. That's what made it entertaining.'

The door opened again, and it was Luna this time. 'Dad, we need to get a move on.' She held out her hand to give him something. 'You forgot this.' He sighed and got up from his chair, took whatever it was. 'While you're doing that,' she murmured, 'we'll go and get everything ready.'

She closed the door again.

He walked back towards her and as he got closer, Anna could see he was holding a syringe.

36

Oh God, this is it. The end.

She didn't know what he was going to inject her with, but she would bet it was lethal. Or maybe it was a sedative, then they would throw her in the water, let her drown. Whatever it was, this was the final act. The end of the drama that she had started. Adrenaline was shooting through her body at an ever-increasing speed, her thought process working so fast she could hardly keep up with all the possibilities her brain was giving her.

She wriggled her left hand again, but it was still stuck half in, half out of the binding.

He saw what she was trying to do and shook his head. 'I'm so sorry, but you're not getting out of there.'

He looked at the syringe and then looked at her and she sensed hesitation. This wasn't his idea, she knew that from the overheard conversation. This was all Luna, her logic and persuasiveness winning the day. She was the one deciding how this was going to end.

'Please,' she begged. 'Please don't hurt me. I'm sorry I tried to fool you. It was stupid. Really stupid. But I wanted justice for Ollie and it was the only thing I could think of.' She was crying now, tears streaming down her cheeks. 'I'll move away, I promise. I won't tell anyone about this conversation. Nobody. Honestly, you have my word.'

He shook his head. 'But you know too much. And Luna's right, we won't ever be able to relax, now we know you have evidence against us.' He sounded weary. 'It gives you the power to ruin our lives, to control us and we can't live with that threat hanging over us.'

He took a step towards her, his eyes closing for a second as he gathered himself. He was clearly finding the task hard, his morals compromised by an overpowering urge for self-preservation. Their welfare was more important than her life. That was the calculation he'd done, and her death was the answer he'd arrived at.

Her brain couldn't cope with the idea she was going to die, whirring even faster as it threw ideas at her. *Don't just let this happen, do something. At least try.*

'It's for the best,' he continued. 'And the more you can accept the inevitable, the easier this will be. I can assure you it will be painless, apart from a little prick when I insert the needle. Think of it as euthanasia. I'm just putting you to sleep.' He gave a sad smile. 'A humane death.'

'I don't want to die,' she gabbled, her eyes locked on his. 'Please, you don't have to do this.' But she knew, as soon as she'd spoken, that her words were futile, the dull light in Theo's eyes telling her he wasn't listening, his mind focused on what he was about to do next.

Her brain popped a new idea into her head, the best she'd come up with yet. And she stilled, concentrating with every fibre of her being. Ready to ensure she took advantage of the only opportunity she would have to save her own life. Her eyes scanned the scene, wondering where he was going to inject her, working out what she had to do. He started tapping at her inner elbow.

'Oh, that's a lovely vein,' he said. 'Very cooperative.'

As he bent to insert the needle, his head hovered over her body, and she reared up and headbutted him, making him lose his balance. At the same time, she pulled her knees up to her chest and swung her feet at him with all the force she could muster. All those gym sessions had been worth it, she realised, being so much more flexible now than she'd been in her life. Ironic, that the process of chasing Theo had given her the means to fight him, to save herself.

He grunted and staggered sidewards, hitting the wall with his shoulder, the hand holding the syringe slapping into his arm.

She watched as his mouth opened, his eyes wide. Then he was staring at his bicep, where she could see the syringe had embedded itself in his flesh. In slow motion, he slid down the wall, his eyes rolling to the back of his head before he collapsed in a heap on the floor.

Anna craned her neck to see if he was moving, but he wasn't. He was completely still.

Instead of humanely killing her, he'd euthanised himself.

37

Anna stared, horrified at what she'd done. She hadn't meant to kill him, just disarm him. Her fear ramped up another notch, clamping her head in a vice-like grip. Because if Luna and Gino came in and saw what had happened, their method of killing would be far from humane. They'd be consumed by rage, and she was still helpless, unable to fend off any sort of attack.

Sweat beaded on her brow, gathering under her arms, her palms clammy. Never in her life had she felt fear like this, making her skin prickle, her mind race.

Ideas. I need ideas. And quick.

The only answer was to pull as hard as she could on her left hand, regardless of the pain, until it was free. Just another inch and she'd be past the hard bit. After a few seconds she could feel it was never going to work while she was lying on her back like this. It was just too awkward. Perhaps it would be easier if she could pull against her bindings in a different way. Maybe if she tipped the bench over? It seemed quite flimsy and had wobbled when she'd lashed out at Theo.

She glanced at the door, listened for sounds that her captors were close, but everything was quiet. If she was going to take that approach, and it seemed the only option, she had to do it now while Luna and Gino were elsewhere, doing whatever it was they had to do. Because there was no way it was going to be quiet and if they were in the house, they'd surely come running.

She hurled her body sideways and on the third attempt, the bench toppled over, sending her crashing to the floor. It took her breath away for a moment but she was fully committed to her escape plan now, her heart feeling twice as big as normal and beating four times as fast. She pushed the bench back against the wall, then tucked her feet under her as much as she could to give her more pulling force. She clamped her teeth together, eyes stinging with the pain as she tugged at her hand.

It took all her willpower to stifle a scream as the skin on the back of her hand was ripped to shreds, the bones feeling like they must surely break with the pressure they were under. She screwed her eyes shut and, in her mind, she had a terrible image of her hand detaching itself from her wrist, but still she kept pulling, desperate to escape. After what seemed like tens of minutes but was probably only seconds, she finally yanked her hand free.

She bent over, gasping with the effort, wincing against the burning pain. But even now, this was only the beginning. She still wasn't safe. All she'd done was free one hand. She was still tied to the bench with the other hand and her ankles were still bound together.

What she wanted was for someone to come and rescue her. Or at least to know where she was, but her phone had been taken. She had no means of communicating with anyone. There was no help on its way, this was up to her and her alone.

She glanced at Theo's body, crumpled and still, lying where he'd fallen against the wall. There was no movement. No rise and fall of breathing and she was pretty sure he was dead. She hesitated for a moment before she forced herself to reach over, patting at his pockets, looking for his phone, but it appeared he didn't have it on him. He must have left it in the kitchen when they'd been talking.

She ground her teeth in frustration, but cautioned herself to stay calm. To think. Because escape was possible if she could find something to cut her bindings.

What she really needed was a pair of scissors. Her eyes settled on the desk. If there was going to be anything useful in this room to help her, it would be over there. She studied the distance. Thankfully, it was only a small room, and the desk was no more than eight feet away. If she bunny hopped, she could get herself over there, dragging the bench behind her. It wasn't substantial or heavy, having hollow tubular legs, and she thought it would be easy enough to do. Difficult to do without making a noise, though, but what option did she have? She'd just have to be quick.

Now she was out of the glare of the floor lamp, she could see a mug stuffed with pens sitting on top of the desk, next to the computer screen. Were those the handles of a pair of scissors she could see? Her breath quickened, sweat sticking her shirt to her back.

It was not a quiet operation, jumping across the room, the bench banging and clanking behind her as she dragged it by her wrist. Thankfully, it only took a few seconds. She lunged at the desk, knocking things flying in her desperation. But it *was* a pair of scissors she'd seen, and she grabbed them, glad to see they were big enough and sharp enough to be of some use. She started sawing at the plastic binding, frustrated tears blurring her vision as she fumbled, her left hand not used to working scissors. Finally the plastic snapped and her hand was free.

A sob of relief caught in her throat and she turned her attention to her ankles. There were two ties to cut and she had just started on the second one when a sound made her look up, her heart leaping up her throat when she saw the door handle turn.

'Have you finished, Dad?' Luna's face appeared, peering round the door.

Their eyes met.

38

Luna did a double take. She stepped into the room, her movements cautious and guarded as she kept her distance from Anna. This was not what she'd expected to see and, while she was still confused as to what was happening, Anna frantically sawed at the last cable tie, willing it to break, only too aware of how vulnerable she was.

'Dad!' Luna screamed when she noticed her father slumped against the wall. She turned and yelled over her shoulder, 'Gino, get in here,' as she ran towards her dad, hunching over him, her hand feeling his neck for a pulse.

At last, the plastic cable tie snapped, and Anna scrambled to her feet. The door was open. She had an escape route and she had to take it before Gino appeared. But in her haste, she stumbled and before she could right herself properly, Luna was on her, grabbing her round the neck with both hands, causing them both to tumble to the floor.

'You've killed him,' Luna sobbed, her face a mask of hatred as she straddled Anna's torso, pinning her to the ground. Her hands tightened, all her weight pressing down on Anna's throat. 'You killed Dad.'

'He killed himself,' Anna snarled, frantically slapping and scratching at Luna's hands, trying to peel her fingers away from her skin. Luna had long acrylic nails, with blunt tips, like ten little spades digging into her flesh. Tighter she squeezed, while Anna tried to buck and twist to throw her off.

Luna's grasp was so tight now, Anna was struggling to breathe, feeling the life draining out of her. But she couldn't let it happen, couldn't let Luna and her crazy family win. Her legs weren't restricted so she drummed her knees against Luna's lower back, throwing herself from side to side, scratching and hitting at Luna's face, but nothing was making her stop. Finally she managed to land a punch to the side of Luna's head that seemed to connect in just the right place, stunning her for a second. Luna's grip loosened and with another thrash of her body, Anna managed to tip her off. There was a clatter as her head whacked against the side of the overturned bench, giving Anna a few precious seconds to wriggle free while Luna was distracted with her own pain.

But it wasn't enough, she didn't have time to get to her feet and get away before she knew Luna would grab her again. She was bigger and stronger than Anna, almost as tall as her father. It wasn't an even contest, and once Gino appeared, which he surely would, then that would be it. No chance of escape.

Anna pulled in a couple of deep breaths, her adrenaline-fuelled brain looking for an answer. *I'm not going to die. I'm not going to let them kill me.* Her teeth clamped tight, her jaw set. She would do whatever she needed to do to survive.

The scissors were on the floor, not more than a couple of feet away by the desk, and she lunged for them, giving a gasp of relief when they were in her hands. Now at least she had a weapon, a means of self-defence. Still on her knees, she opened them, hoping they would be enough of a deterrent. At least sufficient to keep Luna at a distance. She held them in front of her, ready to use like a knife. A scuffling noise made Anna spin round just in time to see Luna launching herself at her again.

A blood-curdling scream filled the air, making Anna wince, her eyes growing wide as she watched Luna clutch at her leg where the scissors were now embedded in her thigh. She hadn't seen them, had jumped right onto the blade in her effort to overpower Anna. Blood was seeping out of the wound at an alarming rate, creating an ever-growing stain on Luna's sky-blue leggings. *Did I hit an artery?* But there was no time to stop and check. This was her chance to escape. She had to get out of there.

She scrambled over the bench, stumbling towards the door, thankful she was still more or less in full working order. But she was exhausted after her fight with Luna and the effort of getting herself free. She wanted to sit down. She desperately needed a drink, but there was no time to stop and collect her thoughts. Not until she was out of this godforsaken house, and away from the nightmare she was living.

'Gino!' Luna shouted, panic ringing in her voice. 'Come here. Now. I need some help.'

Oh God, Anna had somehow forgotten about Gino, but suddenly he was there, blocking the doorway, his hands on the door casing, his body practically filling the gap. She let out a whimper, unable to see how she could possibly get past him. He stared over her head, taking in the carnage she'd left in her wake.

'What the hell?' he growled, his eyes on her now. 'What have you done?'

She backed away, putting space between her and the two siblings as she tried to work out her next move. There was only one weapon in the room and before she could stop to think about consequences, she clambered over the bench, and yanked the scissor's blades out of Luna's leg.

Luna's scream was so shrill and piercing it could have broken glass. She stared at her leg, then at Anna, horror in her eyes. 'Look what you've done now.' A sob burst from her throat, her face screwed up in agony. 'I'm going to bleed to death.'

'That's not my problem,' Anna snapped, her eyes on Gino, who seemed to be stuck in the doorway, his mouth hanging open, eyes as round as saucers. He looked as if he was petrified and rooted to the spot, not moving, his eyes fixed on Luna. But he was acting as a blockage, stopping Anna's escape. There was no other way out. Somehow, she was going to have to make him move.

He was starting to look a bit peaky, she decided, maybe nauseous at the sight of the blood pumping from Luna's leg, colouring her leggings a deep scarlet, the patch growing by the second.

'Call an ambulance,' Anna shouted, trying to break him from his trance. 'Look, she's going to die. I don't have a phone or I'd do it.' Still no movement and she injected more urgency into her voice, hoping her words would strike home. 'You've got to save your sister.'

Gino took a step into the room, leaning against the wall, a hand covering his mouth as he heaved, like he was about to be sick. At that moment, she watched his eyes settle on the still form of his father, crumpled against the wall. The door had been blocking his view of him before, but now he was in the room, there was no missing his collapsed body. And then Gino actually *was* sick, vomit dripping between his fingers, the stench making Anna's stomach roil. Still heaving, he staggered out of the room, presumably towards the bathroom, which was only next door.

This is my chance, Anna realised and she ran from the room, the sound of Gino still retching, giving her confidence that she was safe for now. She hurried into the kitchen and spotted a phone on the worktop. It looked like Theo's and although it was fingerprint protected, she could use it for an emergency call. If Gino wasn't going to get help for Luna, then she would, because she didn't want another death on her hands.

Her fingers hovered over the keypad, something stopping her from making the call.

They'll blame you. If you call an ambulance, the police will be involved. You're going to prison.

She stared at the keypad, the sound of Gino retching in the background, the sour smell of vomit permeating the air.

Should I just run away?

Although she'd acted in self-defence, the idea of killing two people in one day was more than her conscience could bear. She had no chance of saving Theo, but Luna she could try and help. And then run away. Two minutes to call an ambulance and she could do that while she was running. She slipped the scissors into her back pocket while she dialled.

But before her call was answered a big hand reached over her shoulder and slapped the phone out of her grasp, grabbing her wrist so tight she squealed.

39

'Your sister needs an ambulance,' Anna said through gritted teeth, his hand squeezing the blood from her veins. 'She'll bleed to death in no time. You've got to help her.'

Gino glared at her and she could tell he was having an internal debate with himself, wondering whether to believe her.

'I'll take her to the hospital,' he said eventually, settling on a compromise. He twisted her wrist, making her yell as he leant towards her. 'But what am I going to do with you?' His face was very pale, his voice shaking and he was clearly shocked by the way his day was turning out. 'You killed Dad.' He blinked, like he was having problems believing what he was saying. 'You killed him.'

'He injected himself,' Anna snapped. 'While I was fighting for my life. It's called self-defence. None of this is my fault.' She winced at the pain in her wrist, would swear she could feel her wrist bones grinding together. 'You were all going to kill me.'

Gino shook his head, eyes narrowed, lips pressed together as he stared at her. 'Not me. It wasn't me. None of this was my idea, but now I'm stuck in the middle...' He sighed and shook his head. 'Why the hell did I move back home?' His grip tightened as he spoke, taking out his anger on her wrist and she gasped as she fought against the pain. 'I didn't want to be involved with any of it. It was all Luna and she convinced Dad it was the only way. She said you'd keep going until you destroyed us.' He stopped then, his chin quivering and it seemed like reality had just hit home.

'He's dead, Gino,' she said, her voice gentler now, deciding that antagonising someone who could wrench her arm out of its socket was not a good idea. 'I can't destroy him, can I? He's managed to do that to himself.'

He blinked a few times, a solitary tear working its way down his cheek. 'You'll start on us now though, won't you? Luna said you know what happened to Mum. That you've got evidence.' He swallowed, looking more distressed by the minute. 'She said we had to do it. Then we'd be free to live our lives without the threat of you giving your evidence to the police. She said it would be like living with a ticking time bomb if we let you live. And she was worried I'd tell the police about Mum if you handed over your evidence.' He heaved another sigh. 'I didn't want them to kill you. Honestly, I'm not that sort of person. But I didn't know what to do. There's no persuading Luna once she's got her mind fixed on something. She's always been like that.'

Anna squirmed, trying to ease the pressure in her wrist. Her fingers had gone a strange colour now and she could hardly talk through the pain. 'Let me go, Gino. I promise you now, I won't go to the police. I'll go home, pack up and then I'll leave. I'll move away and you won't hear from me ever again.' He twisted her wrist and she screamed, thought she felt something pop. 'Please Gino,' she begged. 'You've got to save Luna. She's bleeding to death in there. Is that what you want? To be on your own?'

She was taking a gamble that it wasn't what he wanted, having seen how much he depended on his family for support. 'Just let me go. I don't know anything about your mother. I mean, how would I?

I made the evidence bit up to try and stop your dad and Luna harassing me. I thought it would act as a deterrent, not a death warrant.' Her mind scrambled for something decisive, something that might tip the balance in her favour. 'All I know about your mum is she died in a tragic accident. And your sister is going to die in a tragic accident too if you don't do something to save her. She impaled herself on...'

She remembered then, the scissors in her back pocket and she carefully slid them out – her body going limp with relief when she felt the heft of them in her hand. Before she could have a debate with herself about the wisdom of her next move, she jabbed him with them, striking him in the midriff. Not to injure him, more to warn him of what she could do.

The effect was immediate. Releasing her wrist, he jumped away from her, holding his hands up in surrender. 'Don't hurt me. I didn't do anything. I swear.'

Wow, this guy is something else, she thought, hopeful now that she had a chance of escape.

'Get a tourniquet on Luna's leg, quickly, before she dies.' He seemed to respond to orders from his sister, so she tried to make her voice hard and authoritative, mimicking the way Luna spoke to him. She spotted a scarf of Luna's hanging over the back of a chair and pointed to it. 'There, use that. Tie it round her leg. Then get her to the hospital.'

Gino looked at the scarf then at Anna, and she could practically see his mind whirring as he made a mental calculation.

'I could kill you,' he said, his eyes travelling to the knife block, which sat on the worktop, although the kitchen island formed a handy barrier, stopping him from getting there. Unfortunately, it was also stopping her from getting to the door. 'Then that would be the end of it. You couldn't tell anyone about Mum.' He frowned at her. 'And nobody would even know you were dead.'

Her heart was galloping faster than she'd ever thought possible. 'Not before I could kill you,' she said, darting forwards and jabbing at him with the scissors again. Harder this time, a spot of blood blossoming on his white T-shirt where it pressed against his stomach. He gasped, staring at the blood before his eyes met hers once more. And this time she saw a flicker of fear, could feel hope stirring in her heart. 'Your sister is dying. And if that happens then it will be on you for not helping her. Do you want that on your conscience?'

She could tell by his face he was conflicted. 'I will walk away from here and pretend that nothing has happened if you promise to do the same. You leave me alone, I'll leave you and Luna alone.'

His Adam's apple bobbed up and down.

'Help your sister, now!' she shouted and finally he grabbed the scarf and ran into the office.

Free at last, she ran outside, past Luna's car, which had the boot open. It was lined with a sheet of plastic and she knew what that had been intended for. Moving her dead body. She shuddered and jogged up the drive until she reached the cycle path that would take her into Bangor. This section was off the main road, bordered with trees on either side, and she could stay hidden, at least for a few miles.

What if he rings for an ambulance? What if he calls the police? Should I find someone with a phone and call the cops, get in there first with my story?

There were so many questions buzzing round her head it felt like she had an angry swarm of wasps in there, the noise of her thoughts so loud she was unable to think clearly. After she'd jogged a way along the path, constantly checking over her shoulder to make sure she wasn't being followed, she saw a bench and sat for a moment to catch her breath. It was unreal what had just happened to her. She'd almost died. Theo *had* died and Luna was in danger of passing away if that feckless brother of hers didn't get her to the hospital pretty quick.

Her life had pivoted in a moment, from a point where she was feeling more positive about her future, thinking all the fuss with Theo and his children was behind her, to this terrible situation she now found herself in. And it was all down to the paint on the car. That's what had changed things. It had made her go to the police and report the crime. And it had made her go up to the hospital to find Theo. And if neither of those things had happened, his children wouldn't have kidnapped her and Luna wouldn't have persuaded Theo he had to commit murder if they were ever to be safe again.

She bent over, resting her elbows on her knees, her head in her uninjured hand, her breath rasping in her throat from running.

There was something about the paint on the car incident that was bothering her. There had been no need for it. Theo had dumped her, humiliated her and they'd seemed to have come to a point where a line had been drawn under all of it. Until the paint. Which had made her go to the police again and wasn't that the last thing they wanted to happen? After everything she'd heard from Theo, Luna and Gino today, they were actually terrified of the police digging around in their affairs. They had no reason to stir things up again.

If her logic was functioning correctly, and of course there was no guarantee that it was, there was something about this whole situation she failing to see. But until she understood what that was, she was never going to feel safe. Yes, Gino had let her go for now. But that didn't mean he wouldn't come for her further down the line.

She sighed, her body feeling so weary and heavy, the thought of walking all the way home was overwhelming. Four more miles or thereabouts. Or she could go to the shop in the village, ask them to call the police and wait for help to arrive.

Her hand buried itself in her hair. That wasn't an option. She couldn't go to the police, not after what had happened to Theo and Luna. And the family had already made her seem an idiot in the eyes of the officers who'd been dealing with her case. Not just once, but several times. The way they'd looked at her, the questions they'd been asking, had made her wonder if they thought she was doing these things to herself. Attention-seeking stunts. It was easy to think they believed she was mentally unwell. Maybe Theo or Luna had even suggested as much.

What am I going to do? Her mind went round in circles, spinning its way through all the events of recent days. There was no easy answer.

* * *

Eventually, she heaved herself to her feet and started walking, shivering in the cool breeze. Her wrist was throbbing and she held her arm against her chest as she walked, supporting her elbow to ease the pain. She didn't think it was broken because she could wiggle her fingers, but the bruising was starting to come out and it was very tender to the touch.

It was getting dark by the time she got home, the walk taking her much longer than she'd calculated. Mainly because she'd taken detours, following the routes that wouldn't be obvious, in case Gino came looking for her. Although he was probably still up at the hospital with Luna.

I've got to leave.

That was the only thought in her head. She'd pack up a few things and visit her parents in Spain, she decided. At least there she'd feel safe, sure nobody would follow her.

She'd never spoken about her parents in any detail to Theo, wanting to keep that part of her life separate. A sudden thought hit her and she pulled to a stop, slapping her forehead when she realised a terrible possibility. Her brain had reminded her of something Theo had said. Luna had done research on her. Was it possible she knew where her parents lived as well? Or if she didn't know now, there could be a way for her to find out.

Oh God, Spain isn't safe either.

Another realisation hit. Her handbag, with her bank cards and ID in it, was still at the Boat House. She had no access to money until the banks opened on Monday morning, today being a Friday. Thankfully her keys had been in her pocket and were still there but her heart sank. She couldn't leave straight away; she was going to have to wait a couple of days.

There was nobody she could ask for help, she realised, a hollow feeling growing in her chest. She was all alone. And scared. Very, very scared.

That fear escalated when she got home and saw that the lights were on. She'd switched everything off when she'd gone out that morning. Somebody had been in her apartment.

So who could her intruder be? Her guess was Gino, looking for her. Her blood ran cold.

Is he still in there?

41

After watching the living room window for ten minutes and not seeing any shadows moving, Anna still couldn't make herself go in. She walked round the back, but there were no strange vehicles parked outside, just her sad little car covered with paint. Finally, she plucked up courage and pushed at the back door, thinking it must be open. But it was locked. Cautiously, she put her key in the lock and turned, being as quiet as possible, pushing it open, while readying herself to run. The kitchen was empty, and she walked in, leaving the back door open as an escape route, just in case. 'Hello,' she called. 'Who's there?'

But there was no answer. Fear crept like icy fingers up the back of her neck. After her long walk and her fight with Luna and Theo, she was a wreck, devoid of any energy. If anyone was in there, she'd have no chance of defending herself. Her eyes settled on the knife block.

She grabbed the carving knife, holding it in front of her as she slowly checked the rest of the apartment. Soon, it was obvious that she was alone and she went back to the kitchen door and locked it before pulling the kitchen blinds and closing all the curtains.

Only then did she feel a bit more secure and able to breathe properly.

Until she realised that whoever had left the lights on had also locked the door behind them. Someone else had a key.

The thought made her feel sick, a weight landing in her gut. Was this ever going to end? She put the knife back in the block and leant against the worktop, head bowed between her outstretched arms as she tried to summon up the energy to go and check the front door, make sure the chain was on. It took a few minutes before she could move and when she did, it was like wading through treacle, her legs heavy, her feet sore with walking so far. But she forced herself to do it, then went back to the kitchen, wondering what she could do about the back door. There wasn't a bolt or a chain, and it was a basic lock, with no means to deadlock it from the inside. The only thing she could do was leave the key in the lock in the hope it would prevent anyone from unlocking it from the outside. It would have to do. She had no money to pay a locksmith to come and change the lock again, nothing she could do until Monday.

The growling of her stomach reminded her she hadn't eaten since lunchtime and food would probably make her feel better. She shuffled over to the freezer and had a rummage for a ready meal, put it in the microwave and leant against the worktop again as she watched it spinning round and round, lost in her thoughts.

It was hard to know what to do for the best. Hard to know how to keep herself safe and, without a bank card, she was stuck for now. She had to get through the weekend unscathed. That was all, just two days.

It didn't sound long when she said it in her head, but the fact someone had been in her apartment and had a key wouldn't stop chewing at her thoughts. The most likely suspect was Gino, looking for her after she'd run away while his sister was being treated up at the hospital. But it was also possible it was someone else.

She frowned, trying to think who would have had a chance to copy her keys. She glanced at the hook by the back door where she kept her spare set. It was empty. So that meant it was anyone who'd been in her apartment recently. Theo and Tanya had definitely been in.

Could Tanya have come over to check on her?

The microwave pinged and she'd just pulled her meal out, spooning the chilli con carne onto a plate when she heard a rattling in the lock. A key. Someone was trying to get in. Her heart leapt up her throat, the serving spoon dropping onto the plate with a clatter as she watched the handle move. Heard the door rattle in its casing.

She was rooted to the spot, unable to move, knowing she was helpless.

A loud bang made her jump, like someone had kicked the door.

Silence, thick and ominous kept her pressed against the worktop, her ears straining to hear. Was that the shuffling of feet? Were those footsteps? She listened for a few minutes but could only hear the faint thrumming of car engines going past on the road at the front of the house.

Have they gone? She turned the kitchen light off and peeped round the kitchen blinds, squinting to see through the blackness. Nobody there.

But they knew she was inside now. Would they come back? Or maybe try the front door?

She waited, but nothing happened. Everything was quiet, just as it should be. Nobody was trying to get in.

Terrified didn't begin to explain how she felt, her whole body shaking. She felt sick and the thought of eating made her feel worse. She left her meal on the worktop and went through to the lounge, perching on the edge of the sofa, not sure what to do. Her nerves were in tatters, and she jumped at every sound, every voice in the street.

With no phone, she felt very isolated. What would she do if they came back? If they managed to get in? Her heart raced, her eyes falling on her laptop which was sitting on the table. She could message her mum and tell her that she needed help, but there was no guarantee she'd see the notification, her mum's mobile generally living on the kitchen table even when she was in other parts of the house.

Her mum wasn't the answer. Neither were the police. She was just going to have to 'think outside the box', as Ollie liked to say. He was a brilliant lateral thinker, always finding a way round problems. Coming up with options her brain hadn't imagined existed.

She sighed, missing her husband more than ever. To think that all this trouble had started with her wanting some justice for him. As if he cared. He was dead. And because of her obsession with revenge, she'd nearly been dead too.

She stared at the wall, no energy to move. Her mind went back over the terrifying day she'd had, and she knew, without a shadow of a doubt, that what she'd promised Gino was true. She wanted to walk away, leave this life and make a new one. Never think about Theo or Gino or Luna ever again. Instead of torturing herself with what should have been, she'd learnt through this ordeal that she needed to enjoy what she'd had. Treasure those times with Ollie, revel in the love they'd shared. Learn to love her own company and find a way to build herself a new life, make new friends and have new adventures.

If only that was possible, she would grab it with both hands, close the door on her stupid actions and the horrifying consequences. Could she really hope to start again?

She decided to message her mum anyway, give her forewarning that she'd be arriving and would need some help with finances in the short term. When she opened her laptop, she found a stream of messages from Tanya.

> Where are you?
>
> I need to speak to you.
>
> Can I call round?

Hmm, Tanya. Friend or foe? If she was a friend, she could definitely do with some help, but if she was a foe, answering would not be advisable. Unfortunately, technology being what it was, Tanya would know now that Anna had read her messages. She would know she was active online.

At the very moment she had that thought, Messenger started ringing, requesting a video call. Talk of the devil. It was Tanya.

42

Anna let it ring, unsure if she was ready to talk to Tanya or not. Her finger hit the button accepting the call, deciding it would be better to get it over and done with, then at least she'd know where she stood and could plan accordingly. The video screen opened and there was Tanya, staring at her through red, puffy eyes, looking thoroughly miserable, her hand messing about with her hair, trying to smooth it down, like she'd just realised how rough she was looking.

'Have you heard?' Tanya asked, with a sniff, a tissue dabbing at her eyes, her cheeks wet with tears. No niceties, no 'hi, how are you?'. Her focus was not on Anna, but on her own misery and whatever had caused it.

'Heard what?' she said, cautiously, unsure where Tanya fitted into the picture. She couldn't know about the kidnap and the mayhem that had followed in the Boat House, could she? No, surely not. This must be a speculative question. Rhetorical. Anna wasn't expected to know what she was talking about. Her heart stuttered, heat suffusing her body, sure that accepting the call had been a bad idea. But then... there was the small matter of Anna's life being in danger, the potential of an intruder and Tanya might be the one person who could throw her a lifeline.

Anna watched her face crumple, her voice wavering 'Theo's... dead.' She disappeared, coming back holding a box of tissues and she blew her nose, closed her eyes and took a deep breath.

'Wow,' was all Anna could manage, wondering where Tanya had got her information and exactly how much she knew. Her shoulders tensed, bracing herself for what was to come. *She can't know the truth. There's no way.*

Anna waited, hoping Tanya would elaborate, half intrigued, half terrified.

'I know. And him so fit and healthy. Who would have imagined he'd have a heart attack, just like that?'

Anna's eyes widened. Right, so that was the story she'd been told. She swallowed, tried to maintain her composure while her heart hammered against her ribs, wondering where this version of events had come from. 'Oh gosh, is that what happened?'

Tanya nodded, her chin wobbling. 'Gino found him. Apparently, Theo went to the Boat House to check how the work was progressing. It's just about finished and he was going to be moving back in. Anyway, he said he was feeling a bit grotty, so he went for a lie down. When he hadn't come down after a few hours, Gino took him up a cup of tea and found he'd...' Her teeth nipped her lip. 'He'd passed away.'

'That's so sad,' Anna said, absently, her mind whirring. 'I can't believe it.' Which was true because that's not what happened. But maybe the authorities would believe the story? Gino must have carried him upstairs and staged it to fit his own narrative. Which made her realise he wasn't as daft as he looked. Although it could have been Luna's idea... The drug Theo had injected himself with had definitely caused his heart to stop. But surely there would be an autopsy for an unexplained death. Would they find toxins in his blood?

When her focus came back to the screen, she noticed that Tanya was frowning at her. 'Are you listening? You don't seem very upset considering you two were engaged only a few days ago.'

Anna shook her head. 'I'm sorry, I'm just shocked. I mean it's so sudden.' She rubbed at her forehead. 'I'm struggling to take it in. I mean... wow. It's hard to believe, but he *was* in a high-pressure job and he did like a drink, didn't he?' She sighed. 'I don't know what to think. Or what to feel for that matter. I'm numb. That's the best way to explain it.'

Tanya stared at her, and Anna realised her reaction was probably a bit lacklustre, devoid of the emotion you might expect when someone was told their ex had died. But then Tanya knew what had really been going on. Looking at her expression now it was as though they'd never had that chat, which made the situation even more confusing.

Anna looked down at her keyboard and cleared her throat while her mind came up with some sort of justification for her response. 'He turned on me, didn't he? I mean, he was truly horrible to me. Those tricks he played. It sort of made me look at him in a different light and altered the way I felt about him.' She studied her hands. 'You know what my plan was, but it turned out he guessed that ages ago and he was playing me at my own game. None of our relationship was real.' She pressed her lips together, ashamed by her part in the whole terrible situation. 'It was a mess,' she sighed. 'And now this.'

Anna sat back in her chair, not sure how to turn the conversation round. Her own agenda had been ripped up and thrown into the wind now Tanya knew about Theo's death.

'Well, I knew him a lot longer than you did, I suppose. He's been part of my life for three years. Obviously, he had his faults, but he could be a fun guy to have around at the gym.'

Anna hated to see anyone upset, and she wanted to reach out and hug Tanya, even though she wasn't sure how she felt about her any more. But she did have to decide whether to trust her or not. Tanya had rung her for sympathy, not to find out how *she* was. Which meant she hadn't a clue what had been going on. She wasn't part of the final plans, hadn't been involved in the plot to kill. And at the moment, she was the only person who could help. She needed to keep her onside and the best way to do that was to look and sound sympathetic.

'Oh, Tanya, I know how you feel. It was awful when Ollie died suddenly.' She stopped, hit by a sudden blast of emotion, still surprised by the power of it even two years down the line. 'It takes a little while to get your head round it. Takes even longer to accept it.'

'God, I don't think I'll ever accept it.' Tanya squeezed her eyes shut and tears leaked down her cheeks. 'Like you say, it's such a shock. Him still in his prime, it doesn't seem fair.'

Anna was struggling with her words. *Fair? Who said life was ever fair?*

'Do you need some company?' Anna asked, thinking she might be safer with Tanya than in her own home alone. 'Shall I come round?'

'Would you?' Tanya gave her a wobbly smile.

'Of course. I'll set off now.' Given how exhausted she was, the thought of walking up to Tanya's place was daunting. But less daunting than staying in her house when someone was trying to get in. And Tanya still had secrets, Anna was sure of it. She could be the missing piece to the puzzle.

They said their goodbyes and Anna grabbed a jacket and left the house, constantly looking over her shoulder in case she was being followed. But the roads were well-lit and there were plenty of students around in Upper Bangor, where Tanya lived. There was safety in numbers and the further she walked, the more confident she was that nobody would be dragging her off the streets. Even so, it was a relief when she reached Tanya's house and rang the bell, eager to get inside.

It was a shared house and the girl who opened the door let her in without a second glance, turning her back and disappearing into her room, which seemed very lax from a security point of view. Anna could be anyone. She headed up to Tanya's bedsit and knocked on the door. 'It's only me. Anna,' she called. After a minute, the door opened. A hand grabbed her arm and pulled her inside.

She gasped, surprised by the firmness of the grip, the suddenness of the pull. The door closed behind her, and her legs threatened to buckle as she looked up into a face she wasn't expecting to see.

43

'Gino! What are *you* doing here?' She gasped, trying to wrench her arm from his grip, thankful he hadn't grabbed the same wrist he'd bruised earlier. To her surprise, he let her go.

Tanya's bedsit was large but cluttered, crammed with furniture that didn't match and didn't quite fit into the space. Gino went to sit on the bed, next to Tanya, his arm draping round her shoulders.

'I came to check on my *girlfriend*,' he said, the emphasis very much on the last word.

Confused didn't begin to explain how Anna was feeling. Tanya and Gino, she hadn't seen that one coming.

'But— I thought—' She looked at Tanya, caught her eye and there was a warning there. Or was she imagining it? She'd got to a place where she hadn't a clue what was going on and decided there was no point second-guessing anything because she'd be wrong. What she did know for a fact though, was the last person she wanted to be in a room with was Gino. Just the sight of him made her stomach churn, her heart race.

'I don't want to intrude,' she said, eyeing the door. 'I only came to make sure Tanya was okay, but if you're here, then I'll come back another time.'

Gino was up on his feet in a flash, his body forming a barrier between her and the door.

'No, don't go yet. I'm glad you're here. There are things we need to... clarify.'

'What things?' It was an odd choice of words, and she wasn't sure exactly what he might be referring to. So much had happened, she was exhausted with it all, her brain too tired to cope with any more surprises. 'Why does any of that matter now?'

'Because this has to be the end of it,' Tanya said firmly, looking from Gino, who was leaning against the door, to Anna and back again. 'Now Theo is dead, we have to stop all the nonsense.'

If only, Anna thought. She glanced at Tanya, noted the determined look on her face, and moved towards the sofa, which was pushed up against the wall opposite the bed. It seemed like the safest place to sit.

'I didn't realise you two were an item,' she said, remembering Tanya's scathing remarks about Gino.

'It's been... on and off between us,' Tanya said, sounding a little wary. Uncertain.

Gino moved back to sit beside her on the bed, took her hand in his. 'I've been an idiot, I know I have. But I went away and got myself sorted out. I promise you I've learnt my lesson.' He looked into Tanya's eyes. 'I'm hoping, now Dad's not here playing mind games, things will be easier.'

Anna wasn't sure what to say, didn't want to speak ill of the dead in case Gino blew up at her. That's how it seemed to work with people. They could say what they liked about their relatives, but if you, an outsider, jumped in with any sort of criticism you'd trigger a defensive mechanism that could let loose the hounds of hell.

'So... tell me, Gino,' she said, carefully. 'What exactly do you want to clarify?'

'Dad's heart attack,' he said, his eyes meeting hers, holding her gaze in a way that made the hairs stand up on the back of her neck. She understood exactly what he'd meant by *clarify* now. He wanted to make sure she knew the story he was peddling to everyone, including the authorities. Ensure she was onside. She gave the tiniest nod of her head and he replied with the same. 'I know everyone will be shocked,' he continued, 'because he was so into his fitness, but he was on heart medication. Had been for years. Apparently, it was a congenital problem, although I've been checked and thankfully it's not been passed on to me.'

'That's funny... he never mentioned it,' Anna said, not intending to make this easy for him. 'And you'd think that would be the sort of information you'd want your fiancée to know.'

But then she hadn't been a real fiancée, had she? And there was so much she didn't know about Theo. He'd never let her see the real man, just as she'd never let her guard down either. Dancing with words that alluded to things but never substantiated with facts. It was all smoke and mirrors, their relationship an illusion.

She knew exactly how Theo had died, but the fact Gino had managed to dress it up as natural causes, with a rock-solid cover story, was intriguing. And genius. The way it worked in her favour was a major bonus. It was convenient for both of them because they were blameless now. No crime had been committed. He was giving her a way out, an escape from any threat of prosecution for manslaughter.

Is that the message he's trying to convey?

She closed her eyes for a second, her shoulders relaxing, the tension in her muscles starting to dissipate. Perhaps Tanya was right. Perhaps this could be the end of her troubles.

'He saw it as a sign of weakness,' Gino said. 'That's why he kept it a secret.'

Tanya nodded her agreement. 'I do remember him mentioning it when I caught him swallowing some pills one time.'

She could be making that up to back up Gino's story. Or it could be the truth. But what did it matter? Gino was telling her she was free from any blame for his death and that was a mighty big weight lifted from her shoulders.

'Who would have believed it,' Anna said, distracted by a sudden thought. She'd forgotten something significant. Or, rather, someone. Luna. 'And how's your sister taking it? Is she as calm and fatalistic about his sudden demise as you are?'

He shrugged, his eyes locking onto hers again and she sensed he was sending her another coded message. 'I haven't been able to contact her.' His jaw moved from side to side. 'And I'm not the emotional type. You won't see me breaking down in tears.' His gaze hardened. 'That doesn't mean I'm not feeling it.'

She decided she should soften her tone. No point causing trouble for herself by being spiky, whatever she might think. 'I'm sorry, I'm sure you're as devastated as Tanya. But Luna...' She raised an eyebrow and he frowned at her. 'I wonder where she could be?'

He must know, so what's he hiding?

In Anna's mind, Luna was safely ensconced up at the hospital having her wound dealt with and her lost blood replaced. But what if that hadn't happened? She thought about it for a moment, tried to imagine how things might have panned out once she'd left the house.

Gino had obviously moved his father's body upstairs and staged a peaceful death in his bed. All well and good. But what had he done with Luna? Had he left his sister to die? Hidden her body somewhere? She chewed on her lip, unease permeating every fibre of her body. She didn't like where her mind was taking her. There were other possibilities too. There was a chance she wasn't as badly injured as Anna had thought. She could be out there, lurking. In fact, it could have been her who'd been trying to get into Anna's apartment. A chill seeped through her body.

Is nothing ever simple?

This whole saga just kept rolling on, seeming to have a momentum of its own, and when she thought she'd managed to get through the worst-case scenario, something else happened.

'I'm sorry you got dragged into this,' Gino said, making Anna snap out of her thoughts. She stared at him. The last thing she'd been expecting was an apology and she studied his face, thought he did look genuinely contrite. Christ, this day was full of surprises and her brain was at a loss to know what to make of it all. She watched as he laced his fingers with Tanya's, like he needed moral support. 'It all got out of hand, and I was pulled along with Luna and Dad. I've never been able to say no to either of them. But it's going to be different now.' There was a determined set to his jaw. 'This is going to be a fresh start.'

He gave Tanya a lingering, meaningful look, and she gave him a warm smile. It was an intimate moment and Anna felt like an intruder, still surprised to find the two of them in a relationship. 'Actions speak louder than words,' Tanya said, and Anna heard it as a warning. A message to Gino that he had to mend his ways. She wondered if he'd heard that, too, if he really could change.

She stood, feeling awkward, not 100 per cent convinced by anything Gino had said. In one way, his cover story about Theo's death had been a major relief. But his vagueness about Luna's whereabouts was a concern because she could still be dangerous and Anna needed to know exactly where she was. And how she was. Because she didn't want to be ultimately responsible if she'd died. Perhaps Gino had been giving her a warning to watch her back because she was out there somewhere? And if that was the case, there was no doubt in Anna's mind, Luna would be intent on revenge.

'I'm going to get off,' she said, edging towards the door. 'Leave you lovebirds to it.'

Gino and Tanya were gazing into each other's eyes, and she wasn't sure they'd even heard her.

'Wait,' Gino said, when she opened the door. 'I've got something of yours. You left it in Dad's car.' She turned and saw her bag in his hand. *Oh yes.* She gave a mental fist pump. *At last, something good has happened.* She took it and peered inside, saw her purse and her phone. Exactly what she needed to make her escape.

'Thank you,' she muttered, before hurrying downstairs and out into the fresh air, needing time to work out what had just happened.

* * *

It had been the weirdest conversation she'd ever had with anyone, the subtext so much more important than the spoken word. He was basically telling her that the real cause of Theo's death was something he wanted to hide. And it suited her for this to be the case. But by blaming Luna and his dad for everything, taking no responsibility for anything that had happened, she had a sneaking suspicion he was deluded. His world bearing no relation to the world everyone else lived in. He'd concocted a narrative that made him blameless, and however far that might be from the truth, he'd convinced himself it was right.

She understood it had been an act for Tanya's benefit, but in Gino's world, life seemed to be very black and white. Simplistic. And who was she to argue if he was going to leave her alone? Perhaps this really was the end of the drama. Especially if his sister had 'disappeared'. All her conscience needed to believe was that she was alive when Anna had left her in Gino's care. Anything that happened after that was not her fault. It was his.

She found herself walking faster as she got closer to home, her mind busy planning what she was going to do next. A move to Spain, to live close to her parents. That was the best solution for now. They would wrap her in their kindness, a blanket of love that would soothe her troubles. She'd resisted their offers after Ollie had died, so intent on finding out the truth and making someone accountable for his untimely death. But now, she knew an escape was what she needed. A time for rest and healing, before she made her own way in the world again.

By the time she got home, she was feeling much better and had decided to call her parents and start making arrangements for her journey to Spain. She didn't have to wait now she had her bank cards and that was such a relief she almost sobbed. At last, she allowed herself to believe the tortuous events of recent weeks had come to an end. It was over and tomorrow she could be gone.

Her mind was busy formulating a list of things to do when she walked up to her front door and went to put the key in the lock. But the door swung open as soon as she touched it.

Her pulse went on overdrive, her hand clutching her keys so tight they dug into her flesh. Having left Gino and Tanya together, there was only one person who could be in her apartment.

44

She listened, but could hear no sound, no movement. No lights were on. Was Luna hiding behind the door, ready to stab her or hit her over the head with something? Or had she been and gone?

With adrenaline firing through her veins, Anna's senses seemed to light up. She could smell Luna's perfume. That sickly scent she seemed to favour, cloying like lilies at a funeral. She stood on the doorstep having a debate with herself about whether to go in or not, looking round to see what she could arm herself with. She adjusted her grip on her keys, slotting one between her fingers like a short blade. It was never going to be terribly effective as a weapon, but it might be capable of causing a distraction, buying her time to get away if there was trouble.

Luna is injured, she reminded herself, trying to think of the positives. Given the state she was in when she'd left the house, Anna doubted she was here for a fight, but couldn't think of any other explanation for her presence. She glanced around again and spotted a big stick on the path of the house next door. Something a dog had probably brought home from their walk. She sneaked over the low wall that separated the houses and picked it up, glad to find it was solid and heavy. Substantial enough to cause harm. Now she felt more confident.

She clambered back over the wall. Cautiously, she pushed the door wide open, glad to see the hallway was empty, wincing as the hinges creaked. She stopped and listened, but still could hear no sound, her heart beating so hard it was making her body shake.

She hesitated, running her tongue round dry lips, fighting her instinct to run away. But what good would that do her? She had to face up to her nemesis if this fiasco was going to be over for good. Luna was a loose end that needed to be tied, a threat that would always be out there unless Anna could persuade her to finally put a stop to her reign of terror.

The absence of sound seemed odd. Surely she'd be able to hear the rustle of clothes as she shifted in her seat, or footsteps on the creaky floors if she was moving about. Wouldn't she feel the presence of another human being?

Finally, she made herself edge forwards, the stick in one hand, the keys in the other, braced for attack, her nerves on edge. Her eyes had become accustomed to the dark now and from the doorstep, she could see through the hallway into the lounge. A shape on the sofa, a person just sitting there.

'Luna,' she called from the doorway. 'We've got to stop this now.'

No answer. The person didn't move.

'Luna? Are you okay?' she asked, reluctant to get any closer. She watched her, warily, but she didn't move, not even an inch, her eyes staring straight ahead. There was a strangeness about her posture, she noticed, something stiff and rigid.

And that's when she realised Luna was no longer a threat. Because Luna was dead.

45

She backed away from the doorway, dropping the stick on her path. Her hand flew to her mouth, bile burning the back of her throat as she stared at Luna's dead body. Sitting on her sofa.

Live by the sword, die by the sword.

The words appeared in her head from somewhere. Anna felt no guilt that Luna had died because it had been self-defence on her part. She'd been fighting for her life when Luna was injured and if she hadn't launched herself at Anna, she wouldn't have ended up with a pair of scissor blades in her leg. And if she hadn't kidnapped Anna, they wouldn't even have been in the house together. She stared at her, unable to tear her eyes away. Two dead bodies in one day. She swallowed, glanced around to see if anyone was watching her, still puzzling over how and why she was there.

Had she come in and died on Anna's sofa, or... had Gino put her there when she was already dead? She chewed on a nail, trying to work it out.

A dead body in my living room.

For crying out loud, what was she supposed to do now? It wasn't like she could move Luna on her own. She must weigh a lot more than Anna, just given their height difference, but she was a more solid build as well. Moving her out of here was impossible. Gino had done this to her. It could only have been him. Heat flushed through her body, her shock replaced with a burning anger.

He's set me up.

And wouldn't the police immediately think Anna had killed Luna when there was a well-documented history of trouble between the two of them? But if that was the case... what was that conversation at Tanya's all about? She was missing something, and knew she needed to give this some careful thought before she acted because her future, her liberty, could depend on it.

She leant against the wall, her eyes still on Luna. How on earth was she going to distance herself from this? Demonstrate to the police that she had nothing to do with Luna's body being in her apartment.

If she went to the police now, she had an alibi with Gino and Tanya, for the time when Luna had supposedly arrived. They could all cover for each other. Was that what Gino had been hinting at? Was his plan to make out that Luna had arrived on her own, let herself in and inconveniently died while she was waiting for Anna to come home?

Perhaps she'd still been alive when Gino brought her in? Forensics would look at lividity, where the blood pooled under the skin to tell them if she'd died in place but there was no way Anna was going anywhere near the body. She wasn't even going to go further into the house. She had to be careful of leaving her DNA. But then she remembered the fight with Luna and she groaned. Her DNA was going to be all over her anyway.

Gino had backed her into a corner, stitched her up.

But what about the blood? There would be Luna's blood all over the office floor in the Boat House. And even if Gino thought he'd dealt with that, there would still be traces. Could she use that as a lever to make him help her? Her head was aching, her brain stuffed full to bursting with unanswered questions.

Top of the list was whether Luna had walked in herself or if Gino had put her there. But Gino was already at Tanya's apartment when Anna had arrived. So he would only have had a very small time-gap between her leaving her apartment and him putting Luna inside. And how would he have done that without being seen? It didn't seem possible. The logistics of it were tying her brain in knots.

She rapped at her forehead with her knuckles trying to think, to work out the logic. If Luna had driven herself then her car must be outside somewhere and there would be keys. In fact, there would be two sets of keys, because Anna's door was unlocked. But she couldn't go inside and check.

She walked up and down the road looking for Luna's car, but it was only when she walked round the back of the terrace that she saw it, parked at the end of the lane. So Luna had come in through the back door, she surmised, either under her own steam or carried by Gino. She tried the handle. The door was unlocked.

She thought back to Gino's cryptic messages when they were in Tanya's room and she understood now what he'd been trying to tell her, what she needed to do. Her story had to be that this was not her problem. She'd come home and found a body in her apartment. That was the truth. And she would deny having anything to do with what had come before. Gino had been at the Boat House, the police knew that. In *his* story, Anna hadn't. Which was why he'd made sure to return her handbag.

She needed to check something. Pulled her phone from her pocket and made a call.

46

Tanya answered on the second ring.

'Is Gino still with you?' Anna asked, her voice an urgent whisper.

'No, so you can talk normally.' Tanya sounded as weary as Anna felt. 'He's had to go and speak to the police. There are lots of formalities to get through when someone dies suddenly at home.'

'Yeah, I'm sure there must be.' She hesitated. 'I— um— I have to say I was surprised when I saw him at yours. I didn't know you two were an item.'

Tanya sighed. 'Yeah, well, it's been on and off for a while.' She was silent for a moment. 'Look, I haven't been completely honest with you. When I was talking about my friend being with Gino, I was really talking about myself. I just didn't think you'd want to spend time with me if you knew we'd been so close. And I wanted us to be friends.'

Anna thought back to their previous conversations and could feel pieces of the puzzle starting to fit together in her brain, the picture becoming clearer. A prickle of annoyance made her rub the back of her neck, but she couldn't argue about dishonesty at this point. Hadn't a leg to stand on, given the games she'd been playing. 'That doesn't matter,' she said. 'But can you be honest with me now?'

'I will be, I promise.' She sighed again. 'We were good together for a while, until his financial problems got out of hand. He was a compulsive spender, always buying things he couldn't afford. Things he didn't need. Theo was a shoulder to cry on when we were breaking up, just as a friend. Of course Luna hated it. Because she hates any attention being taken away from her relationship with her beloved father. Honestly, she's obsessed with him. It's not normal but he can't— couldn't see it. And in turn, she could do no wrong in his eyes. Anyway, Gino moved away for a bit and started going to therapy to get a handle on his compulsive behaviour. But his job didn't work out and as soon as he was back, he called me, and we started seeing each other again.'

Anna was still a little confused, the picture not yet clear in her mind. Tanya had been quite disparaging about Gino so it seemed odd that they would suddenly be back together. And there was another thing bothering her.

'I saw you kissing Theo in Gethin's video. That was only a few days ago. And when you called me earlier to tell me Theo had died, well... you looked and sounded genuinely upset.'

Tanya gave a dismissive snort. 'Yeah, well you can't believe everything you see and hear. It's not always what it seems. As I learnt recently, Theo was not a nice man underneath the smooth façade. But you know that already. He made me kiss him. He wanted you to be jealous, to think he'd moved on. And what would be more hurtful than moving on with your best friend?'

'Really?' Anna decided she was more gullible than she'd thought. But then we all see what we want to see, our minds making up a narrative that suits our beliefs. Wasn't that what her therapist had told her? 'It was an act?'

'I was coerced into kissing him.' Tanya sounded frustrated. 'I've already told you this.'

Anna hadn't believed Tanya the first time she'd told her but now she was wavering. *Is Tanya on my side?*

'I'm so sorry, Anna. I know I haven't been a good friend to you recently, but I did warn you about Luna early on. I should have been more specific, made it clear that Luna could manipulate her father any way she wanted. It was the weirdest father-daughter relationship. It was like he was bewitched by her, and she knew it.' Her sigh crackled in Anna's ear. 'It's all ended so horribly, but I had to do what he asked with the kiss and the pranks, otherwise he was going to ruin Gino's life. That's what he said. He forced me to do it.'

Anna wasn't convinced. She'd been tricked one time too many and it was vital she get her next move right. 'So why ring me in tears like that, if he was so awful to you?'

'Because Gino needed to speak to you before he got tied up with all the police stuff and statements and everything. He knew he would be unable to talk to you for a while, so it had to be then. It was his one opportunity. And after all the... unpleasantness between you, he didn't think you would speak to him if he approached you directly. So he gambled that you would want to come and check that I was okay.'

Her words had a ring of truth about them.

'Hmm, he's right. I don't think I would have spoken to him.'

'Are you okay though?' Tanya asked. 'I mean this has been an awful time for you too.'

Anna huffed. Tanya didn't know the half of it, and she was hoping she never would. It was clear Gino hadn't told her the truth, otherwise they wouldn't have had that cryptic conversation. Was it possible Gino's version of events would work? If it had only been one dead body to deal with, then maybe, but now there were two, it was a different matter. But she needed help and Tanya was the only person she could ask.

'Umm... I've got a situation.' She took a deep breath. 'You're not going to believe this, but I came home, and the door was open, and... Luna was sitting on my sofa.'

She heard Tanya gasp. 'You're kidding me.'

'No, I'm really not. But the worst part is... I think she's... dead.'

'No! Oh my God, you didn't—?'

'No. Honestly, I didn't touch her. She was dead when I came back to the apartment. At least I think she is. I haven't been in to check. But she's just sitting there and...' her voice cracked. 'I'm not sure what to do.'

'Ring the bloody police, you idiot. They know she's at large somewhere. Gino's already told them she was distraught and dashed out of the house when she found out Theo was dead. He said he hoped the police would find her before she did something stupid. Well, it looks like she has done something. Just leave her where you found her. Don't touch anything. Call the police.'

Anna knew this was the only option, but having someone else confirm it, was the spur she needed to actually go ahead and do it.

'Okay. Yes, I will.' Her heart started racing at the thought of speaking to the police again, especially after all the trouble she'd had with Luna. She'd be the prime suspect. They'd be treating it as murder from the get-go.

She was walking round to the front of her property now, and as she drew closer she saw the glow of her video doorbell and she realised it would all have been recorded. Her going to Tanya's. Her coming back from Tanya's. Hovering around outside. There would be video. Time-stamped video. Anna felt her body crumple with relief when she realised there was solid evidence of her movements and her reluctance to go inside. It would all be recorded. Every movement, every word. Hopefully it would be enough.

'Shall I come round?'

'Would you?' Tanya was exactly the person she needed right now. Someone who'd known Luna for a while, who could testify to her difficult nature and corroborate what Gino had been saying. Between them, there was a slim chance they could get through this. 'Then you can tell the police I was up at your house with Gino when she arrived.'

'Okay, yes, I'll do that. Just keep calm and remember you've done nothing wrong. This is just something awful that's happened in your apartment, okay? You are not to blame.'

They said their goodbyes and Anna sat on the wall outside her front door, going through the conversation. It sounded like Gino had already laid the groundwork with the police. Tanya was going to back her up. *We can do this.*

She looked at her phone and called the police.

47

THREE WEEKS LATER

Anna stood in the queue at Malaga Airport, waiting for her passport to be checked. Her hands were slick with sweat, and she wiped them on her jeans, hoping she didn't look as nervous and guilty as she felt. They'd stop her, she was sure. Sit her in a little room for hours while she was questioned, then handcuff her, and stick her on a plane back home, no doubt escorted by a police officer.

The queue inched forwards, some sort of problem with two young men now resolved. She kept her eyes on the floor, talking to herself in her head, telling herself to stay calm, that it would be okay.

Finally, it was her turn and the woman in the kiosk looked at her passport, stared right at her, through her, inside her. Anna swallowed, forced a smile while trying not to squirm, hoping she'd hidden her discomfort. The woman asked a few questions, then handed Anna her passport and she was through, almost running to the arrivals hall and the exit. Elation exploded in her chest, making her feel light, so light she almost felt she could fly if she wanted to.

A cluster of people stood waiting for passengers, hugging their loved ones before leading them away towards waiting transport. Her eyes scanned the crowd, her mind expecting someone to be running after her, a hand on her shoulder stopping her, telling her they'd made a mistake.

Her mum saw her and started waving, her dad rushing towards her to grab her case, wrapping her in a hug. And then the three of them were clasped together, laughing and crying and she finally allowed herself to believe she had escaped from the madness. This really was the end.

Her parents chattered away to her, one on either side as they led her to the car and she tried to answer their questions, but they were both talking at once and it all felt a little overwhelming. She was glad when they'd left the airport and her dad was too busy driving to speak, her mum too busy giving him directions.

She gazed out of the window, her mind reliving the past three weeks and her miraculous escape. It was still a shock to her that she was free, but here she was, in Spain and she wouldn't be going back to the UK anytime soon. Of course she'd have to return for the inquest, but that could be six months away, the police had told her. For now, though, their investigation was over. There was nothing to suggest Luna's death had been suspicious.

A lot of blood had been found in Luna's car, like she'd been sitting in it for quite some time before she'd made her way to Anna's apartment. There was a pair of scissors on the passenger seat which fitted the stab wounds in her leg. They only had her prints on them and looking at the nature and angle of the wound, their conclusion was it was self-inflicted. A reaction to her father's sudden death. They were very close, and the police had told Anna that Gino had said she was beside herself with grief when he'd told her the news that Theo had died.

Apparently, Luna had a history of self-harm, with several stays in private mental health clinics. Their diagnosis of her was enlightening and Tanya had passed on what Gino had learnt from the file he'd found locked in the filing cabinet in his mother's office. The psychologist's assessment was that Luna's relationship with her father was unhealthy and she was totally dependent on him for self-validation, constantly needing his attention and approval. And she was unreasonably jealous of anyone who got close to him, including her mother. She'd learnt to use the threat of self-harm as an attention-seeking weapon, but had also used it to manipulate him to do what she wanted. Gino had said it had been going on since she was a child, but it had got worse since their mother's death. Now, with her father gone, the police theory was that she felt she couldn't exist without him.

The question of why she'd ended up at Anna's apartment had been a tricky one to answer. Nobody knew for sure, so they could only make an educated guess. It had been fortunate for Anna that she had an alibi at the estimated time of death. She could prove she'd been with Tanya and Gino because witnesses saw her arrive and leave and her doorbell recording had proved invaluable in confirming her movements. A theory had been put forward that Luna blamed Anna for Theo's heart attack because of all the stress she'd caused him. Ending her life in Anna's apartment was her final act of revenge, hoping Anna would be charged with her murder.

Gino's evidence supported this theory. He'd said he heard Luna saying it was all Anna's fault, telling him she would make her pay. Those were her last words before she took off after they'd found Theo dead. He'd been to look for her but hadn't been able to find her and although he'd checked at Anna's apartment, nobody had been home. He'd tried to call his sister, but he quickly realised she'd left her phone at the Boat House when he heard it ringing in her bedroom, so there was no way of contacting her.

The only grey area had been those hours between Anna speaking to the receptionist at the hospital at lunchtime and when she'd arrived home that evening. She told the police she'd gone to see if she could speak to Theo, but he'd been delayed. She got tired of waiting and went for a long walk along the cycle path before returning home. There was nothing to suggest this wasn't the truth and she was confident it sounded believable. After all, her car had been ruined that morning, so she wasn't going to be driving anywhere.

It had been difficult for Anna to unravel her feelings about Tanya and Gino. They had spun a very believable tale and, without them, Anna knew, the outcome would have been very different for her. But she also knew she was a mere pawn. A means for them to get what *they* wanted. She had been used to fit into their narrative, rather than them actively trying to get her out of trouble.

After a while, she realised it didn't matter. The important thing was to put a distance between her and them, both physically and emotionally, so she could be rid of the stain of their influence.

Looking back at it now, her ill-conceived plan for getting justice for Ollie had backfired in ways she never could have imagined. It had traumatised her emotionally and physically and put her in life-threatening situations that still gave her flashbacks. The silver lining to this big black cloud though, was an enforced change and as she watched the beautiful Andalucian countryside go by, she thought she might like it here. Rather than seeing herself in exile, this could really be her chance to let go of the past and create a new life for herself.

Ollie's wedding ring was back on her finger, and she turned it round, feeling his love in her heart. She would always have that, whatever happened, and it was more than enough to give her the strength to move forwards rather than looking back. Revenge was not a dish best served cold, she decided. Revenge was a dish that should never be served at all.

48

Gino held Tanya's hand as they walked down the jetty outside the Boat House. It had been a tricky few weeks, but thankfully Anna and Tanya had both understood the assignment and played their parts to perfection, leaving his story untouched and believable, just as he'd constructed it.

He'd always been good at stories, he thought, as he gazed out over the calm waters of the Menai Straits. He remembered his mother saying to him once that he'd never had a solid relationship with the truth. He smiled to himself. The truth was for dummies. For people who had no imagination. Oh, the scrapes he'd got himself out of in his lifetime, with a few well-placed lies. He knew people liked to say the truth was stranger than fiction. But his truth was never strange, he kept it simple. That was the way for it never to be questioned. People liked boring. They liked familiar.

His dad's death, for example. Not a whisper of doubt about that one from the authorities. Honestly, he couldn't believe it when he'd burst into his mum's old office and seen him collapsed on the floor. That eventuality had not been in his thinking at all, but it had suddenly opened an opportunity to him. One he'd never thought possible. The idea that the Boat House would be his, along with his father's bank account, substantial investment portfolio, life insurance policy and generous pension.

At that point, his mind had been a whole whirlwind of thoughts, the main problem being Luna. He didn't think she'd been badly injured. A pair of scissors couldn't do that much damage, could they? Initially, he'd thought Anna was bluffing and he'd been panicking to the point of making himself sick, unsure what he was supposed to do once Luna's plans had gone so badly wrong.

He was so used to doing what he was told when Luna was around, he'd almost forgotten how to think for himself, keeping his seething resentment bottled up inside. But, for once, he'd hit on his own plan, a whole narrative playing out in his head, and he knew it would be better to let Anna go. What was he supposed to do with her anyway?

He'd kept himself at a distance, on the periphery of the plans, so the worst he could be was an accomplice. But now those same plans had died along with his father, and with Luna out of action, he could choose a different outcome. He'd realised that Anna wasn't going to be rushing to the police to tell them she'd killed a man and stabbed his daughter. No, if he played his cards right, Anna could be his biggest asset, a great big stepping stone to a bountiful future he'd never imagined possible.

When he'd gone to check on Luna, he'd been shocked at how much blood she'd actually lost. Her face had been deathly pale, and she was hardly able to move, let alone speak. He'd had the scarf in his hand, about to tie it round her thigh to stem the bleeding and then something had stopped him.

Because if Luna was dead, he would get his life back.

He'd no longer have to be at her beck and call. He'd no longer owe her anything. He'd no longer be second best. Never again would she make him do things he didn't want to do, using that threat she had hanging over him all the time. But more than that, everything that belonged to his father would be Gino's and his alone. He wouldn't have to share. He could have a proper fresh start and concentrate on rebuilding his relationship with Tanya.

There was plenty of evidence that Luna had been unhinged for years, getting herself hysterical about their dad's relationships with any woman who'd got close to him. She'd wanted him all to herself. Unnatural really, but his dad couldn't see it. He'd doted on her, always had, meaning Gino had been second best all his life. He would admit that it had tortured him, and he'd constantly sought his father's approval. That's what he'd been doing the day his mother died.

* * *

His mum hadn't known their dad had been having a long-term affair, but it hadn't been surprising, given they'd rarely been in the house at the same time. They'd worked different shifts, become different people. When she'd found out, there'd been lots of rows and it had seemed obvious to both Luna and Gino that their parents' marriage was on the rocks. His mum had wanted a divorce and she'd wanted to sell the house so she could return to her home-town in Italy and buy a property of her own. Luna had been unbearable, doing whatever she could to get their parents' attention and the atmosphere in the house had been toxic.

Gino had been unable to bear it and one day he'd confronted his mother. She'd been standing in her favourite spot at the end of the jetty, looking out over the Straits, the place where he could always find her if she'd wanted some time alone. He'd challenged her about the divorce and her plans to split up the family, sell their home and move away. He'd asked her to put her family first.

She'd spun on her heel to face him, anger sparking in her eyes.

'I've been putting your father and you children first for over a quarter of a century, Gino. Don't you think it's about time I got to do what I want for a change? Your father doesn't love me; our marriage is just a convenience for him.' Her gaze had softened. 'It's not that I don't love you and Luna, but you're old enough to look after yourselves now. I've always been homesick, you know that. I want to go back home. Especially now Mamma and Papa are slowing down. They need my support more than you do.'

'No, Mum, you're wrong, we still need you.'

'I'm leaving,' she'd said. 'I'm booking a flight for tomorrow but you know you can come and visit whenever you want. I honestly can't bear to stay here a moment longer. Not with your father messing about with other women. Have you any idea how humiliating that is for me?'

'But you can't, Mum.' He'd choked back tears, desperate for her to stay. She was the stabilising factor in the family. The voice of reason. 'You can't.'

Her jaw had tightened. 'Just watch me.'

She'd tried to push past him, and he'd grabbed her hand, trying to stop her from going. She'd yanked her hand from his grip and lost her balance, toppling over the side of the jetty and into the water. He'd known from the red bloom that spread around her head that she'd hurt herself.

He could have waded in and tried to save her, but he hadn't. Because if she didn't want him, if he was such a burden to her, then he didn't want her either. His hurt had burned in his heart. It had been her choice, and it was better for all of them for it to end like this. Then at least they'd still have a home.

What he hadn't realised was Luna had seen everything out of the bedroom window. But by the time she'd come running out of the house, their mother's body had been taken away by the current. She was gone.

Luna had taken charge. She'd found a hand-written report in their mother's office and practised her handwriting and signature before she'd forged a suicide note. It was a believable story, given his mum had been on sick leave for mental health issues, and the fact their father had been having an affair. They could all attest to talk of divorce. Yes, it was obvious it added up to a situation that had overwhelmed her. And that was what everyone had chosen to believe.

Ever since then, Gino had paid a high price for Luna's assistance. His sister was highly strung at the best of times and prone to obsessions. Once his dad had started dating Anna, she'd been furious and when she'd found out exactly who Anna was, it hadn't taken her long to decide she was faking and that Anna was tricking their dad into a relationship as some act of revenge. Their dad hadn't wanted to believe her, didn't want to listen, but eventually the evidence was there and he'd had to take notice. Luna had been right.

That's when the madness had really begun. She'd roped him into behaving like a stalker to try and freak Anna out, getting a dodgy acquaintance – Adam – to ransack the apartment and give Anna a kicking. He'd thought that would be it. Then his father had taken the baton after the engagement day debacle, when Gino had got overenthusiastic in his role. It was supposed to have been play acting when he'd attacked his father for Anna's benefit, an attempt to scare her away from the family, but old resentments had bubbled up and he'd found his anger was real. They'd had a major row about that afterwards, but Luna had calmed them down, told them Anna was trying to create bad feeling between them. They had to keep their eyes on the prize and not get mad with each other. Unfortunately, nothing had worked, and they'd had the unnerving experience of several police interviews.

Everything ramped up several notches when Anna had

announced she had evidence that would make the police ask questions about their mother's death. At that point, Luna had become demonic, scary in her assertions that Anna had to die, or their lives would be ruined for ever more. She'd spotted that the top sheet of the blotting pad on their mother's desk had gone and had guessed what Anna's evidence might be. She'd been frantic and her hysteria had transferred itself to Gino and their father.

All of that had gone through his head as he looked at his dying sister. He could have helped her, but decided, on balance, his life would be so much better if he didn't. He'd pretended to, of course, just to keep her placated. He'd told her he'd rung for an ambulance, but they didn't have one to send. He'd have to take her to hospital himself. He'd covered the passenger seat of the car with plastic and with his support, she'd managed to get herself inside. He'd fastened her in and driven the car down their track to an old barn which the farmer no longer used. It was a handy hiding place while he'd set up his dad's death to look like a natural one.

It was amazing how sharp his brain had been when he'd needed it to be. Luna wasn't going anywhere, and he'd told her his plan to cover up their father's death. Telling her he had to move him now, before rigor mortis set in. He wouldn't be long. She didn't even protest, and at this point she'd been too weak to do anything to stop him.

Then he'd carried his dad upstairs to the bedroom, arranging pillows to make it look like he'd died in bed. Once that had been set up, he'd called emergency services. Said he'd just got home and found his father unresponsive. While he'd been waiting for the paramedics to arrive, he'd quickly changed his clothes, putting his soiled ones in a bin bag, and hiding them in the grounds of the house.

It had taken an age for the police and paramedics to sort everything out and leave. Gino had felt he'd been convincing and when he'd produced his father's heart medication, it had all seemed more straightforward. Once he'd been sure they had definitely gone, he'd walked back up the track to retrieve Luna's car, finding his sister unconscious, but still alive, in the passenger seat.

Darkness had fallen by that point and he'd been sure Anna must be home. His first task was to speak to her and make sure they were on the same page about what had happened at the house. He'd also wanted to feed her the story about Luna running off. Unfortunately, he'd not been able to get his key to work because she'd left her own key in the kitchen lock, and he didn't want to walk round to the front of the property because he knew she'd had a video doorbell fitted and he'd be caught on camera. He'd kicked the back door in frustration, but she didn't come to open it and he'd not been sure if she was even in. Calling out to her would have only drawn attention to himself so that hadn't been an option. So then he'd devised a new plan to get her to meet him at Tanya's and he'd had a brainwave about what to do with Luna's body.

As agreed, Tanya had called him to let him know when she'd persuaded Anna to walk round to her bedsit. He'd tried his key in the back door again and it had worked. He'd picked up his sister and carried her into the lounge, putting her on the sofa, happy to find she was not yet dead, and her wound still seeping blood. Perfect. He'd opened the front door to give Anna warning that something wasn't right when she got home later. Then he'd switched the plastic cover from the passenger seat to the driver's seat to make it look like she'd driven there. In all, it had only taken a few minutes. Once that had been done, he'd taken off the boiler suit he'd been wearing, stuffed it in a carrier bag in a bin, and he'd legged it up to Tanya's, arriving a few minutes before Anna had.

It had been risky, and a bit too close for comfort, but he'd done it. Looking back, he was proud of himself and the way he'd confronted every problem, finding solutions that had slotted into place as if it they were meant to be.

* * *

The gentle evening breeze on his skin brought him back to the present and he looked around him, breathing in the briny tang that hung in the air. A little group of oyster catchers waded by the water's edge, a tinge of pink in the sky as the sun started to set. He smiled to himself thinking he could never have seen it ending like this.

He was free. Anna was free and he was sure things would stay that way. Only they knew the truth, but he trusted her to keep it to herself. If she ever decided to tell the police what had really happened, she was making herself a murderer. No sane person would do that, so he felt secure. It was perfect like this. Everything was in balance. He had what he wanted, and Anna had a chance at a new life, no need for either of them to muddy the waters.

Everything of his father's was now going to be his, once all the legalities were squared away properly. He was wealthy beyond his wildest dreams and could take some time to decide what he wanted to do next.

He chuckled to himself, thinking it was the first time in his life he'd actually won. And in a way he had Anna to thank. If she hadn't have thought up her scheme to get revenge on his father, none of the recent events would have happened. His father wouldn't be dead, and neither would his sister. Yes, he had a lot to thank Anna for. But Gino knew his quick thinking had given her what she needed too. He thought it was a fair trade.

He smiled to himself and drew Tanya close. This was it, the perfect moment. He felt in his pocket, his hand closing round cold metal. He dropped down on one knee, looking up at his love as she gazed at him, puzzled. He pulled the stunning antique engagement ring from his pocket. The same one that his father had given to his mother all those years ago.

'Tanya, my darling.' He took her hand. 'Please would you do me the honour of becoming my wife?'

Her mouth dropped open, tears springing to her eyes. 'Yes,' she gasped, and he couldn't tell if she was laughing or crying when he wriggled the ring onto her finger. He clambered to his feet, and they shared a lingering kiss. She was his one true love, his future and now he would have the means to give her the life she deserved.

A new beginning, born out of untimely endings. Everything in balance, just as it should be.

ACKNOWLEDGEMENTS

This is my first book with my new publishers, Boldwood Books and I would like to thank the whole team, staff and authors alike, for the wonderful warm welcome. I'm sure this is going to be the perfect home for my stories!

I am back working with my wonderful editor, Isobel Akenhead, who picked up my debut when she was working for Bookouture six years ago. I've missed you! Thank you for the brilliant edits and the gorgeous cover. You have put the fun back into my writing and I can't wait to see what we can do together over the next few years.

Thanks also to my trusty group of beta readers who have given me some great feedback and made this book so much better. Mark, Wendy, Kerry-Ann, Sandra and Chloe, thank you all from the bottom of my heart.

Finally, my thanks to my family, Kate, John, Amy and Oscar for keeping me sane. My friends for being lovely and enthusiastic about my writing. And to my dogs, Maid and Evie, for being my writing buddies, making sure I have a daily fitness regime and evening cuddles.

ABOUT THE AUTHOR

Rona Halsall is a #1 bestselling author of psychological thrillers including, most recently, *The Bigamist* and *Bride & Groom*. She lives in Wales with her mad little Border Collie, Maid and Romanian rescue dog, Evie.

Sign up to Rona Halsall's mailing list for news, competitions and updates on future books.

Visit Rona Halsall's website: www.ronahalsall.com

Follow Rona on social media here:

THE

Murder

LIST

**THE MURDER LIST IS A NEWSLETTER
DEDICATED TO SPINE-CHILLING FICTION
AND GRIPPING PAGE-TURNERS!**

**SIGN UP TO MAKE SURE YOU'RE ON OUR
HIT LIST FOR EXCLUSIVE DEALS, AUTHOR
CONTENT, AND COMPETITIONS.**

SIGN UP TO OUR
NEWSLETTER

BIT.LY/THEMURDERLISTNEWS

Boldwood